CIARA HALL

SHE GETS WITCH SHE WANTS
Copyright © 2025 by Ciara Hall
Published in Houston, Texas

Editor: Andrelle Quammie
Proofreader: Tee Tate

The Library of Congress Cataloging-in-Publication
Data is available upon request.

Paperback ISBN: 979-8-9989920-0-1
eBook ISBN: 979-8-9989920-1-8

*To those with big dreams, please trust and
be patient in the process of your life.*

Don't let your desires consume you.

PROLOGUE

"There's nothing wrong with wanting more, but when you force things with magic, it has a way of snapping back when you least expect it," my dad said. It was something he often reminded me. Today, his words were quickly followed by my mother's: "Yes, Chyna, you do have magic, and with that magic you have the power to make a real impact, to truly help people. So why are you wasting your time chasing after some fairytale lifestyle? Seriously, what more could you possibly want?" she asked, slapping her thighs for emphasis.

"I want a lot more, Ma! What's the point of having the ability to reach the stars if all you're going to do is sit on earth and forever gaze at them! We are blessed that we can do anything we want! Why not take advantage of that?" I pleaded.

"Look child, just because you can do something doesn't mean you always should. Everything you do has consequences and karma! You need to seriously humble yourself or the law of things will do it for you! Yes, we are special, but we are still humans, and we must abide by the laws of society in order to fit in and not be outcasts."

"This isn't ancient times, Ma! We're in the twenty-first century. No one burns witches at the stake anymore!" I let out a soft chuckle.

My mom gave me a cold-eyed stare. "That's not funny, Chyna. That history is real, and the past can always repeat itself. Even worse, you could be kidnapped and used for evil."

"Oh please! Dad, console your wife." I looked at my dad for backup. "Ma, you can be so dramatic sometimes."

"Dramatic! Ha, look who's talking!"

My dad walked up behind my mom and placed his hand on her shoulder, indicating whose side he had taken.

I scoffed and ran upstairs to my bedroom, slamming the door before throwing myself onto the bed and wailing into my pillow. I couldn't wait to move out of this house!

I loved my parents, but I couldn't stand my mom's old school way of thinking. And I couldn't live like this anymore.

Here I was at twenty-two, full of dreams and desires just waiting to burst out of me while living in this tiny-ass town in the middle of nowhere. How the hell was I supposed to become a famous hairstylist in this country bumpkin town?

I stroked the soft fur along the back of my beloved cat, Neli, a beautiful black Bombay with bright yellow eyes and a white patch resembling a full moon on top of her head. In response, she rubbed her back against my arm.

"Damn, if only you could talk. But I know what you're thinking: *we gotta get the hell outta here and chase these dreams before it's too late.* Am I right? Okay, just give me ten more minutes of sulking."

Meow.

A few minutes later, I opened my laptop and got to work. First things first, I had to figure out where I needed to be.

Honestly, it didn't even matter. As long as I was in a big city with lots of opportunities, I should be fine.

I started to revamp my resume. I graduated with a bachelor's degree in political science and was currently working as a paralegal at a small law firm owned by one of my dad's childhood friends. I should have been trying to get into law school but forget that. Law is not my passion.

Ever since I was young, I wanted to own a hair salon.

Growing up, I used to love watching TV, not just for the entertaining plots but to marvel at the actors' hair and style. I used to study the popular hair shows for inspiration and to learn about the hair industry.

While frequenting hair salons with my mom, I loved watching how everything was done, from the perms and silk presses to the sew-ins and braids. I needed to learn it all. And when I wasn't following the stylist's every move, I was reading up on all the latest styles in the hair magazines. I would take a mental picture of the hairdos and try to recreate them on myself.

I loved going to my cousin's house to practice different hairstyles on her—not just for the little tip my aunt would give me, but for the experience, so I could try them on myself later.

Why didn't I go to hair school? Why did I give in when my parents pressured me to pick a career that would be reliable and guarantee me a steady income?

Now, here I was with this law background trying to pick up the pieces of my childhood dreams.

Should I just move to a big city and become a hairstylist? I did have some experience as a hairdressing assistant/apprentice. I often snuck into the salon after school or on weekends to help out and, more importantly, to learn some valuable skills. But since I wasn't officially an assistant, no beauty school would consider me accredited.

I sighed, as I drummed my fingers on the bed. I could move to Los Angeles and work under a big stylist as an apprentice. But how would I get those connections? And where would I live once I got there? I logged into my Zillow account to look up homes in LA.

DAMN!

Two million! I didn't need a house yet, though, so, I concentrated on looking for a high-rise apartment.

OH, HELL NO!

The only acceptable high-rises with enough space to fit my big dreams cost more for one month's rent than my total savings. It looked like I would be stuck in this small ass town forever.

I fell back onto my bed feeling defeated.

I had to come up with a plan or my dream of becoming a big-time celebrity hair stylist would never happen.

How would I pull it off? It definitely wasn't something I could make happen overnight. But...I stared at the lamp sitting on the desk in front of me. With one blink, I turned it on. Cue devious smile.

Of course it was going to happen! I'm a witch, and with my magic, I had the ultimate cheat code to attract whatever I want!

CHAPTER 1

I could feel the hair on the back of my neck rising as I sat uncomfortably in front of my parents. I had just broken the news to them that they didn't have to worry about their only child anymore, because she was moving a few states away.

"Ha! I know that's a lie! Ain't no way!" My mom chuckled as if I was telling a funny story.

"What do you mean you're moving? Where could you possibly be moving to?" My dad had such a worried look on his face.

"I'll be fine. I'm grown, and it's about time I moved out of the nest and made a life for myself. I found a nice cheap little apartment in LA, and I've saved enough to cover my move and at least three months' rent," I reassured them.

"But, if you want to help me cover more than that, then it would be highly appreciated." I gave my dad the biggest, sweetest puppy eyes I could muster, hoping to secure more money for another month's rent and a few necessities for my new place.

"Chyna, we don't mind helping you out, but how are you going to afford to live on your own?" He furrowed his brow in concern.

"I got a job, Dad."

"How?" My mom jumped up, startling Neli, who ran under the couch.

"Oh, it was easy. I had two virtual interviews, and they loved me. I'm going to be a paralegal at a law firm." I looked away from my mom's glaring eyes and started to pick at the peppermints we had in a bowl on the living room table.

"Oh? How did you pull that off, Chyna?" My mom's tone of voice and the stern look she gave me told me she understood exactly how.

"With my amazing charm and top-notch personality, which I inherited from my beautiful mom and charismatic dad." I stretched the corners of my mouth into a big, adorable smile in the hopes it would minimize my mom's anger.

"I know you didn't do what I think you did! Tell me you didn't use magic to secure a job! That's wrong! It's against the rules and out of pocket!"

"What rules, Ma? Why should I be *in pocket* when I have the ability to be out of it? What's the point of having magic if I can't use it for my own benefit?" I stomped my foot like the disapproving child I was.

"It's not to be used to manipulate and…what's the word you kids say now a days? Finesse. You can't finesse the natural way of the world. You can use your magic to help others. You just can't use it for yourself."

"Oh, like you do?" I asked, cutting my eyes at her.

"Exactly!" she said, cutting her eyes right back.

My mom had a real smug look on her face now, as if she hadn't used her magic to fund our current lifestyle. No, we weren't living it up in a mansion, but we were pretty well off. We were able to afford a nice house in a great neighborhood plus three cars. We didn't want for much.

And how did she do it?

Magic!

That's right. My slick and sly mom was a seasoned therapist. Well known and appreciated in this small town, she had worked as a therapist for over two decades and was in high demand.

The way she used her magic?

Whenever she had a patient, she counseled them just like any other therapist. But near the end of the session, she always encouraged her patients to take a few minutes to meditate on what was just discussed.

While her patients were busy meditating, she would conjure up a spell to heal, or I should say "temporarily heal", any major issues they were having at the time.

The result? Her patients tended to leave each session feeling like a huge weight had been lifted off their shoulders and they were ready to take on the world. That is until a few days later when the weight and pressures of life returned. She couldn't heal them fully because then there would be no more income.

"In order to keep my steady income, I need my patients to always feel the urge to return and vent about their problems because it relieves their stress. It works for them, and it works for me. I'm not God. I can't heal them. But I can help a little." My mom believed that this was very helpful and in no way harmful.

"This is honest work, Chyna, and it's similar to other types of therapy too. No one can help someone fully heal from trauma or erase their stress, but I help them work through it easier. They might be able to fully heal one day, but it would take a few sessions. But that doesn't change the fact that what I do is normal and honest work."

She was doing some real verbal gymnastics to convince me.

Well, that was just fine. Because if what she was doing could be considered honest work, then that meant that me finessing my way into a job to save my employers the time and stress of doing more interviews was honest work as well.

It was good magic, which was what my mom liked to call hers.

"It's okay Ma, I took a page out of your book. Good magic was used to secure me a stable job to make me an honest salary. At least I'm not using magic to rob a bank." Although, life would be so much easier if I could use my magic to rob a bank.

My mom let out a deep sigh and shook her head, raising her hands to her temples.

"Well, I guess what's done is done. I'm happy you found a job and I'm glad you're going to continue being a paralegal. That's what pays the bills, honey. Now, I know that you have big dreams about being a hairstylist, but you can still pursue those hobbies while making a living."

My dad gave me a big hug. "Don't worry too much about your expenses. I'll send you some money to get you on your feet."

"Thanks, Dad!"

"I'm kind of sad, you know? My only child, my only daughter, moving away to a big city by herself. Not gonna lie, I'm worried. I guess I just have to trust that I raised you right," my dad said.

My mom let out another sigh and joined in the hug. "And I know that when you make your mind up, that's it. There is no telling you to reconsider. But I think this will be good for you. It'll give you time to grow on your own and learn some valuable lessons. It'll also give me and your dad a chance to take some baecations."

"Uh-uh, who taught you that word?" I tugged my lips into a smirk.

"My younger patient, Vanessa. She keeps me up to date with all the new lingo."

I stepped back and took a good look at my parents. My dad was tall and lean with a shiny bald head. I don't know when I stopped paying attention, but now I noticed he had quite a few sprinkles of gray hair on his beard.

When I looked over at mom who was rocking her luscious fro, I noticed that she had a few gray hairs too, but not as many as my dad. And even though she was in her early fifties, she looked so good for her age. Her toned, radiant, brown skin shone today just like it always did when I was a child. And as her daughter, I knew I was going to age just as gracefully.

I bent down and scooped up Neli, who was trying to sneak off.

"I won't be alone, though. I'll be taking Neli with me."

"That's perfect. I've been wanting to get a dog for the longest time," my dad said, raising his hands into the air as if he'd just won an award.

"Ohhhh, I'm going to miss my baby. Please take good care of her."

"Ma, who are you talking to? Me or Neli?"

My mom chuckled and left the room with my dad. I could hear him discussing what kind of dog he was thinking of getting as I stood rooted to the spot, holding Neli.

Bittersweet feelings swept over me as I realized that in two weeks, I wouldn't be here anymore.

Those two weeks flew by so fast I could barely remember them. I had a dim memory of my dad discussing my lease with my future apartment manager. I also had faint memories of my mom trying to toss out all my favorite items in order to make everything fit into the moving truck. She even tried to throw away my old spelling bee trophies from middle school.

"Uh-uh Ma, I need those!"

She huffed. "For what exactly? You're turning into a hoarder. These are too old for you to be hanging onto. Save some room in your new apartment for new rewards and memories. Besides, I'm not sure you can fit much into that new place of yours."

"Fine, just keep them here for me."

"Nope. Once you leave, I'm converting half of this into my meditation room, and your dad wants to turn his half into a movie room."

"I can't believe it! Y'all have been waiting for me to move out, huh?"

A few days later, we placed the last box on the moving truck.

"That's all of it," I said as I looked back at my home, feeling a tug at my heart.

"You sure you don't want us to drive up there with you?" my dad asked as he finished hooking up my car to the truck with the help of one of the movers.

"No, it should be fine. Once I have my apartment all decked out, I'll send out your invites." I gave my dad a big hug before turning to my mom.

"Oh my…I can't believe this is happening so fast."

My mom ran toward me and held me tightly. Even though she could really work my nerves, and we always butted heads about how magic should be handled, I would deeply miss her wisdom and her sense of humor.

"I love you so much."

"I love you too, Chyna. I know you're going to make us proud and have an amazing life. I can't wait to come visit. I'll be checking for flights ASAP."

"A broomstick would be quicker," I said. We both let out a snicker.

We'd often watch movies about witches and make fun of some of the stereotypical tropes that we would see.

"Ha! Imagine flying a broom to another country. Must be nice!" My mom loved mocking fake witches on the big screen.

"Neli is a sensitive little thing, so please take care of her. Make sure to feed her a balanced mixture of wet and dry food. Use the organic brands so she'll be healthy."

"I know, Ma. Who do you think took care of Neli while you were working? Certainly not dad."

"Neli will be fine. That cat has a few more lives left in her," my dad joked as he rubbed my mom's shoulder.

Once inside the truck, I took one last look at my home in the rear-view mirror before turning down the street and heading toward my new life.

Thanks to my mom, I wouldn't have to make any stops on this fourteen-hour drive. She had put a nice little spell on the vehicle that would prevent it from needing gas. I had my favorite podcast downloaded, and I was ready to go.

I made perfect time. I arrived right when the leasing office opened and waited outside the truck for the manager to prepare my keys.

From where I was standing, I had a good view of my apartment, unit 2212. It wasn't a high-rise, but it would do.

The apartment was very small. 560 square feet to be exact. It was a renovated studio with a big window and hardwood floors.

I wasted no time in figuring out where I wanted everything to go. I still needed to buy a cute curtain to separate my bedroom from my living room, but my bed would go in the corner, and a small café table with two chairs would be squeezed in near the kitchen to serve as my dining table. I even had a tiny balcony to enjoy whenever I needed some fresh air.

"I know it's smaller than the big spaces you're used to in the country, but this is a really good deal. I think you could make great use of the space," the tall blond apartment manager said before handing me my keys.

"Thank you! I think I'll be just fine," I said.

Correction, I didn't think it. I knew it. This tiny closet of an apartment was a temporary stepping stone. I had a master plan, and I didn't plan to stay here longer than a year.

The men my dad hired to bring in my heavy items like my dresser and bed arrived an hour later. While they were setting up my bed, I grabbed one very important box from the back of the truck and placed it on the kitchen counter. Neli sat beside my feet, staring up at me curiously.

"Don't worry, Neli, we won't be here for long. I promise." I opened the box and carefully removed a large, dark brown book that had gold and red detailing on the sides. The cover of the book was blank, but the insides held my future.

This book—the very book my mom had kept hidden away in her secret room in the basement—was now mine.

The room, undetectable by regular eyes, looked like a simple wine cellar. But with the right words and knowing which wine bottle to push, a passage behind a row of bottles opened, leading into a classic witch's lair full of spell books and potion-filled glass bottles, a few of which I had snagged along with this book, right here.

I flipped through the pages and landed on the spell I was searching for. There in deep red ink it read, "The Love Spell." I hopped up onto the kitchen counter and began to study the pages as if I had midterms tomorrow.

Four hours later and my new home was finally starting to come together. My bed was exactly where it should be with Neli's right beside it, and my TV was firmly mounted on the wall. The antique rug my grandmother had purchased on a trip to Morocco was laying in the middle of the living room surrounded by three ottomans. I still needed to make a run to the store to get a few things, but that could wait until tomorrow.

My Uber Eats order had an ETA of thirty minutes. So, I turned up the volume on my speaker which was playing my favorite song before hopping into the shower to wash the grime from the move off of me.

As the water ran down my body, I began to imagine what my life would look like in the next year.

I couldn't stay in this tiny, cramped apartment. I was in LA. I needed a high-rise with a view. I needed to be in a furnished modern suite that screamed luxury living. And I had the perfect plan to pull it off.

I stepped out of the shower, dried myself off, and immediately applied my favorite vanilla-scented body butter. I removed my shower cap to let my leave-out from my sew-in breathe.

The twenty-six-inch Cambodian kinky straight hair extension bundles I had bought from hairstylist, Hairoholic, that I found on the popular social media app, Pic-Talk, matched my silk-pressed hair perfectly.

As I examined myself in the mirror, admiring my beautiful brown skin and my dark brown eyes, I noticed a few pimples on my cheek starting to show. So, I repeated the spell that my mom had taught me when I started going through puberty in middle school.

"Place your finger on the pimples you want to erase and repeat after me," my had mom said in an all-knowing tone.

Once I removed my fingers, the bumps were gone, and my skin looked as radiant and dewy as ever. No need for a skincare routine if you had magic. Despite this, I followed up with some self-care to wash away the makeup and keep my skin in good health.

I relaxed on my bed and began skimming through the book of spells to learn some new tricks.

In order for this love spell to work, I needed to strengthen my magic. You couldn't just recite spells in your head or even out loud without practice. You needed to give your magic a workout just like you gave your legs a workout at the gym.

Magic needed to be toned and developed to make your spells strong, and you needed to practice avoiding any backfiring. I learned that lesson very young, and I was not going to make the same mistake again.

Okay, this one is doable. It was a simple levitation spell that could move items and even open doors. I'd had some practice with it, but I needed to be sharper.

I started to practice on some cups that were sitting on the kitchen counter. I said the spell out loud and used my pointer finger as a guide.

"There we go."

The red coffee mug lifted an inch off the counter.

"Now come to me."

I flicked my finger toward myself and watched as the mug shakily moved toward me.

"No, that's not it."

I plucked the mug from the air and placed it back on the counter to try again. After five tries, I was able to move it toward me without any wobbles.

So next, I filled the mug with water. My mind focused intensely on the mug as it floated its way toward my open hand.

"That's it!"

There were a few ripples in the water, but it had landed in my hand with no spills, and even better, with no vocal spell.

Don't get me wrong, a vocal spell could be powerful. But who wanted to announce to the world that they were using magic?

Hey everyone! Look at me! I'm a witch using magic. I'm casting a spell on you!

Nope! I couldn't have that. I needed to be sneaky and calculated to pull off my ultimate plan. And I also needed a target.

I ran over to my computer and started looking up NBA players in LA. For close to two hours, I did nothing but familiarize myself with the sport, because I was clueless when it came to anything sports related. I vaguely remembered watching some games with my dad, because it was his favorite way to unwind after a long day at his thriving barbeque restaurant.

I checked each player's stats, income, and even their Pic-Talk pages to narrow my search down to three potential targets.

One was a white guy, who wasn't bad looking at all. He didn't post much on his Pic-Talk, but he had just signed a half-a-million-dollar contract.

The other guy was cute, extremely tatted. But his red flag was that he had recently had a baby.

Now the last guy…I'm not sure if it was how fine he was, the way he carried himself, or the fact that his net worth was $15 million and he a rising star that everyone had their eyes on, but he lit my interest like a new candle from a sale at Bath and Bodywork's.

His name was Chicago Moon, and he was a twenty-four-year-old from Houston, Texas, who had just posted a picture from his high-rise two days ago with a gorgeous view of downtown LA.

CHAPTER 2

Navigating the streets of LA was hard. The city was huge compared to my small town. I won't even start on the traffic. It was insane.

The thing that really got me was the easy access to stores on almost every street you turned. That might sound totally normal, but my hometown was so small, there were only about ten stores within a ten-minute drive from our house. If we needed anything niche, that meant at least a twenty-five-minute drive to a larger—but still small—city.

So, being in LA surrounded by clothing stores, endless restaurants, and even a variety of grocery stores had my mind blown.

I spent hours visiting every store I could find until I was finally able to complete my apartment shopping list.

My home was ready, and I was looking forward to cooking a nice meal and putting my new fancy stoneware to use.

I even did a little shopping for Neli, getting her some new patterned ribbons to tie around her neck along with some treats.

I pulled out the new fishy smelling treats and shook the bag, waiting for her to jump for an opportunity to taste.

"Neli, come try your new treats."

Silence.

"Neli?" This was odd. Where on earth was she? I checked under the bed, in the closet, and in the bathroom.

She was nowhere.

Panic washed over me once I noticed the window cracked open with just enough room for a cat to squeeze its little ass through and make a break for it.

"No! She wouldn't," I whispered in a hushed voice.

Neli did have a tendency to casually waltz out of the house back home, but it hadn't been a big deal.

We'd given her the freedom to explore because there wasn't much trouble she could get into. We knew all our neighbors and they adored Neli. Some even purchased their own cat food for when she visited.

Neli had known where home was, so she would wander for the day, but would always come back for dinner and evening cuddles.

I took a deep breath to calm myself, before realizing we were in a new city now, and I wasn't sure if she was even familiar with the scent of our new home yet. I didn't know how these LA streets were going to treat her.

Fear erupted inside me again, and I rushed out of the apartment with her favorite toy, ringing it frantically while screaming her name. My embarrassment was nonexistent. I was more concerned about losing a member of my family.

"Neli, where are you?" I screamed like a mad woman.

I ran down the stairs and began searching the bushes beneath my window and under the nearby parked cars.

Gone.

My only family member in the city was gone.

Hot tears ran down my face as I remembered the first day I had held Neli when I was a child. She looked exactly the same now as she did then.

No one in my family really knew how old Neli was, as she had been with us since my mom was a child. The perks of being a cursed cat assigned to a witch were that they never aged. Instead, they became a family heirloom, passed down with every generation.

I walked back to my apartment feeling defeated and trying to decide what my next steps should be. My mom might have a spell that could track Neli down or make her come back home.

"Um, hey girl, is this the Neli you've been crying about?"

I looked up to see a young woman with deep brown skin and a full head of bouncy tight curls staring down at me from the top of the staircase. She sported a pair of chic red, cat-eye glasses. She looked about my age and she was holding Neli.

"Does this little cutie belong to you?" she asked as she rubbed the top of Neli's spotted head.

"Oh my God, yes! That's my Neli! I've been looking all over for her!"

She sucked her teeth and said in a teasing voice, "Dang! I thought I was going to be able to keep her."

"No way. That's my only family here. I need her. But if you want to co-parent and help with her expensive organic kitty food, I will gladly grant you weekends," I joked.

"Now, how expensive is this organic kitty food? She better not be eating better than me!"

I giggled and reached out to rub Neli's head.

"Oh, you must be the new person who moved in across from me. I'm Cali, what's your name?" she asked.

"My name is Chyna, and yes, I did just move here. Are you from LA?"

"Nah, I'm from H-town, but I've lived here for about four years now."

"Really? How do you like living here?"

She shrugged, "I can honestly say it's very different from the South. The people here aren't as friendly, but the opportunities and the beaches are something special. I moved here for work opportunities. I'm an apartment finder, but I'm trying to get into selling homes, million-dollar homes. What better place to do that than a city where the majority of the residents are famous people with money."

"Oh, that's cool. I work as a paralegal, but doing hair is my passion. I want to open a hair salon one day and become a celebrity stylist."

"You can definitely get connected with some celebrity stylists here if that's the avenue you want to take."

"I hope so, girl. I don't even know where to start. I'm from a small town so I'm kind of already overwhelmed just being here. I've traveled to big cities before but living in one day to day is a different story. I'm ashamed to admit I haven't been to the beach since I was little. So, I'm excited to go do that soon, but I'm also a little nervous."

"Wait, hold up." She stepped back. "Going to a beach is a must here. It's so pretty and clean compared to what I'm used to seeing back home. You've got to go. It'll become your new weekly thing."

She shook her beautiful curls. "We are going!" she said as she wagged her finger back and forth. "What are you doing tomorrow? It's Saturday, you don't work, do you?"

"No, I don't start until next week."

"Perfect! Take my number down. I'll be your personal tour guide."

I raised my eyebrow, "For the free?"

Cali narrowed her eyes, "You can pay me in food. I can always eat."

I walked back into my apartment smiling from ear to ear. I'd just made a new friend. I felt like a kid again, making friends at school.

Well, at least trying to make friends. I had had a hard time making friends growing up because I knew I was different. With my mom constantly reminding me that I had to be careful, it made it really difficult for me to grow close to anyone.

I did my best to learn boundaries so I could avoid any magical mishaps. I never attended sleepovers and only went to birthday parties when I could be strictly supervised by my mom.

But some shit happened anyway, and I had to move to a new town and start making friends all over again. This hindered my ability to make long-lasting connections and friendships. I found myself in a friendless slump most school years. I was a loner, never feeling comfortable enough to open up to any one at school.

So, after a while, people stopped trying to befriend me. But I wasn't completely alone. I had my cousins, who I would visit regularly.

Having magic was a blessing because it enabled me to make things happen, but it was also a curse because it made me an outcast.

I had a hard time fitting in with people because, according to my mom, I couldn't just tell everyone I was a witch who knew magic spells. Most people wouldn't have accepted that. They would have circled me as if I was a freak and chastised me like they had before.

Times are absolutely different now. There's an entire category on Pic-Talk called Witch-Talk, which is dedicated to witches and witch admirers who watch and save videos of spells and potions they want to try.

Even I would occasionally jot down spells I'd found on Witch-Talk and send them to my mom to confirm whether they were valid. She would respond with either: "That's bull crap. They don't know what they're talking about!" or "Oh yeah, that's what my mom used to do. Who taught them that?"

If I wanted Cali to know my secret, I wasn't sure how the subject would even come up. I had a good feeling about her, though, so I felt like she might just laugh it off.

But I didn't know her at all, so who knew how she would react.

Maybe it was best to let this little friendship fizzle out. That's what I usually did because I didn't know how they would react.

Besides, I had a bigger mission on the horizon than cultivating a friendship. I needed to make money and make my real dreams come true: marrying a rich man and becoming a successful hairstylist. And yes, he had to be rich, because that would make it easier for me to achieve my goals.

I poured myself a glass of wine, sat on my bed, and began scrolling through Highrise.com to find my dream high-rise condo.

A few minutes later, I got a text from Cali, "Hey girl, what time do you want to head out to the beach tomorrow? Do you want to do brunch first? I know some good spots close by."

I tried to squash my smile as I read the message.

I needed to be cautious, but going to brunch and having a new friend to get mani-pedis with would be awesome.

That set my smile loose, and I immediately texted back, "Yes! Brunch, please! Mimosas, chicken, and waffles, I need it all!"

The next morning, we were clinking our mimosa glasses over a table filled with our brunch favorites.

"I'm so happy you're a foodie like me! So many people here act like they don't like to eat anything but salads, and I can't stand it. Back in Houston, we go down on brunch! Food in general. We like to eat!" Cali said before taking a few more gulps of her mimosa.

"My dad owns a barbeque restaurant, and he loves to cook. I miss his food, especially his Sunday funday breakfast: cinnamon French toast, cheesy eggs, candied bacon, skillet potatoes, and grits."

Cali raised her eyebrows, "Dang! Every Sunday?"

"Yep!"

"I haven't been able to find anyone that makes grits like they do back home. I miss my catfish and grits with a side of hookah." Cali shook her head as she reminisced.

"Catfish and grits? Y'all eat that together?"

"You never had catfish and grits before? Girl, you are missing out!" Cali threw up her hands in shock.

"We do catfish and spaghetti, not grits," I said in a matter-of-fact tone.

"Spaghetti? Oh, I've heard about that but never tried it."

We talked more about food until the bill arrived. We discovered similarities and differences in our tastes and even exchanged recipes.

Then the next thing I knew, we were going on about fashion.

"I used to want to be a fashion stylist when I was younger, but I realized I enjoyed doing hair way more. Unfortunately, my family wasn't going for it because they didn't believe if it would bring me steady money like being a lawyer would," I said during our walk to the beach.

"I can definitely see it. I love the outfit you're rocking now."

I was wearing a short-sleeved shirt with pink and white flowers which was partially unbuttoned to show my white bikini top. The shirt was half tucked into the light denim shorts that made my butt pop, along with a pair of pink kitten heels. I was dripping with layers of gold jewelry, some with gems that matched colors in my shirt.

"Thanks, girl. I like your style too."

Cali wore khaki shorts that accentuated her long, thick, toned thighs, a beige funnel-neck tank top, and brown sandals. She was also adorned with gold accessories: long layered necklaces and bracelets. She had a somewhat preppy style to her. She wore her curly hair in a high puff ball with gold bobby pins on each side of her head.

By the time we arrived at the beach, we were discussing hair.

"Nothing is better than a fresh hairstyle! I would change my hair every week if my paycheck would allow it," Cali said with a laugh.

"Same! My coworkers at my old firm loved it when I changed hairstyles. They would eat it up: 'Wow, Chyna, you just had a short bob, and now you have long braids. How long did that take?'"

"Oh, my God, it's so annoying. I get braids every summer and they still ask the same questions each time! 'How long did it take this time? How many people worked on it? How long are you going to keep it in?' Like shut up please. Go ask Google, not me!"

Once we got to the beach, we found an empty, flat patch of sand and sat down to soak in the beautiful view and perfect weather.

A few people were scattered nearby, reading or sunbathing, but not close enough to disturb us.

"This is so nice and peaceful."

I slipped my shades on and took in a deep breath.

"Yes, it is. I try to come out here at least once a week. It really helps me to relax. I love coming on Sundays to meditate too."

"Thanks for inviting me out. I really appreciate it. I was a little worried it might be hard to meet people to hang out with, so I'm glad we were able to connect so easily." I smiled at Cali before looking back out at the view.

"No problem, thanks for coming. I know it was a random invite, but you seemed cool, and I don't know, I had a good feeling about you. Besides I know how it is when you move. It's hard to make friends especially when you're out of school. I've been lucky enough to make some new friends out here, but it took a while. I was lonely for a bit before I found some cool people."

I rose from my spot and started to take off my top and jeans. "Well since we're here, let's get in!"

Cali twisted her face up at me as if I'd made a bad joke. "I'm not getting in there. I don't know how to swim."

"I don't either. So, you just come here all the time and sit on the beach? You've never gotten in the water once?"

Cali got up from her spot and put her hands on her hip. "Nope. But fine, for you, I'll put my feet in."

The water felt great as it splashed over my body. I submerged myself, being careful not to lose my balance and get dragged out to sea. Cali went in up to her knees, kicking and splashing with her feet.

I had always loved the water; maybe it was the water sign in me. I moved my fingers in time with the waves, making little ripples in the water.

I turned my back to Cali and performed a spell that I used to do while taking bubble baths when I was younger. I grabbed a handful of water and molded it into the shape of an orb. I was amazed that I could still do it.

While holding the orb, I used my pointer finger to pull spikes of water from the orb, making it resemble a morning star ball.

"Did you find something?" Cali walked up behind me so suddenly that I gasped, and the orb spilled through my fingers and back into the ocean.

"No, no, I was just playing with the water."

That was a close call.

"Look what I found!" Cali held up a large, iridescent pink seashell the size of her hand.

"Wow, that's so pretty. Where did you find that? I want one."

Cali pointed to a spot in the water. "Over here. There's a bunch more."

There were so many shells in different colors, sizes, and shapes. I collected about fifteen before finally calling it quits.

My hands were full as we walked back to Cali's car.

"Did you really need to grab that many?"

"Yes! I'm going to put them in a bowl in my bathroom and give some to my mom and dad when they come to town."

"So, your bathroom is going to have the typical sea theme?" Cali teased.

I rolled my eyes with some embarrassment and mumbled, "Maybe."

The next thing I knew, my seashells were flying toward the ground. Momentarily distracted by Cali's comment, I had tripped on a rock.

Before I knew what I was doing, I said a spell in my head; the same one my mom used when she accidentally dropped a dish or her phone.

The spell causes the surface of the ground to soften and lessen the impact when something falls.

Sure enough, the seashells fell to the ground without shattering or sustaining a single crack.

Phew!

As I bent down to pick them up, Cali came over to help.

"It's crazy that they didn't break." She picked up a shell and studied it.

"Oh yeah, that is crazy. These shells must be super durable," I said, letting out a soft giggle.

"No way. Seashells can be fragile, especially on concrete like this. That's so weird. I guess you're lucky."

"Yeah, lucky me."

I took the shell from Cali and placed it with the others in my towel to keep them secure and prevent them from falling again.

Another close call.

We arrived back at our apartment building and said our goodbyes before separating in the hallway.

Once inside, I found a glass bowl to display my shells on my bathroom counter, and I hopped into the shower, taking a few minutes to reflect on the close calls I'd had today.

I enjoyed hanging out with Cali, but I definitely needed to do better at masking my magic. She had been really confused and weirded out by the shells not breaking.

As I got out the shower, I reached for my towel.

I glanced at the water dripping down my body and recited a spell out loud to gather all those water droplets in the palm of my hand.

I fashioned the water into a big ball, tossed it back into the shower, and watched as it burst and flowed down the drain.

Perfect, no need to use a towel now.

CHAPTER 3

"Here I go," I said in a hushed voice as I pushed my way through the revolving glass door and stepped into the lobby of my new workspace. It was a huge, forty-two-story glass building located in downtown. I walked over to the receptionist to let her know where I needed to be.

"Someone will be down to get you," the main receptionist said as she hung up the phone. She was middle-aged with a cute short bob and a kind smile.

My eyes surveyed the lobby.

There was a small sitting area that was decorated in a modern style including a beige couch, a couple of tan-colored patterned chairs, a few small coffee tables, and various plants. Across from the reception desk, people were congregating in front of a row of elevators. Beyond the elevators were stairs leading down to a large pit area, but I couldn't see into it from where I was standing.

"Is this your first day? I've heard good things about the law firm here, so I think you'll like it," the receptionist said before glancing toward the stairway.

"Down those stairs, you'll find the food hall. There are a bunch of little restaurants down there where you can get breakfast and lunch. I believe the law firm provides a stipend for you to use at any restaurant here."

"Really? That's great! It's my first day and I'm a little intimidated already. It's way bigger than my old law firm."

I was fiddling with my fingers, displaying my nervousness. I stopped myself then placed my hands on my thighs to calm my nerves.

"Don't be nervous. You look great by the way."

I was wearing a midnight blue blazer with a long satin tie wrapped around the waist, and pants in the same satin fabric. Around my neck was a gold pendant necklace that had a cluster of small diamonds on it, and my hair was in a long, low sleek ponytail with my baby hairs in simple swoops. She was right, I did look great. So, there was no reason to be nervous.

"Thank you," I said with a newfound confidence.

"Chyna Cole?" I turned my head and saw the same woman I had interviewed with, the lead paralegal, Sasha Mackie. Her hair was styled in a natural twist out, and she was wearing a brown plaid suit.

"Nice to finally meet you in person." She extended her hand, and I did the same, giving it a firm shake like my dad had taught me.

"Hi, it's so nice to meet you. I'm very excited to meet the team and start working," I said, code-switching seamlessly.

"Great! Everyone is excited to see you. Follow me."

The mass of people milling around the elevators had withered out by the time we got to them. Sasha pushed the button for the thirty-first floor, and we shot up.

"How was it getting settled in? Are you liking LA so far?"

"I'm loving LA. It's far more expansive than my hometown, so I'm looking forward to exploring it."

"That's great. There's so much to explore in this city, so once you've checked a few spots out, I'm sure you'll get familiar with where everything is," she said while fixing her blazer.

We arrived on our floor, and she led me through rows of white desks separated by dividers. Some of the dividers were decorated with pictures of children, spouses, and pets. When we got to the end of the floor, we entered a meeting room where five other people were present.

"Hey everyone, this is our new paralegal, Chyna Cole!"

Everyone rose to shake my hand and introduce themselves. After the introductions, we discussed the current cases they were working on. Sasha was appointed to integrate me into two of their ongoing cases. After the meeting was over, she showed me around the office and then led me to my desk.

"Don't worry about the cases for now. We're going to set you up with a few training modules for the next few days. When that's completed, we'll dive into it," Sasha said while helping me set up my work computer.

This place was so much better than my previous job. Not only was it bigger, but it was more professional and had better benefits. My team was only made up of six people, but there were about forty other employees on the floor working for other teams. Each team handled different cases for different industries and types of law. My team focused mainly on tax law for the technology and software industry.

Two weeks in, I was fully acclimated to the new work culture. I was now friendly with the receptionist, Shelly, who would often keep me up to date on the latest gossip in the building. She was a real comedian, who kept me laughing during my breaks.

I was getting to know my coworkers and quickly determining who I liked and didn't like. Sasha, our lead paralegal, was great to work with. She was funny and the queen of code-switching.

"Sure thing, John. I'll get that motion drafted and sent to you shortly." Sasha lit up a bright smile before closing the door of the conference room she and I were sitting in. As soon as she closed the door, she turned to me and rolled her eyes. "Girl, I can't wait to hurry up and get the hell off this case! I can't stand working with John's annoying ass."

I leaned back in my chair and shook my head. "I bet! That man looks like a headache."

We stared over at John through the window while he was talking to another attorney. He was a short white man with a bald head that didn't help to hide the large green veins constantly popping out of his temple. It could have been because of the tight button-down shirts and slacks he wore. If he bent the wrong way, he would lose a few buttons.

We looked back at each other and burst into laughter.

"I'm so happy you're here at our firm. If you couldn't already tell, we needed some more seasoning on our team."

She wasn't wrong. Aside from myself, Sasha, and one Black attorney, James, we were the only Black people on our team. Added to the three other Black employees who worked on different teams, we were the only speckles of brown in the entire firm.

Although I wasn't working on James' cases, we had brief chats in the break room. He was married to a Black woman and had two beautiful daughters. His wife was a food influencer in LA, who I followed to get the latest news on the new and yummy restaurants around the city.

As I left the conference room to take a bathroom break, I bumped into the other attorney I was working with on a different case, Sarah. She was a petite white woman with long blond hair and pale blue eyes.

"Oh, your shoes are so cute, Sarah."

She was wearing a pair of bourbon-colored kitten heels that paired really well with her cream-colored slacks and oversized white blouse.

"Thanks, Chyna, yours are too," Sarah replied while slowly turning red.

Sarah was easy to work with. Even though she was timid, she was straightforward with what she needed and expected. Rumor had it that in the courtroom, she turned into a completely different woman. Her whole demeanor would change into an extremely confident woman who would not back down, even toward the judge.

As I walked back to my desk, I was stopped by Richard, a fellow paralegal with a permanent stick up his ass.

"Chyna, I'm not sure what you used to do at your little old firm, but at this firm we really like to focus on neatness."

He pulled out the binder of exhibits I had worked on the other day. It was a big binder filled with over 500 exhibits that I had printed, hole-punched, and put in the binder with labeled dividers for each exhibit. He opened the binder and flipped through a few pages. "Look here."

"Um, what's the problem, Richard?" I asked, not bothering to hide my irritation.

"You don't see that?" He pointed to the punched hole.

"The hole on this page is slightly off. The page is practically sticking out of the binder. I think you should reprint this page." He flipped through a few more pages. "Look, these are sticking out too. I really think you should reprint and re-punch these again."

"Richard, you're making it seem like the page is falling out of the binder or something. It's slightly off, but it doesn't look bad at all. But if it bothers you that much, then I can send you the pages so you can fix it." I sat down at my desk and turned to face my computer.

"No, sweetheart, I'm not going to do your job for you."

I slowly turned my chair around to face him again, letting out a sigh. "Richard, *sweetheart*, if you are looking for perfection in the pages of this binder, I think it would be best to take matters into your own hands and *perfect it*." I gave him a soft smile and he shot back a nasty glare.

Just then, John walked past, and Richard signaled to get his attention.

"John! Excuse me, but could you take a look at this binder?" He explained that, in his opinion, the binder had been "poorly" made.

John looked up from his paperwork, glanced at the binder, and then at Richard. With a stone-faced expression he said, "It looks fine, Richard."

Then he marched off to his office, shutting the door behind him.

Richard looked over at me, pursed his lips, and walked away.

Prick!

"He is such a dick. I don't know what his problem is with me," I ranted to Cali at dinner that night while stuffing my mouth with a piece of sushi.

"Mm-hmm, he sounds like one. Probably mad 'cause you look good and he doesn't," Cali said with a nod.

"You're right. He better leave me alone before he gets what's coming to him." I let out a chuckle thinking of all the spells I could use on Richard to keep him away from me.

"Girl, you're not going to do anything," Cali said, unaware of what I was capable of.

"You're right," I said while reading a text message from my mom, who was insisting I give her and my dad the green light to come visit. I shot her a text back letting her know I wasn't quite settled yet. I needed more time alone to explore and find my people.

"So, how is your boss? Are you getting along with him?" Cali asked as she dipped her sushi into an illegal amount of soy sauce.

"I mean, he's alright. He barely talks to me. I think he's awkward around bad bitches."

"Makes sense," Cali nodded.

"So how are things with you? Were you able to get that beauty influencer to move into that condo yet?" I asked.

Cali shook her head. "No, not yet. She's definitely stalling because of the price. She's from Alabama, so she isn't used to things being this expensive. But I think she'll sign the lease eventually."

I nodded in agreement, "She will. She doesn't want to miss out on that view. Girl, that commission is going to be crazy good."

"Right." Cali raised her sake cup, and I clicked mine with hers.

"But don't worry, once I get up there, I'm going to hire you as my realtor for my million-dollar property."

Cali raised a brow, "You want to be an influencer?"

I shrugged. "Yeah, I could do that too. But my main job would be celebrity hair stylist and basketball wife."

"Hold up now! You want to be a basketball wife? Oh girl, when you find one, please hook me up too," Cali joked.

"I got you, girl."

"Yeah, right," Cali laughed.

"I'm serious, Cali. By this time next year, I'm going to be the wife of an NBA champ." I gave Cali a serious look, letting her know this was not a game.

"Chyna, if that's your dream, then I say go for it. But how are you going to make it happen? You know those guys usually go for…" she flashed her eyes at a table of white women clinking their cups of sake. "Unless they met you in high school, your chances are very slim."

"Not mine," I said, showing my confidence. "I have a grand plan. Don't worry about the details, though. Just get ready because when it happens, I'm taking you with me. Shopping at all the designer stores, riding in sports cars, and sitting courtside."

A spark of excitement flickered inside me as I saw all my wants and desires flashing through my mind. Cali smiled and played along.

"A girls' trip to Turks and Caicos doesn't sound bad at all. Okay, Chyna! We're in LA. Anything could happen."

We continued eating and discussing what our lives would be like if we both dated successful basketball players. Our fantasies were as high as a skyscraper. We listed the type of cars, homes, jewelry, and luxury designer bags we would have.

"I definitely need a red and a pink Birkin!" Cali screamed in excitement.

"Girl, why just two? You could have a whole collection of Birkins and have your purse closet looking like a rainbow."

We might have been laughing and having a good time letting our imaginations run wild, but as I said earlier, I was serious. Dead serious. These weren't just dreams for me but manifestations.

CHAPTER 4

B y week three, I was tired of Richard's bullshit. He had messed with me long enough to give me ample time to practice and perfect my spells. After his latest rant about how "messy" my work was according to him, I'd had enough.

"You should make sure your handwriting is up to par when writing on these legal documents," Richard said in a matter-of-fact tone that made my stomach churn.

"I think my handwriting is just fine, but if you have a problem with it, then I would be more than glad to let you handle it," I said with a scowl on my face.

"Once again Chyna, I will not do your work for you." He had a smug look on his face, confirming that he enjoyed pestering me with silly issues.

He seemed intent on putting me in my place to show me that he was above me because he'd been at the firm longer than I had. He had automatically ranked me, my knowledge and experience beneath his from our very first encounter.

This, despite me implementing a new tracker system for our cases that helped us stay up to date with our tasks and on top of our deadlines. This, even though our boss had raved to our team about the great research I had conducted that had helped us push our case further. This, even though I had worked diligently with our most difficult client, who had bragged to our boss about how easy I had made the process for them. Despite all this, Richard refused to see me as an equal on the team because he still had the mindset of a teenager who didn't want a newbie to upstage his tenure with the company and the team. But at this point, I was sick and tired of it.

I tried to befriend him by inviting him to have lunch with me in the hopes that he would get to know me better and back off, but that failed! He was too uptight to have lunch with, since all he wanted to do was talk about work and boast about his extensive knowledge of our cases.

So, I tried a new tactic and complimented his fashion choices, even though I thought they sucked.

"Nice tie, Richard."

"Love the suit, Richard."

"Your haircut looks great, Richard."

"Those socks are so cool, Richard."

My reward: nothing but a cold, flat "thanks." There was no winning with this guy. My last resort was to just let him think he was a top-notch paralegal by gassing him up.

"Wow, Richard, you're so smart."

"You're so right about doing it this way."

"I need to take notes because you're obviously amazing at this kind of stuff."

That only made his remarks more condescending and annoying. I was fed up with his bullshit. Now it was time for payback, my way.

"You need to rewrite this Chyna, and make sure your handwriting is legible." Richard took a sip of the freshly brewed coffee he had poured into one of the paper cups from the break room.

"Sure thing, Richard."

He took another sip as he walked, and then I began to work my magic, literally. I closed my eyes and recited the same spell I had practiced many times before at home.

That's when I heard him scream. I opened my eyes to see Richard's coffee spilling down his neck and onto his crisp white shirt. The spell I used was a simple "hole in the cup" spell that created a tear in the cup, allowing the hot coffee to run out.

"OW! SHIT!" Richard yelped as he dropped the cup on the floor and ran to the restroom to clean himself up.

"Oh my God, how did that happen?" Sasha grabbed his cup and inspected it. "There's a hole in the cup. Be careful when using the cups, you all!"

"Oh wow. I hope he's okay," I said, turning to face my computer to hide the big smile on my face.

Richard returned to his desk an hour later, now wearing a company T-shirt he probably got from HR. I walked over to his desk to hand him the edited documents.

"How are you feeling? I hope you didn't get burned too badly." I gave him a soft smile while trying to hold in my laughter.

"I'm fine. I don't know how that happened."

Richard's face turned red as he grabbed the documents and turned his back to me.

"You oughtta be more careful, sweetheart."

After a full month of living in the city and starting my new job, life had been moving nice and steady. Cali and I had grown closer, which meant I had almost slipped up and gotten caught doing magic around her a few times.

Back at home, it was easy to use magic around family because they already knew and had magic themselves. So, it had been pretty difficult hiding it from her.

It was so convenient to use magic on a daily basis. The more I used it, the better and stronger it became.

I'd gotten so good now that I didn't even have to get out of the car to pump my own gas. I usually went to pump gas at night to avoid any spectators. I used magic to insert my card into the pump, enter my pin, open my gas tank, and lift the pump. I was able to do all that while scrolling on Pic-Talk, occasionally peeking at my mirrors to make sure no one was watching.

Meanwhile, at home things were constantly floating through the air: bottles of water when I was thirsty, household cleaning sprays and paper towels when a mess needed clearing, and my duster wiping things down before the dust even settled. It was truly amazing. I could be as lazy as I wanted, because I honestly didn't have the time to spend my days cleaning, especially when my cleaning tools could clean by themselves. I had more important things to focus on like finding a way to meet my target and making Richard's life at work hell. Out of the two, only one had been successful.

If making Richard's workdays a living hell was a class, I would have passed with flying colors. Now, I hadn't been a complete bitch, messing with the man for no reason. He had started it, but I would finish it. Even with all the coffee spills I created, he still managed to find time to piss me off.

He was pissing me off even more now because he was no longer using the paper cups. Instead, he was bringing in his own ceramic mug. It was a lot harder to create a hole in ceramic undetected even with magic.

But I'd found alternatives such as summoning spiders to appear in his desk. He hated spiders, but I loved his screams. I'd also managed to splatter him with bird poop a few times when he went outside for a smoke break. Lately, however, he'd been taking his break in his car. Maybe, I should set his car on fire.

Just kidding.

That would be taking it too far. Plus, I was having way too much fun as it was. And he was a dick, so it made me feel less guilty. Besides, technically, *I* wasn't doing anything. I was just sitting at my desk working while my magic had all the real fun.

I did start to feel a little guilty once, when I overheard him and Sasha talking.

And when I say overheard, I meant used a spell to increase my hearing range. With this spell, I was getting all the tea at work, from who was sleeping with whom to who was getting fired this week, to who was making bank. Spoiler: it was my boss with his fifth raise this year.

Anyway, I overheard Richard ranting to Sasha about how he'd been feeling cursed lately. He was thinking of having his reverend pray for him.

I did feel bad when I heard that.

But like I said, if he hadn't been such a dick then this wouldn't have been happening.

Richard plopped a fat binder onto my desk. "Chyna these need to be re-punched. You would think that after a month, you would be better at this by now."

"Yeah, I'm not that good at punching holes because I'm too busy helping win cases!" I said giving him a cocky smirk.

That's right, your girl had won a case! Not by myself of course, but with my team, Sasha, and our attorney Sarah. My co-workers were right, Sarah was badass. In the courtroom, she was a completely different person. She didn't look timid or smile once. Even after our win. Not until we left the courtroom.

"Wow, I can't believe we got that one. I was really scared the judge was going to rule in favor of the opposing counsel. He had a really good case," Sarah said with a big smile on her face.

"Sarah, you were amazing! It was so intense in there, and you took control of the judge." I was excited and full of adrenaline after seeing her win.

"Thanks, but I really couldn't have done it without you or Sasha. You both did the majority of the work. All I did was present it."

"I think I speak for both of us when I say that we couldn't have done that. I still get nervous just being in a courtroom, never mind presenting a case and going back and forth with opposing counsel. You did that, Sarah!" Sasha gave us both a high five, and we walked out of the courthouse like it was the final scene of a movie.

After our win, Sarah bragged about me and Sasha to the whole floor. Everyone was congratulating us, and Richard was big mad! It felt good.

"Technically, only Sarah and Sasha won. They were working on this case longer than you. You can't just show up when the work is practically done and take credit," Richard said with a sour face.

"No, it's not like that. Chyna really helped us out. She stayed here late with me to help crank out stipulations and motions. She even helped us get all our exhibits in order when some went missing. She helped a lot," Sasha said.

"Thanks, Sasha."

I gave Richard a stank look before picking up the binder and plopping it on *his* desk. "These papers look fine to me."

"It looks sloppy." He started to flip through the pages and accidentally gave himself a paper cut. "Shit! See, if these were neat, I wouldn't have cut myself!"

I didn't do that, but I wish I had. I needed to learn a paper-cut spell. It would definitely come in handy when dealing with Richard. I would use it so much that his finger would fall off.

Minutes later, our boss walked into our sector, and Richard jumped up to flag him down. "Jerry, what do you think of this binder? It's not that neat, and the holes aren't punched evenly, so the papers are halfway to falling out. I think it should be redone, what do you think?"

Jerry skimmed through the binder. "Yes, I see a few papers that need to be reprinted and re-punched. We want it to look neat and professional in a courtroom. Chyna, could you please?"

I closed my eyes so he wouldn't see them rolling. "Sure thing, Jerry," I said. I snatched the binder from Richard and went back to my desk.

Ugh! They made me sick. I needed to quit and find a new job where I was appreciated. Correction, I didn't need to work at all. I had magic. Someone with magic like me shouldn't be working.

I should rob a bank!

CHAPTER 5

I'd often contemplated robbing banks but could never quite execute a good plan. I may have shoplifted a few times in the past using magic, but nothing on the scale of robbing a bank. With that kind of job, I'd really need to train my magic to be top tier, and I didn't have time for that right now. I needed my dreams to come true fast.

Besides, if I did rob a bank, I'd probably have to give up being a stylist or basketball wife because I'd have to go into hiding or change my whole identity. That was too much work. Not to mention the work of planning it all out.

Shoplifting at a single store was way easier, and I had done it before. I had used some light interference magic to blur the cameras while I pocketed makeup from the beauty stores. I had also used a magic spell that made me insignificant to people. I wasn't invisible. That took more skills than I had. But I was insignificant enough to grab a few snacks from a coffee shop and slide past the checkout line without having to pay and without drawing anyone's attention.

As my tastes grew more expensive, I knew I had to sharpen my skills even more. So, when my mom was out, I would sneak into her lair and learn a few new spells to help me out. I had learned a new one that allowed me to put people into a temporary trance that froze them long enough for me to exit the store before they even noticed. I could only hold them for a mere ten seconds, though, and only up to three people.

In college, my tastes peaked, and I started stealing designer items. My first score was a Chanel bag.

I had walked into the store with so much confidence, you would have thought I was a billionaire. I knew the exact purse I wanted, and I had the lady bag it up all nice and pretty for me.

Then once I grabbed the bag from her, I used two spells: one to block the multiple cameras in the store, and another to make me insignificant so the employees and security didn't notice me. Luckily, there were only two people nearby, the employee and one security guard. So, that Chanel bag and I walked right out the front door.

It had felt good, but I had been nervous as hell. I did this a few more times but always at different stores just to be sure I wouldn't get caught.

I really thought I was invincible. I thought I could rule the world. Inevitably, I got too cocky and started slipping up.

The last time I did it, I'd had my eyes set on a cheetah print designer purse that I saw my favorite singer, Beyé, wear to an award show. I couldn't wait for people to see me walking to class with that purse swinging from my shoulder.

That wasn't the only thing I snagged, of course. I got a few shoes, some jewelry, and a dress. Everything had been going according to plan, that was until I ran into a classmate who ruined everything.

"Hey, I think I know you," a familiar voice said. I turned to see a young woman walking over to me holding a pair of boots that I had been eyeing earlier but had convinced myself not to get. It was Shanti Miller, the captain of the cheer squad and daughter of a judge.

We'd had a few classes together but barely spoke to one another. I was surprised she even knew who I was, let alone decided to speak to me that day.

Her timing couldn't have been worse. I was at the cash register, and she startled me just as I began working my magic. "I don't think we know each other. You have the wrong person," I said trying to get her off my back so I could get my things and leave without breaking the spell.

"Aren't you Chyna Cole from my Business Law class?"

Unfortunately, she wasn't backing down.

I turned and gave her a confused look as if I was trying to remember where I knew her from.

"It's me, Shanti Miller. I'm captain of the cheer squad. We're in the same class. My dad is Judge Miller. You know who I am." She was annoyed that I had the audacity to claim I didn't know who she was.

"Right! Yeah, I know who you are. Maybe I'm just a little shocked that you know me. We've never really spoken before." My acting skills were impeccable. I knew I'd played that off pretty well.

"You don't really speak to anyone. I'm surprised to see you. I always shop here, and I've never seen you here before. What are you doing here?" She sounded like a suspicious teacher who had just caught a student roaming the halls during class, acting as if I wasn't supposed to be here.

"Shopping. I usually go to a different mall, but they didn't have what I wanted in stock."

"You couldn't get it online?"

"Yeah, but I'm sure you could have gotten those boots online too." I shot her a look, warning her to back off.

She raised her hands in mock surrender. "True, but I like to see things in person. I'm sorry, were you checking out?"

She looked at the clerk who was standing frozen in a trance. Then she looked at me in confusion.

"I was, but I think I might want to look at a few other things," I said as I walked over to a clothing rack and started sifting through the garments.

The lady at the register woke from her trance. "Oh hello, Ms. Miller. I didn't see you walk in. What can I help you find today?"

I grabbed a few more dresses and requested a changing room so I could try them on as I pondered how I was going to get out of this situation. My spell was limited because there were too many people I would need to use it on. There was Shanti, the two clerks, and the security guard. The only other option was to wait her out. Hopefully, she would leave before me.

"Chyna, let me see how the dresses fit! This is so cool! We can have a little shopping date together. Not many other girls from our school can afford to shop with me."

This bitch! We weren't even friends. So why the hell would she want to shop together?

Did she know that I couldn't afford this stuff? Was she trying to call my bluff? DAMN IT! I didn't know what to do other than play along.

Thirty minutes later, after we had both taken turns in the dressing room trying on dresses, she was finally ready to check out.

"Oh no, I hope I don't go over my limit! My dad will kill me if I do that again. You ready?" She motioned me over to the checkout counter.

"Um no, I think I may stay a little longer and try on some shoes. You go ahead."

"No, it's okay. I'll wait with you. I can tell you which ones look good on you."

"It's fine, Shanti, go ahead." I waved her away, hoping she would actually leave.

"No, it's okay." She plopped down on a couch, making herself comfortable.

I groaned internally. I spent another hour trying on multiple shoes and then jewelry.

"Alright Chyna, I think we've done enough damage to our credit cards. Especially you. I mean damn, how much do your parents allow you to spend?" Shanti said while rolling her eyes.

"You go first." I nodded toward the register.

The clerk rang her up and she swiped her card, paying a balance of $9,700 as if it was light work. Then she turned to me, eager anticipation written all over her face. She was absolutely on to me and knew I was stalling to avoid paying.

My palms were dripping with sweat as the clerk rang up my items.

"Okay, your total is $28,000 even. How will you be paying?"

I slowly closed my eyes, took a deep breath, and said my spell out loud. I reached for my bags and walked toward the door, holding my breath and counting the seconds in my head.

10...9...8...7...6...it was eerily silent like it usually is after I use the spell. The gut feeling in the pit of my stomach was dangerously intense. I was just a few steps away from the door now. 5...4...3...2...

"Ma'am! Excuse me, ma'am!" the clerk cried.

I kept walking. My intentions were strong, but my spell was not.

"Chyna, where the hell are you going?" Shanti yelled. "I am so sorry, ma'am. I am not associated with that girl at all!"

Just keep walking, just keep walking. I finally made it out of the store! Then a firm hand grabbed my shoulder and pulled me back in. I watched as my door of freedom that led to my life two hours before I walked into this store became smaller and smaller until it was nothing but darkness.

Next thing I knew, I was cuffed and sitting in the police station waiting for my parents to arrive. I wasn't a minor anymore, so the cop could have easily thrown me into the cell without letting me see my parents, but he didn't. Maybe it was because I was crying so hard and he felt bad for me, but he allowed me to call them.

I'm very lucky he did. My mom and two aunts used their most powerful magic to clean my record and erase everything that had happened from the memories of the cops, the security guards, the store employees, and even Shanti Miller.

The next time I saw her at school, she walked right past me as if I was invisible, just like she always had.

I was indebted to my aunts. So, until I graduated from college, I constantly ran errands for them and babysat for free on the weekends I was home.

And my mom? She never let me forget it. She forced me to sell every designer item I had stolen—after my aunts got their pickings—and donate the money to charity. It made me sick to give up my designer bags. I actually threw up twice.

Because of that incident, no amount of begging would convince my parents to let me change majors. They held firm and forced me to stay in the political science program.

But those days were in the past. I'd learned my lesson and I'd grown.

As a paralegal, I could now afford the things I needed. Plus, my skills had sharpened, and I no longer needed to engage in petty thefts. And once I got my big baller NBA husband, I'd be able to afford all my needs and desires.

CHAPTER 6

Cali and I were enjoying our weekly dinner date at a nice upscale Mexican restaurant. It was decorated beautifully, and it felt like we were literally in Tulum. There were plants all around us, and Cali was trying to pocket a few of their leaves so she could grow them in her apartment.

"Cali, stop! You're going to get us kicked out," I said, laughing while Cali was taking a small snake plant that she had been eyeing the whole night.

"Girl, no. I need this! I've been wanting one since forever," she said sliding the pot into her medium-sized purse.

"You are too much!" I screamed. "But this place was really good. We've gotta come back."

We paid the check and headed out of the restaurant. Our apartment wasn't far, so we had elected to walk and save ourselves a hefty parking fee.

It was only a fifteen-minute walk each way, and we figured it would count as our exercise for the day since neither of us had been to the gym in a while.

During the day when we made the walk, it wasn't bad. There were plenty of other people out and about, and we were so deep in conversation that it felt like we'd only walked for five minutes.

But now, it was dark out. And by the time we were halfway to our apartment, we noticed that there weren't a lot of people around.

"Damn, I didn't realize how sketchy this area looks at night," Cali said as she surveyed our surroundings nervously.

"Yeah, maybe we shouldn't walk in this neighborhood this late at night anymore. I know parking can be difficult, but we could split an Uber or something."

We noticed two men emerge from an alley and walk in our direction. I looked over at Cali and motioned to her that we should cross the road to avoid having to walk near them. We began to cross the street when we heard the men's footsteps speed up behind us.

"Hey! Gimme me your fuckin' bags right now!" one of the men screamed from behind me.

I felt something cold and hard touch the side of my rib. He had a gun! I looked over and saw the other man pointing a gun to Cali's head as he ripped her bag from her hands. She was screaming and crying hysterically, but I was frozen to the spot and couldn't move.

"Did ya hear what I fuckin' said? Gimme me your fuckin' bag or I'm gonna shoot the fuck out of you!"

I turned my head to face the man who was demanding my belongings…the things I had worked hard to get. He wore a ski mask and hood over his head, but I could still tell he was a white man, probably in his thirties, with dark brown eyes and severely chapped lips.

He raised his gun to my head, placing the end of the barrel against my skull.

"I will blow your fuckin' brains out if you don't give me that bag, bitch!"

I could still hear Cali crying and screaming. I couldn't tell what was happening, but I heard what sounded like clothes rustling. Then I heard a ripping sound.

I was pissed. How dare these assholes think they could take advantage of us like that? Just because they had guns.

Well, little did they know, I had magic on my side. They didn't know who they were fucking with. They didn't know how happy I was for this opportunity. This was the moment I'd been waiting for to display my magical growth. They'd picked the right one. My mind was churning with images of what I could do to thank them for this inconvenience.

"Please don't touch me! Please don't touch me!" Cali cried, pleading with the jerk who was ripping her shirt.

I slowly held my bag out toward the scumbag next to me. As he reached for it, I said the spell, freezing both men in place. I ran over to Cali and helped her up, snatching her bag back then hitting them with another spell.

Crack! Crunch! Crack! Their fingers bent and cracked as they watched in horror, helplessly frozen. The spell continued up their arms, breaking wrists and elbows. Splintered bones were popping out through their skin, and their arms were glistening with blood. Damage they wouldn't be able to fix easily even with the best of doctors.

I wanted to keep going, but I saw the bewildered look on Cali's face. I grabbed her hand, and we ran. Not stopping until we were in the lobby of our apartment building.

"Hey girl, are you okay?" I asked Cali as I caught my breath. I could see her shirt was ripped, exposing her bra.

"Chyna, what the hell just happened?" Cali said in a quiet voice that I had never heard her speak in before.

At that moment, I realized I had exposed my secret.

I didn't even think back there. I had simply reacted. But I had to. I had no choice. Who knows what would have happened if I hadn't done what I did.

But what consequences would my actions have?

I'd just shown my only friend in the city that I was a weird witchy freak.

I'd made a mistake, but I could fix it. If I explained the situation to my mom, I'm sure she could teach me that mind-erasing spell she'd used on Shanti Miller.

"Chyna, did you...did you do that? Did you make them freeze and then break their bones? I heard you saying something...like a spell or something."

I couldn't think of a lie to tell her. Besides, hopefully by tomorrow morning, with my mom's help, Cali wouldn't remember anything that had happened.

"Yes, I'm a witch," I said in a matter-of-fact tone. "I come from a family of witches, and I know many spells. That's how I got my job. I put a spell on my interviewer and made them think they should hire me."

I chuckled, remembering how the interview had lasted only five minutes after I put my interviewer, Sasha Mackie, in a trance and gave her all the reasons why she was going to hire me.

"What the hell, Chyna? Are you for real?" Cali had a dazed look on her face as if she was lost for words. "Did you use a spell on me?"

"No, girl. I've genuinely been vibing with you."

Cali took a step back "So, you know how to freeze people?"

"Mm-hmm, I learned that spell some years ago."

"And you never thought to tell me about this?"

I took a seat on the couch in our lobby, let out a sigh, and looked up at Cali. "No, I wasn't going to tell you. I don't go around telling everyone I'm a witch. Do you know how crazy that sounds? I'm only telling you this now because you're not going to remember it tomorrow after I have this erased from your memory."

"Oh, hell no! You're not erasing shit from my memory! I need to remember this for the next time we go shopping and you freeze them people so I can get my shit for free!"

"Girl, what?"

"Don't tell me you never did this to get some free shit?"

I laughed out loud when I realized that shop lifting was Cali's only concern. She was reacting the same way I had when I realized the potential of my powers.

"Hell, yeah, I did it before. But that was years ago before I got a real paying job. I learned my lesson. Trust me, with the plan I have, we won't need to steal ever again."

Cali took a seat beside me on the couch. "With what plan? You mean when you said you want to be a basketball player's wife?"

I leaned in closer to Cali. "Freezing people isn't the only spell I know. I've been practicing toward something bigger and stronger. A love spell that would guarantee me shopping sprees on his dime. I used to shoplift in college, and yeah, it felt good to walk out with free stuff. But imagine the salesclerks already knowing your name and treating you with the utmost respect." I was having flashbacks of how Shanti Miller was treated at the store because she was a frequent customer using her dad's credit card.

Cali had an amazed look on her face. "Damn, I like how you think. How are you going to do it, though? Who are you going to do it to?"

I pulled out my phone and showed Cali the newest post from Chicago Moon's Pic-Talk. He was walking to his dark green Corvette wearing the latest designer clothes.

"I want him."

"That's Chicago Moon! He is fine and loaded. Not only is he a really good player, but he also comes from money. His dad was a former NBA player too."

"I didn't even know that."

"Girl! An old friend that I went to school with is a DJ at this club that all the celebrities go to. He said he's seen Chicago and some other players there a few times. Chicago usually rents a section in the club, so my friend will know when he's going to be there next. So, I can get you into the room with him! But you'll have to work your magic for the rest." She grabbed my wrist as if we were plotting a heist.

"And Chyna, all I need is one of his friends, okay? I need to be in that circle too. Imagine if I could sell one of those guys a multi-million-dollar house! I'd be set!" Cali was bouncing up and down on the couch now. "Come on, Chyna, you can't erase my memory. We need each other, girl!"

"How do I know I can trust that you're not going to tell the whole world who I am? This is serious. Yes, being a witch can be beneficial, but it has its downsides. Not everyone is cool with it."

I took a deep breath, assessing the situation. I was really hoping I could trust Cali with my secret. I needed someone here that knew who I was and would have my back. I couldn't do this alone. Besides, she'd been a great friend so far.

"Girl, your magic just saved my life! Do you see me?" Cali pointed to her exposed bra. "That man was going to steal my shit and try to have his way with me, and you stopped that with your magic. I owe you big time, so I'm not going to blast you. I love hanging out with you. You are my only real friend out here. Trust me. And if I do, *which I won't,* but if I do slip up, feel free to turn me into a frog. A pretty frog."

We both burst out laughing. I gave her a hug. I was happy I had found someone I could trust. Someone who could help me achieve my dreams, and in return, I would help her achieve hers as well.

CHAPTER 7

Operation Bag the Ball Player was set and ready.

I sat at my desk, trying to contain my excitement about meeting Chicago Moon at the club tonight. For the whole week I'd been reciting what I would say. How we would meet. How I would smile. What I would wear. And what magic spell I would use to start things off with.

What would I wear? That was the easiest part. I know I said I was done with the shoplifting, but this was an exception because this time would truly be the last. I needed an expensive show-stopping dress to catch this man's attention and secure my future. And I found that dress on Tuesday night about thirty minutes before closing time.

The store was pretty empty with only a few people near the exit, three clerks and two security guards.

Even though I hadn't shoplifted since getting caught, I had practiced my spells and could now hold up to six people in a trance for three whole minutes. This was the perfect opportunity to test my new skills.

I jammed the cameras before walking in to stop the recording, then told the salesclerk I would only take ten minutes to pick out the items I needed.

I grabbed a red, strapless minidress, a pair of black heels, and a small bottle of the most expensive perfume. I even grabbed a denim minidress for Cali. I had the clerk bag my items, then I cast my spell to freeze her and walked right out, waving goodbye to the frozen security guards.

Afterward, Cali and I got ready at my place. There were makeup pallets, brushes, and curling irons flying across the bathroom.

"Girl, this is so freaking cool! If I had your powers, I would be so damn lazy I wouldn't lift a damn thing," Cali said, plucking an eyeshadow palette from the air as it sailed from the bedroom into the bathroom.

"Yeah, it definitely comes in handy," I said while curling my last curl. "How do I look? Do you think he'll be all over me?"

"Girl, if he isn't, I will be! That dress is sooo freaking sexy! I love it!"

"Thank you, girl!" I chuckled.

I knew I looked good, but I was nervous. I was sure there would be other beautiful girls at the club, and I needed to stand out so I could get close enough to Chicago to cast my spell.

My repertoire of spells for tonight was another thing I had worked on. There was no way I could start with something too strong off the bat.

According to my spell book, in order to fully bewitch Chicago and keep the love spell strong, I had to work my way up. My first step would be to captivate him by keeping him wanting more. Keeping me on his mind 24/7.

"You ready, Chyna?"

"Yes ma'am. I just need two shots of tequila and I'll be ready for the mission." I winked at Cali as we walked out the door.

I hopped out of a black SUV feeling like a billion bucks.

The club was in a black brick building, and as club-goers entered and exited, I could see the interior neon lights pulsing each time they opened the doors. There was a long line, people were bopping to a rap song that was playing on the exterior speakers.

"Dang, we gotta stand in that long line?" I asked Cali as she closed the door to the SUV behind us.

"Nope. I told you I know the DJ, and he said he put us on the list." Cali linked arms with me, and we marched up to the bouncer blocking the front door. She pulled out her ID and gave the man a flirty smile.

"DJ Kenny put us on the list," she said.

"Okay, you're good," he said after checking her ID and looking her up and down with a lustful eye.

He then turned to me. I flashed him my ID and a big smile. He scanned my ID then winked. I did my best not to gag.

As we stepped into the club, we scanned the room before entering further. It was packed, but of course, no one was really dancing. Most of the girls were either standing around drinking or sitting pretty in a section, and the men were bobbing their heads to the music while pouring themselves drinks. So, although the club was packed, it felt pretty dead.

We found a spot to stand behind a section. The women in the section were eyeing us up and down to make sure we didn't enter, while the men kept eyeing us in the hopes we would give them the green light. A section filled with jealousy and lust.

I didn't blame them. Cali and I looked damn good.

I was on the short side at five-feet three-inches, but I had an hourglass figure most women would pay for. My hair was extra curly and bouncy, blending perfectly with my leave-out. You couldn't even tell it wasn't really mine.

And my makeup? Beat to perfection, thanks to a little help from my magic spell.

Cali was on the taller side at five-feet eight-inches and with her thick hips, popping ass, and full breasts, she was built and stacked like a stallion. Her natural curls were also juicy and bouncy, and her makeup was flawless.

We were both wearing designer dresses and looked like two Black goddesses. If I didn't look like us, I'd be jealous too.

Even though we looked good, we were standing, not sitting pretty as we should have been. I was grateful to be in the same room as my future husband for free, but I wished Cali's friend could have thrown us into a section or rustled up a couple of chairs for us to sit on.

I scanned the room and clocked my man—who didn't yet know he was my man—at ten o'clock. He was standing in the front of his elevated VIP section holding a bottle of liquor and rapping along to the song that was being blasted on the speakers throughout the club.

Chicago was tall, about six-feet four-inches, with a muscular build. He wasn't too ripped or stocky, but he had nice thick arms that showed he could bench over 130 lbs. His braids were freshly done, and he had a confident smile on his face.

I bit my lip while staring him down, and nudged Cali to let her know my target was on lock.

"Whew, he looks even better in person!" Cali said.

I raised an eyebrow, and she laughed.

"Girl, I don't want your man! But there he is, so what's the plan?"

"I don't know, and I'm getting really nervous now after seeing him. He looks too good!" It felt like a bunch of butterflies were having a gathering in my stomach.

"Okay, let's go get some drank in you."

Cali linked arms with me again and guided me to the bar, where we got two shots that we threw back immediately, along with two sugary cocktails that we held on to as we walked through the club.

We managed to circle the dance floor twice without me making eye contact with Chicago, before Cali finally pulled me to the side.

"Look girl, we're not going to keep walking around this club without you making any moves. He's right there! Make eye contact. Wink. Wave. Blow a kiss! Do something to catch his eye!" Cali said, her tone tense. Her feet must have been hurting and making her cranky.

"Okay! Damn!" I took a deep breath and looked over at Chicago. He was sitting and chatting with his friends. I turned back to Cali and pouted. "Shit, I'm scared girl. I don't know what's wrong with me!"

I started to wave my hands to dry off the sweat that had accumulated on my palms. The butterflies in my stomach were now on crack and having a mosh pit.

"Chyna, calm down. You're a witch bitch!" Cali said as she laughed at her own joke.

She was right, though. I was a witch bitch. I was THE witch bitch.

I'm going to make all my dreams come true. And my dreams are right there in that section, waiting for me to take control. I turned to look at Chicago. He was just a fine man with money. No big deal.

I took a big gulp of my drink and nodded for Cali to follow me. We found a spot right in front of Chicago's section to stand.

The DJ was playing a song that had gone viral on Pic-Talk. I started moving my hips to the rhythm and soon Cali and I were singing and dancing to the popular song.

Our drinks were kicking in, and we were both feeling it. I attempted to whine my hips, but Cali shook her head in disapproval. She then demonstrated how to do the dance correctly, and I caught on quickly. We were dancing, raising our drinks to the roof and having such a good time that I even forgot why we were there.

After the song ended, I gestured for Cali to come sit with me, as some stools had become available at the bar. We were just about to head over when a buff security guard tapped my shoulder.

"Excuse me, miss? Y'all want to sit down?" he asked, pointing to the section behind him where Chicago Moon was sitting.

I glanced over and saw Chicago gazing at me. He raised his eyebrows before taking a swig from his bottle. I looked over at Cali and saw the big grin on her face that she was struggling to hide.

We nodded, and the security guard led us into the section.

I spotted a seat next to Chicago, and eagerly took it as if my name was on it. I watched as Cali sat across from me in between two of Chicago's friends.

As I scanned the seats near me, I noticed two familiar faces. They were other members of Chicago's basketball team.

I must have looked nervous as hell because Chicago placed his hand on mine.

"You good, shawty?" he asked.

I turned to face him, and my heart skipped a beat. His face, his smile, his cologne, that deep county voice of his. All of it was making me melt inside. The butterflies were holding a fight club in my stomach, and I wanted to throw up.

But this was my time to shine, and I was not going to mess this up. I was not about to go home empty-handed and full of regretful thoughts like *I should have done this. I should have said that.*

No regrets tonight.

I steadied my breathing and activated my inner witch bitch. I also said a spell inside my head to give myself a confidence boost. It was one my mom had taught me when I was in school and had to do presentations in front of the class.

"Yeah, I'm good. You good?" I asked, trying to sound cool and collected.

Then instantly wanted to slap myself. Why would I ask him if he was good?

Chicago chuckled. "Yeah, I'm feelin' real good. You nervous? Don't be. I should be nervous around you. You're fine as hell. What's your name?"

Heat rushed to my cheeks as I released an internal squeal.

"Thank you. I'm Chyna. What's your name?" I asked as if I didn't already know his name, the condo he lived in, the car he drove, and his zodiac sign.

"Chicago," he said, smooth as ever. "Like the city."

I smirked. "That's funny. Both our names are places."

"Guess it was meant to be," he said, flashing a grin.

I laughed. "Is this your section?"

He nodded.

"Well, I appreciate you for inviting me and my girl in. Our feet were starting to hurt."

"Not a problem. What are you drinking?"

"Amaretto sour."

"Never had that before."

"What do you usually drink?" I asked.

"Tequila. Wine. Champagne. The good stuff." He raised his bottle. "You ever had this?"

I shook my head.

"Here, try it."

He tilted the bottle toward me, and I opened my mouth wide, letting the liquor slide down my throat with a smooth, tingling warmth. Definitely the good stuff. No burn at all.

"It's smooth. I like it," I said, patting the droplet that had fallen onto my chin.

I leaned a little closer to him as I felt the confidence spell finally working its magic. "You like wine, though? I wouldn't have taken you for a wine connoisseur."

Chicago let out a light chuckle. "Why not?"

"You definitely give tequila straight with no salt or lime. You just seem really hard and tough," I said as I ran the tips of my fingers over his rock-hard arms.

"Shit, I am tough. But this nigga got layers," he said, shrugging. "My mom owns a winery back home in Houston. She always had me trying all her new stuff, so I really am a wine connoisseur."

"Oh, that's dope! My friend is from Houston too," I said, pretending to be shocked.

I pointed over to Cali. "Cali, y'all are both from Houston. Small world, right?" I cringed at my corniness.

Cali was having what looked like a deep conversation with the guy next to her. "That fool was really trying to convince me that hot sauce was not needed for fried fish or chicken. No matter how good the seasoning is, hot sauce is a necessity," she would later tell me.

Cali leaned forward to join our conversation. "Oh yeah? What part?"

"South. Mo City."

"Okay! I see you. I'm from Humble."

Chicago cocked his head to the side and sounded off like a buzzer. "AAANNHH Wrong answer. You ain't from Houston."

"Boy stop! That ain't nothing but a quick little drive to the city."

"But you outside the loop, though."

"Man, whatever." Cali leaned back in her seat and dismissed herself from the conversation.

Minute by minute, I started to feel more comfortable around Chicago. Even though his exterior was a little rough, I could tell he was a big tender and charming teddy bear inside. He had an enticing smile that was warm and sweet like heated syrup on a fresh batch of French toast. I wanted more of a taste, so I made cute corny jokes to get him chuckling.

The conversation really began to flow when we discussed the fact that we were both new to LA. I told him where I was from and how I missed my family. He could relate because he'd moved to LA by himself "for work" a year ago.

I didn't want to pry into his career, but I did poke at it, and he opened right up. He told me all about being a basketball player. I played it smoothly as if it was really cool but not that big of a deal, and I think he appreciated that.

Somehow our conversation eventually turned to aliens, and we both revealed our quirky love for conspiracy theories. I, of course, believed full-heartedly that aliens were real. I mean, I was a witch with magic powers, so aliens couldn't be that farfetched.

Chicago also believed they were real because one of his uncle's swore he was abducted by one in the early 80s.

I was enjoying the conversation and wanted to know more about his thoughts on everything and hoped that one day, I might even learn what he thought about witches.

I stole a glance at Cali and saw the annoyed look on her face. She was sitting next to one of Chicago's friends, who was talking her ear off. I raised a brow, signaling that I was ready to leave if she was, and got a quick nod in reply.

"My friend is getting a little tired, so I think we should head out," I said in a disappointed pouty voice.

"Damn." Chicago had a somber look on his face. "It was good talking to you. Can I text you later?"

"Of course. What's your number?" I pulled out my phone, trying to act nonchalant while my insides bubbled with excitement.

This was it! I'd done it! And I didn't even have to use that much magic. I could feel multiple pairs of envious eyes scorching the back of my neck as I walked away from Chicago with the biggest smile on my face. My head was ten times bigger leaving the club than it had been entering it.

As soon as I got home, I sent a text to Chicago to let him know that I made it back safely and how nice it was to meet him.

"It was good meeting you too. I really enjoyed your company. Hopefully I can see you again soon," he replied with a blushing emoji.

"Yes, I'd like that. I might be free this weekend," I texted back, smiling so hard my face started to hurt.

I slept great that night, knowing I had secured my husband and his bag.

CHAPTER 8

He ghosted me!

"I'm serious, Cali! He ghosted me! It's been two days since I texted him. I know he's alive because I watched his story from my burner account. He bought a new Rolex just the other day!" I shouted in disbelief.

"Damn! I can't believe he played you like that!"

She could have at least fed me a few delusional excuses. Said my texts hadn't gone through or something. My stomach was in knots, and I felt sick with despair. I'd already planned our wedding, the dress I would wear, and the venue. I wanted Beyé to serenade us during our first dance. Every detail had been saved to my Pic-Talk board, but now my dreams were crashing and burning.

"Can't you use a magic spell to get him to text you back?" Cali asked, wriggling her fingers as if she was casting a spell.

"I'm not that skilled. For me to use stronger magic on someone, I need to be in their presence."

"Well, that's unfortunate. How are you going to be in his presence if he ain't text you back to set a date?"

Dejected, I collapsed onto the couch. Cali was right. I had to come up with a plan. A few minutes later, the idea hit me like a basketball to the face if you were sitting courtside. I summoned my laptop and flung the screen open.

"They have a home game tomorrow night. Want to go with me?" I must have looked deranged because Cali had an odd expression on her face when I looked up at her.

"What are you going to do? How you going to get his attention from the stands?" Cali asked.

I pressed my lips together and twisted my mouth to one side. She had a point.

"Girl, I don't know, but I'll figure it out when I see him. I should be able to plant a spell on him if we're in the same room."

Cali rolled her eyes. "Should I be the voice of reason here and tell you how crazy you sound and look, or should I be a good friend and feed into your delusions?" Cali gestured with her hands as if she were weighing her options.

"I could use a good friend right now, Cali."

"And I could use more celebrity clients. So fine. Let's do it!" Cali wiggled her body in excitement, and I joined in, letting out a squeal.

Within a few minutes, our tickets were secured.

The next night, I walked into that stadium like I was already the wife of an NBA star. I was wearing a cropped black puffer jacket, a pair of very short shorts, and black thigh high boots. My jacket was unbuttoned to display the perfect amount of cleavage laced with stacks of silver necklaces. My bundles were long and pressed straight. I deserved to have a hundred paparazzi snapping pictures given how good I looked.

Cali and I grabbed our snacks and drinks then headed to our seats. We were late, so by the time we sat down and got comfortable, the game had already started.

I desperately scanned the court for Chicago, and my heart fluttered when I finally spotted him.

He looked good!

Sweat dripped from his meaty biceps, and I could see the hunger to win in his eyes. I was in awe.

He wanted to win badly, and I wanted him to win too.

I let out a whoop to cheer him on, hoping he would look up and notice me, but the roar of the surrounding crowd drowned me out.

Then I remembered that this man had ghosted me. I hated to admit it, but it still stung. He obviously didn't want anything to do with me, yet here I was ducked off in the crowd watching him like a rejected stalker.

Not gonna lie, I felt some shame. But I couldn't let it go. Why didn't this man want me?

I looked down and saw a few groups of women occupying the courtside seats. The majority were young, pretty, and wearing designer clothes from head to toe.

Could one of them be here for Chicago? His main girl who he paraded courtside?

Why couldn't that be me? I mean look at me! I was stunning. I was a catch. I deserved to be in those courtside seats cheering my man on.

Rage ran through me. How dare he ghost me! How dare he hinder my dreams, my goals! I was starting to see red, and before I knew it, I was chanting a spell in my head, begging him to look at me.

He did.

He looked right at me, staring so intensely that the ball he was taking a shot with slipped from his hands, missed the hoop, and landed in the lap of a fan in the stands.

The crowd collectively groaned, and Chicago dropped his head walking over to his coach.

Damn. Did I do that?

I glanced over at Cali, who was giving me the eye.

"Did you do that?" she asked between mouthfuls of popcorn.

"Shit, I think so. I don't know. I just got upset for a moment."

I glanced down at Chicago. He was definitely looking at me now. He had a blank stare on his face. I wasn't sure if it was because of the spell or because he was annoyed to see me.

The shame returned and lingered, even after I was home in bed.

Just as I was about to nod off, I got a text. I figured it was Cali again telling me not to be discouraged and that there were plenty of other players we could go after.

I rolled onto my side and grabbed my phone off the bedside table. My jaw fell to the ground when I saw who it was.

"Hey, my bad for the late response. Were you at my game tonight? I could've sworn I saw you," Chicago wrote.

I flipped onto my back and tried to think of what to say. I was happy he'd texted, but I was also nervous, just like I had been the night we met.

"Lol, you probably just missed my pretty face," I replied, sending him a winking emoji.

"I sho' did. You free Friday? Let me take you out."

CHAPTER 9

Okay, this was it!

I was finally going on my first date with Chicago, and it would be my best chance to secure my future.

I wasn't going to let this opportunity pass me by again. I had been practicing my spellwork for the past week to make sure I would stay on Chicago's mind and clinch my courtside spot.

Once again, I had to make a special stop at my favorite store. I picked up another designer dress that would showcase my assets perfectly on our date at Nobu.

Chicago picked me up in his Corvette. He had a small bouquet of red roses waiting for me in the car. He was definitely the romantic type, and I loved it.

I kissed him on the cheek and complimented his good taste to let him know he'd done good. He gave me a cocky smile, but I could see the warmth and sincerity beneath the macho facade.

The drive out to Malibu was about an hour. I figured it would give us enough time to get comfortable around each other again. We were listening to a playlist Chicago liked that featured a variety of popular rappers.

"What type of music do you like?" Chicago asked, keeping his head straight and eyes focused on the road.

"I'm more of an R&B girlie. I have love for the new school and especially the old school. I love a good love song that I can sing along to."

"Who's your favorite singer?"

"Beyé! She's an icon."

"She's cool. My mom's a huge fan. You like rap?" Chicago turned his head to me, showcasing his beautiful brown eyes.

"It's cool. I think I prefer female rap over male rap."

"What? That's crazy!"

I reached for his phone that was connected to his car so I could search for my favorite female rap artist to play for him. He studied me up and down with a quizzical expression before giving in.

I put on some of my favorite female rappers and started throwing my hands up rapping along. After a few songs, Chicago took his phone and put his music back on.

"What? You didn't like it?" I asked.

"I mean it's cool. Female rap is just different. All they rap about is sex."

"So do the men," I said matter-of-factly.

Chicago sucked his teeth and continued to defend the male rap industry.

"Take for instance, Jalen Cole. He has a whole album rapping about how beneficial therapy is for people and how it can prevent people from letting their emotions ruin their life."

"I really did like that album," I said, reluctant to agree with him. "'He had Beyé singing on one of the songs, and her vocals were perfection.'"

"Did you only listen to Beyé, or did you listen to the message of the song?" Chicago asked, giving me a deep scan when we stopped at a stop sign.

"She was a bonus for me. But I did enjoy his message because it was needed. I think it had a positive impact on a lot of people and encouraged them to take that initiative to tend to their mental health. You know, I encourage therapy because my mom is a therapist," I said.

"Really? That's what's up."

"Have you been to therapy before?"

Chicago took a left at the intersection before answering.

"Not until recently. Being famous has been kind of stressful for me, so I go to therapy every other week and it helps keep me present and focused."

As we continued our drive, Chicago pointed out restaurants, shops, and other areas he had visited, offering to take me the next time he went.

My eyes were glued to the window as we drove along the Pacific Coast Highway. I was in complete awe of the view.

Not to be a cliché, but as a Pisces, seeing such a vast stretch of water was captivating. It was different than sitting at the beach because I could see nothing but water for miles along with various mountains and rock formations.

This feeling was magical. I could tell Chicago was loving how impressed I was. He just knew he was racking up brownie points. He was romantic and thoughtful, and I truly loved that. It made me want him to fall in love with me. If he was doing all this for a date, just imagine how sweet life would be once he was deeply in love.

We arrived at Nobu and were seated right away on the patio with a full view of the beach. The ambiance was elegant, and the dishes were scrumptious. He let me order whatever I wanted, and I did. I may have gone a little crazy, but he didn't judge me.

Chicago was big on seafood, and so was I. We indulged in oysters, a variety of sashimi, and caviar. We both felt adventurous enough to try tartare which neither of us had before.

As we enjoyed our food, I decided to take a chance and begin working to open Chicago up so I could intertwine my essence with his mind. I needed him to let me in so I could place my love spell roots deep into his heart, so it would be mine.

I gently placed my hand over his and said my spell in my head.

"How are you feeling right now, Chicago?"

He dropped his eyes and tilted his head, then peered up at me with a slightly intoxicated look in his eyes. He had only indulged in one glass of wine, so I was sure he wasn't tipsy yet. It was definitely the magic starting to take effect.

"I'm feeling good, Chyna," he said in a low, husky voice that wove its own spell, sending sensations through my body. "I'm enjoying myself with you right now. I like being around you. I like hearing your voice and hearing you laugh. You're beautiful."

"I like being around you too, Chicago. Could you see yourself being with me long term? Marrying me? How do you feel about marriage?" I asked while tightening my hold on his hand and pouring more of my spell into him.

Chicago's eyes became intense. He opened his mouth then paused, collecting his words before speaking. "I think…marriage is beautiful. I've seen it a lot of times in my life, and it's amazing to see people finding partners that…understand them and can be honest with them. My parents have been married for over thirty years. They look so happy and peaceful knowing that they have someone to come home to that they can trust. I want that."

He looked into my eyes for a few seconds then curved his lips and gave an enigmatic smile. "Could I see myself with you? I think we'd look good together. We'd have some pretty babies. I think the media would like you too. You would look good for my image."

I smiled and giggled like a child. Not only because of what Chicago said, but because I knew the spell was working.

"I think we look good together too. We don't have to rush, but we shouldn't take long to decide. I think we should—"

Chicago pulled his hand back and began eating again.

"This shit is fire," he said with a whole piece of sushi in his mouth.

I sat there slightly puzzled. Did the spell wear off that fast?

I pulled out my phone and searched through my photos for the ones I had taken of the love spell to make sure I'd done it right. This wasn't going to be easy. Right now, I just needed to keep giving him small doses of the spell so I could grow and strengthen my roots inside of him.

"You good, Chy?" Chicago asked.

"Yeah, I'm good," I said as I slid my phone back into my purse. "Oh, are we using nicknames now?" I asked, a smile teasing the corner of my lips.

"Mm-hmm. You wanna give me one?"

"Let me think on it."

After our dinner, Chicago led us down to the beach so we could walk and talk some more. The sun was setting, and the sky was a beautiful blend of blue, orange, pink, and purple.

The sound of the waves crashing against each other was soothing. We took off our shoes as we walked along the shore so we could feel the sand and water between our toes.

I held Chicago's hand, his grip warm and firm as our fingers intertwined.

"What made you want to become a basketball player?" I asked, breaking the silence.

Chicago leaned his head back and let out a breathy sigh. "Um, I was really good at basketball when I was little. My dad was a former pro player, and we had a court in our backyard, so my cousin and I played every weekend. One day, my dad noticed I had 'real talent,' so he enrolled me in basketball camps and made sure I practiced every day. From then on, I loved it. I played through middle school, high school, and college before getting scouted."

"Wow, that's dope that your dad supported your hobby like that. It really paid off. I saw you play. You're really good."

"You be watching me?"

"Of course, I do. I want to support you."

Chicago gave me a cute, shy smile which set off warm tingles in my heart. "I appreciate that. I look forward to seeing you in the crowd the next time I play."

"You would be able to see me better if I was sitting courtside." I glanced up at him.

"I got you. So, Miss Cole. What are your dreams? I know you told me you're a paralegal. Is that what you always wanted to do?"

"No." The word escaped my mouth so quickly, it almost came out like a bark.

"Damn!" Chicago said, making both of us laugh.

"I mean, it's a cool job, but it wasn't what I wanted to do. It's what my parents pushed me to do because it's a stable career. Everyone needs a lawyer."

"Man, that sucks. In a dream world, what would you want to do?"

I looked out at the ocean. The sun was gone, but there was a bright moon instead, illuminating the waves.

I was on the fence. Did I want to tell Chicago about my dreams of being a hair stylist? I wasn't sure how he'd react. Maybe he'd think it was stupid and feel I should stick to something reliable like my parents wanted.

When I turned back to face him, I realized he was staring at me with an intrigued expression. I returned his gaze, and, in that moment, I knew I could trust him with my dreams and goals.

So, I gave in.

I told him I wanted to be a hair stylist and own my own salon. I shared everything with him: how much I loved doing hair, the TV shows that had inspired me, and how often I daydreamed of working with celebrity clients and seeing my work on the red carpet.

He didn't laugh or belittle my dreams. Instead, he encouraged me.

"Yo, I think that's dope! I could definitely see you having your own shop and having a bunch of stars in there all lined up. Your hair always looks good, so I think you'd kill it."

I smiled a little too hard in response to Chicago's uplifting and positive attitude. He really made me believe I could do it.

My dream seemed attainable now. Especially if he was going to be by my side funding me and putting his big name behind my projects.

"Thank you, Chicago. Your words of encouragement are truly appreciated. This means a lot to me because it's one of the big reasons I moved here. I know I'm getting close to my dreams. I can feel it," I said, squeezing his hand a little tighter. "Talking with you makes me feel really motivated and pumped up." I turned to face him, practically levitating with excitement.

"I got you, Chy. I'll keep motivating you." He grabbed my chin and leaned down.

I rose up onto my toes and held onto his chest as our lips pressed together in a fervent embrace.

I stretched my arms up above his head to grasp his broad neck while he placed his hands on the lower part of my back just above my ass and pulled me against him. Our bodies were pressed so tight, he could probably feel my heartbeat.

His kiss was mesmerizing and activated every inch of my body. His lips were soft and warm as they danced with mine and elicited a tingling sensation that spread from my mouth to my thighs.

I wanted to melt into his arms and live in this position for the rest of my life.

I was about to lose my mind and my willpower as sweat began to pool between my legs. He must've cast a spell on me to make me this weak. That's the only explanation, right?

It made me realize this was the perfect time for my spell. I began reciting the spell in my head, but it was hard to stay focused.

Reluctantly, I slowly pulled my lips from Chicago's, then I placed them on his neck, kissing him with soft and gentle pecks. My tongue glided down his skin, leading my lips to new places.

"Damn, Chyna." Chicago said with a low moan that made my eyes roll back.

I continued to kiss his neck and in between each peck, I said my spell in a whisper that probably sounded seductive.

Chicago caressed me more eagerly now, even reaching down to hold my ass.

"What's up, Chy? What are you saying?" he asked in a hushed tone.

I didn't respond.

I finished my spell, then grazed his neck and chin with my lips until I found his, brushing lightly against them before locking in.

I repeated the spell again in my head to give him the finishing blow.

When Chicago came up for air, there was a soft and gentle look in his eyes. They were unfocused as if he wasn't fully there.

I broke out into a mischievous smile. Even though Chicago was winning my body, I knew I was winning the war.

CHAPTER 10

O n our first date, I told Chicago we didn't have to rush into things, but in the back of my mind, I needed everything to move quickly.

And it did.

After a steady stream of dates, late-night phone calls, and, of course, my constant use of magic, it wasn't exactly a surprise when it only took one week for us to make it official.

Sure, my spellwork helped move things along. But the way he made it happen? That was all him.

From the moment he picked me up that day, I knew he had something special planned.

We were heading to Long Beach. It was a long drive, but we enjoyed every minute of it.

We turned the car into our own private karaoke show, singing along to all our favorite songs. I found myself feeling more and more comfortable with Chicago, absentmindedly stroking his neck, running my thumb from his jaw to his clavicle as he drove. In return, he gave my thigh a gentle squeeze.

We pulled up at a red light and made intense eye contact, our eyes communicating what we wanted to do to each other in the privacy of a bedroom.

The next second, our lips were locked, and I was melting into him until I heard distant honking and realized it was the car behind us letting us know the light had turned green.

Once we arrived at our destination, Chicago led me onto a small yacht. It was lit up with tiny electric candles and rose petals that had been spread all over the deck. He took my hand and guided me to the front of the boat where a huge heart made of red roses stood on a stand.

Surrounding the roses were pillows, blankets, champagne, and a large charcuterie board. Chicago stood near the heart and asked me out officially. It was like a mini proposal. A taste of what our future could look like. I ran over to him and jumped into his arms.

"Hell yeah, of course I'll be your girl!" I said, trying not to cry.

"Oh, my gawd!" Cali screamed when I dished all the details about my big date, especially when I got to the part about Chicago asking me out officially. "That is so sweet and romantic! But GIRL, it actually worked! That's so good!"

We grasped each other's hands and started jumping around in a circle.

I was officially the girlfriend of a popular basketball player. The spell was working, and I was one step closer to my dreams.

I could already envision the ribbon-cutting ceremony for the soft launch of my hair salon. Surprisingly, I hadn't even thought of a name yet.

Chyna's Hair Salon. Hair by Chyna. Fine Chyna Hair Salon.

Honestly, I was fine with any name as long as my name was buzzing in the rooms of influential people who would keep my business thriving.

"It's so crazy! Even better than I imagined it would turn out!" I said.

"So, what's the next move? How are you going to get your salon?" Cali asked as she leaned toward me, craving the mastermind plan.

I sat there, eager to tell Cali the next steps, but every time I opened my mouth to speak, I found myself speechless.

My mind was blank.

My goal had always been clear—date Chicago, get my salon. I just hadn't figured out the next part of the plan to actually secure the salon, mostly because I didn't think the "dating Chicago" part would happen so fast.

And sure, I could've worked hard and made my salon happen myself, maybe even sped things up with a little magic. But why settle for one path when I could have it all? A relationship, funding, instant fame. It was a win-win.

Plenty of people did this…so why should I feel guilty?

It's not like I was hurting him. If anything, this was beneficial for Chicago just as much as it was for me. He got a beautiful girlfriend to parade around for the media and even a little magic boost in his confidence when he was around his fans.

Often when we went out, he was swarmed by fans and the paparazzi, both groups hungry for photos. Chicago would become instantly cold and not even smile for the photos. He wasn't rude. He would occasionally dap up a fan, but most fans wouldn't even approach him due to his icy demeanor.

Once we were alone in the car, he had to take several deep breaths until his protective armor melted away and he could be himself again.

"I just want to play ball and make money while doing it. This fame shit sucks. I get nervous around a lot of people," Chicago confessed.

"Even while you're playing ball with all those fans cheering you on?" I asked, while taking hold of his hand.

"Nah, that's different because I feel more comfortable on the court. When I'm playing, I'm usually able to cancel out all that noise, so I forget people are even there sometimes. But when I'm out in public and people are in my face talking to me…that shit is so weird to me. But I have to get used to it, especially if I want to work with more brands," Chicago said, nodding his head.

I placed my palm against his cheek to reassure him. "It'll eventually get to a point where you won't feel anxious around people anymore, but if you ever do, you can always confide in me. I want to support you in any way I can."

I said a spell in my head to give him a confidence boost to ease some of his anxiety.

"I for sure feel better when I'm with you, Chy." Chicago leaned over and planted a sweet kiss on my lips.

CHAPTER 11

S ince meeting Chicago, I had never been to his place, although I would see glimpses of it when we were on the phone.

I took it as him being very respectful by not rushing me over to get me undressed.

But after we became a couple, he gave me the invite, and I gladly accepted. He had just gotten back into town from an away game and was heading home. He wanted to see me, and I wanted to see him too.

I was bubbling over with excitement and slight panic knowing I was about to stay over at Chicago's place. I made sure I had my kitty appointment the day before so I could be prepped and ready for whatever.

I loaded up my pink spinnanight bag with all the essentials: toothbrush, extra pair of sexy underwear, perfume, deodorant, lotion, and a few other items. I grabbed my bag and stopped in front of the mirror for one last fit check. I looked good, as per usual.

I had a sleek ponytail with a black catsuit that squeezed my stomach, accentuated my ass, and perked up my boobs. My lips were extra wet and glossy, and my fragrance was delicious.

Before I headed out, I glanced over at Neli's empty bed, hoping she and Cali were enjoying movie night at Cali's place.

Once I arrived at Chicago's condo, I was greeted by the valet, who took my keys to park my car. I walked into the lobby, and my interest immediately piqued as I admired the huge chandelier hanging above my head.

It reminded me of those movies I had seen growing up, where the prince and princess would dance in a ballroom beneath a chandelier while everyone gawked in admiration. I got goosebumps imagining Chicago's and my fairy tale moment dancing beneath the chandelier at our wedding reception.

My high-heeled boots clicked against the marble floor as I made my way to the concierge to let her know who I was there to see.

She called Chicago then led me to the elevator. I stepped in, pressed the button, and the elevator shot up to the forty-second floor.

The mirrored doors opened, and there stood my man, tall and fine with a fresh line up, single plaits, and a cheeky smile. He stood there wearing a long dark green robe with matching pants. His robe was open, exposing his chiseled chest and a thick gold rope chain.

He grabbed my waist and pulled me into his chest with a warm and burly embrace. His cologne wrapped around me, making my knees quiver.

"You alright, baby?" he asked in a low mumble.

"Mm-hmm," I said as I tilted my head up and puckered my lips. Chicago leaned down and surrendered to my silent request for a kiss.

Our lips pressed together and began moving to their own rhythm of passion and longing. Chicago squeezed his fingers into my waistline, pressing my body into his, which shot a fiery rush to my head. I slipped my tongue into his mouth and twirled it against his, not even noticing that I was standing on my tiptoes. I slowly began to pull away and then licked my lips to let him know how much I had enjoyed my welcome gift.

Chicago squeezed my waist playfully before grabbing my bag and walking me down the long hallway.

We stepped into the living room, and there it was—the same astonishing view of downtown LA I'd seen in his post. Only now, seeing it in person, it was even more breathtaking. The lights across the city twinkled like glitter, it felt almost unreal.

"Dang, Cago. I love this view! You're going to make me want to move in," I said glancing back at him as he placed my bag on one of the chairs in the living room.

His condo was sleek and simple. Almost too minimalist, but it worked.

The big gray couch looked surprisingly cozy, draped with a fluffy white throw blanket and white and black pillows. Two matching chairs sat across from a glass coffee table, where a candle burned like it had been lit just for me.

Abstract art in matching tones hung on the walls. It was obvious an interior designer had decorated the place, and a professional cleaner kept it spotless. Everything was perfectly in its place.

"Shit, you can. I could use some permanent company," he said as he hugged me from behind and stared out at the view.

Chicago brushed his lips against my neck. Gently, he began to kiss me there, sucking with each peck he planted.

A warm shiver ran through me. I rolled my head to the side to give him better access, and he took full advantage, sliding his tongue up my neck to my ear. I let out a soft moan and rubbed my hands up and down his arms.

He began to kiss my neck more aggressively as he glided his hands up from my stomach to cup my breasts, squeezing them tenderly. I let out another moan. Louder this time, my body writhing against his, signaling that I wanted more of his touch.

Without warning, he turned me around and hoisted me up onto his waist, holding me tight. I wrapped my arms around his shoulders and looked into his eyes. His gaze was hot and intense. I felt as if he was undressing me with his eyes.

Lust thickened the air, and I couldn't resist any longer. Our lips met once again, but this time it was an urgent and desperate union.

Chicago carried me to his bed and laid me on top of it gently as to not disturb our moment.

He unzipped my catsuit and peeled it off my skin, kissing every inch of my body as it was uncovered. I was burning from the inside out. The ceiling fan above us and the silk sheets beneath me tried to keep me cool, but Chicago's sweet kisses ignited a fire within me all over again.

His lips made their way down the inside of my thighs then crept between my lips. A delicious euphoria washed over me, leaving me dizzy and breathless. I was panting to cool myself down, but Chicago kept firing me back up. I moaned loudly as I dug my nails into his sheets.

"Chicago!" I cried.

I could feel the pressure between my legs building up. Chicago let out a deep groan that vibrated throughout my body, making me buckle and shiver. I let out one last yelp before my body caved and released itself. My eyes rolled into the back of my head, and my legs dropped, completely limp.

Pleased with his performance, Chicago lifted his head and let out a cocky chuckle before climbing on top of me and planting a kiss on my lips.

"You good? Are you tapping out?" he asked, a note of disappointment in his voice.

I gasped for air then brought my hands to his head, running my fingers through the parts between his braids.

"No, I need more, Cago," I whispered, my voice soft and breathless.

He pressed his lips against mine and kissed me deeply as he slipped his pants and robe off. Then he slowly slid himself into me, and we made love passionately.

After an hour of our bodies merging together, we laid side by side, panting. I was spent, and all I wanted to do was nuzzle his chest and go to sleep, but my work wasn't done.

I flipped over and mounted him. Chicago was resting his eyes, but they flickered open with curiosity as I straddled him. He was still firm, so I slid him back in. I stared into his eyes as I slowly grinded my hips.

"You like me, Chicago?" I asked in a soft whisper.

"Yeah, I like you, Chyna. A lot," he said, raising his hands to hold onto my waist.

"I like you too, Cago. I want to be with you for a long time."

Chicago raised his eyebrow. "For real?"

"Mm-hmm." I grabbed his hand and kissed each finger playfully, letting out a soft giggle.

I saw Chicago's eyes light up as he snickered at my playfulness. Once I got to his thumb, I pressed my lips against it for a few moments, closed my eyes, then took a bite.

"Ow! What the fuck are you doing?" Chicago shouted.

I sucked in some of his blood then quickly bit my own finger. I brought my bloodied finger toward Chicago's and unsurprisingly, he resisted.

"Chyna! What the fuck!" He fidgeted beneath me, trying to push away my hand.

I mustered all the energy I had left and poured it into this spell. I said my spell out loud and felt his body tense and then freeze.

I placed my bloodied finger into his mouth and said the spell one last time. Chicago moaned and groaned a few more times before his eyes closed and his body relaxed. He fell asleep, and my job was done.

That love spell had taken a lot of energy. So, I cuddled up beside Chicago and soon slipped into a dream.

In my dream I was in a kitchen holding a beautiful baby boy who looked just like Chicago. He had the same warm smile.

The kitchen had an upscale, Tuscan-inspired design. It looked like it belonged in a magazine. I looked down and saw I was wearing a long, delicate white silk dress, clearly crafted by a luxury designer. The dress was high quality and screamed rich housewife.

I looked at my finger and clocked a ginormous glittering diamond on my ring finger.

I heard Chicago's voice coming from the patio door which led to a beautifully decorated back yard with a pool and a huge lake view. I followed Chicago's voice outside.

I found him standing in front of the grill, wearing nothing but swim trunks. He looked like he had just gotten out of the pool to check on the food he was grilling.

His skin was glistening with water which dripped off his body onto the grill, making it sizzle.

The baby boy in my arms let out a coo, which caught Chicago's attention. He turned his head and waved me over.

I walked toward him and noticed an older woman standing to the side of him.

She had a sweet face and warm, inviting eyes. Her light brown hair was styled in a finger coil updo, with curls cascading down both sides of her face. She wore a blue gown and, now that I was really looking, I could see a slight resemblance to Chicago.

I tried to say hello, but no words came out. I couldn't speak or move, yet I was captivated by this woman's eyes. She lifted the corners of her mouth to give me a dubious smile.

I could smell bacon, but when I glanced at the grill, it was empty. Somehow, it was smoking, but there was no food on it.

The woman was moving her mouth, but I couldn't hear a word she said. I listened closely and heard the sound of music playing in the background.

I took a deep breath and gasped as I woke from my dream. There was so much light spilling into the room from the floor-to-ceiling windows that I almost went blind.

I sat up in bed and smelled the same strong scent of bacon that I had smelled in my dream.

What the hell had that dream been about?

I got out of bed, put on the robe Chicago had worn last night, and made my way from the bedroom.

Bleary-eyed, I shuffled into the kitchen to see Chicago pouring batter into a hot waffle maker while singing along to my favorite song.

"Good morning, handsome," I said, leaning over the breakfast bar.

"Good morning, beautiful."

Chicago closed the lid of the waffle maker and walked over to give me a morning kiss before pivoting to the stove and flipping the bacon, all the while continuing to sing and dance to the rhythm of the music.

I laughed as he grabbed a spatula and went into full karaoke mode, singing into it as if it was a microphone.

"Chicago, what is wrong with you?" I asked, giggling as I covered my mouth with my hand.

Chicago grabbed my hand and continued performing his serenade.

"Last night with you was amazing, I think I'm...I think I'm in loooove," he belted out with the singer while bopping his head and tapping his foot to each beat.

I'll admit, I was cheesing so hard my cheeks were hurting. He was so cute and goofy that I couldn't help but sing and dance along. Chicago sang the last part of the song as he slid back over to the bacon to remove it from the pan. "I think I'm...I think I'm in loooove.

CHAPTER 12

Two days later, Chicago packed his bags to head to his away game in Cleveland.

"I'm missing you already, Cago," I said truthfully with a hint of sadness in my voice.

I was seriously going to miss him. Even though we'd only spent a few days together, I had already grown attached to his presence.

I liked the way he slept so peacefully on his back, letting me hog the covers while I snuggled against his chest. I also couldn't help but notice how he watched me intently as I went through my morning routine—washing my face, making playful faces in the mirror. And I loved the way he held me while we watched movies in bed, wrapping his arms and legs around me like a sloth hugging a tree.

He was only leaving for three days, but the way my heart was aching, you would have thought he said he was leaving for three years.

Chicago gathered his duffle bag and suitcase and headed for the door. He had given me a key earlier that morning so I could come and go as I pleased while he was away.

He even gave a thumbs up to Neli having a spot in the living room.

I decided that while he was away, I would move my things in and officially make myself at home.

"Man, I'm gonna miss cuddling in bed with you," Chicago said with a pouty face as he stood by the door.

He grabbed me and pulled me into a tight bear hug. "I wish I could fit you in my suitcase, but that ass is too big," he said, squeezing a handful of my ass which made me giggle like a schoolgirl in love. "My hotel bed is gonna be all cold'n shit."

"Hell yeah, it will! Don't think of sneaking no hoe into your room either. You better call me every night!" I threatened.

I knew how some girls could be—sneaky, bold, and ready to pounce the second they saw an opportunity. Hell, I was the same way, so I knew the game.

There were plenty of girls in his DMs and comments trying to shoot their shot at this tall, fine, and paid man, and I wasn't about to lose my spot.

I wasn't that worried, though. I knew my spells were stronger than any big booty hoe. None of them stood a chance when my magic was involved.

Though, I was a little bothered that he hadn't posted about our relationship yet to let the world know he was off the market. I knew that announcement better come soon.

We shared one last passionate wet kiss before he walked into the elevator.

Not even a second later, I hit up Cali to come visit me at my new home.

She arrived quickly despite the LA traffic, which meant she had probably sped like a bat out of hell to get to Chicago's high-rise. She came with my baby Neli, hot wings, and a bottle of tequila.

"Damn! Girl, this is everything!" Cali said, in awe as she walked around the living room. "I like this! I'll be up in here every time Chicago is on away games!"

I laughed as I showed her around the condo. "You're really going to fall in love with this place. Wait until you see the rooftop pool!"

"This is so much space. Y'all can put a few walls up in the living room and let me live there."

"Girl, bye."

We stepped out onto Chicago's large balcony which spanned the width of the building. It had been decorated professionally too with a super cozy bamboo daybed covered with white pillows, a hanging egg chair, a bamboo table, a rug, and plenty of plants.

Cali made herself comfortable on the egg chair and began to dig into her food. I sat on the daybed across from her stuffing my face with fries and telling her all about my first night with Chicago.

I didn't have to hold back any details because Cali already knew I was a witch, which made it easy for me to open up to her. I was so happy that I had decided to trust her with my secret.

Cali dropped a devoured chicken bone back into the container, her face scrunched up like she'd just seen the chicken she ate being slaughtered right in front of her.

"What's wrong? Why are you making that face? Did you bite into something?" I asked, ready to jump up and call the wing restaurant to make a complaint.

"Bitch." Cali turned toward me, pure disgust in her eyes.

"What?" I was annoyed now.

"Bitch. You drank that nigga's blood."

I let out a long sigh and relaxed back into my seat. "Yes, Cali! I did what I had to do."

"That's nasty as hell! No, absolutely not!" Cali shook her head in disapproval and gagged.

I'm sure she was starting to regret knowing I was a witch.

I narrowed my eyes at her childish reaction. "That's what the spell book required of me. It's not like I wanted to just be out here drinking nigga's blood like a damn vampire."

"I couldn't tell! You were excited as hell to tell me all that just now. As if you really liked it or something."

I wasn't ashamed of what I had done. It had been a necessary step. And maybe, just maybe, I had enjoyed it a little. I definitely enjoyed taking charge and taking control of him. It felt good to know I had Chicago Moon wrapped around my finger.

"I didn't like it! His blood tasted like metal. It was gross and nasty," I said with a hint of sarcasm to reassure her.

Cali gave me the look of a tired and concerned parent. "Look Chyna, I understand that you're a witch and this is what y'all do. Just don't lose yourself. Don't lose your humanity for some man. It's not that serious."

"Noted," I said before taking a bite of my chicken wing.

I was feeling a little disappointed that my friend wasn't being as understanding and open as I thought she would be. In that moment, I seriously considered erasing her memory.

CHAPTER 13

C hicago raced out of the elevator with his luggage in one hand and a bouquet of red roses in the other. I ran up and jumped onto him, my legs wrapping around his waist.

"Welcome home, baby!" I screamed and kissed his cheek. "I'm so happy you're home! I missed you! And I'm so happy you won that game! You did that!"

Chicago dropped his luggage, wrapped his arms around me, and planted a soggy wet kiss on my lips that made my insides melt.

"Thank you, baby." He looked up and sniffed the air. "It smells good. What you cook?"

I rescued the bouquet, which was getting crushed against my back, and buried my nose in them before taking his hand and leading him into the kitchen where a feast awaited him.

Spread out on the kitchen island were lamb chops, baked macaroni and cheese, and broccolini.

"Oh, shit! Hell yeah. I'm hungry as hell." Chicago rubbed his palms together eagerly.

"All for my man. Let me make your plate."

I set the roses down on the counter and fixed Chicago a big plate of the dishes I had just spent two hours making. My dad had sent me his recipes after I told him I was making a dinner for my "friend." He didn't question it, but I knew he was aware that I was doing this for someone special.

I watched with a big grin on my face as Chicago dug into the meal, moaning and grunting as he devoured the spread. When his plate was half empty, he lifted his gaze to me with a dazed look on his face.

"I think I love you, Chyna," he said in a quiet voice before returning his attention to the meal

It had worked. The spell I had infused in the food had worked.

I sat next to him and rubbed his muscular arm. "Baby?"

"Mm-hmm," Chicago mumbled.

I reached up and gently turned his face toward mine. His head was turned but his hungry eyes were glued to the plate that now only held a few spoonfuls of macaroni and cheese and a couple of bites of lamb.

"Look at me, baby."

Chicago sighed before shifting in his seat and giving me his full attention.

I batted my eyes and spoke in a honeyed voice. "So, I know you have a game here tomorrow night, and I really want to watch you play. I watched you play on TV, but I'm sure it's not the same as being in the stadium with you. I want to be there to support you. Can I come watch you at the game, baby?"

"Yeah, baby, of course you can come," Chicago said nodding his head.

"But I have to sit courtside. I need to be able to see you work up close."

"I got you, Chyna." Chicago let out a chuckle. "You're my girl. I want you there."

"Can Cali come with me, so I don't feel lonely?"

"Yeah, baby, that's fine."

I wrapped my arms around Chicago and let out a short squeal. "Aw, thank you baby!" Then I dropped my arms abruptly and began to pout.

"Oh no! I don't have anything to wear. If I'm going to sit courtside to support my man, I have to have something good on, you know? And I'm sure Cali needs something to wear too." I bit my bottom lip and looked up at Chicago, seeking a solution for my problem. "Shit, I don't know what to do, Cago."

Chicago sucked his teeth and cocked his head to the side to get a good look at my performance before bursting out laughing.

I was taken aback.

Did my love spell stop working? Did my pouty face not work?

Damn, maybe I needed to use sex magic for this.

"Maaannn, Chyna. If you need some money to go shopping, just say that. You don't have to put on all the theatricals and shit. I got you, baby. Anything you need," He said, placing his thumb under my chin.

Wow, it did work!

Or was he actually having feelings for me now? Because that wasn't the response of someone under a spell. He didn't have that dazed look in his eyes. His eyes were clear.

Was he actually falling for me? My heart started to flutter at the thought of Chicago actually liking me. Not to say there wasn't plenty to like. But if he could fall for me without the magic, then maybe I could actually tell him about it. If he truly liked me, he wouldn't care, right?

It made me think of my dad and my mom. He loved her for her. She never had to use magic to capture his heart.

Although she claimed she had used a little to capture his attention.

"Girl, ya mama is fine and very confident. I only needed a little boost to catch his eye when we were in school, but I did the rest all by myself," she would proudly boast whenever I asked how they met.

My mom was a very charming person.

Not only was she a wiz at magic, but she also had a natural talent for connecting with others. Magic was my one struggle, though.

My aunt blamed my mom for conceiving a child with a man who had no magic in his bloodline. I blamed my mom for not teaching me pride in my magic.

She had always taught me that having magic was a privilege and I should handle it with care. This was totally unlike my aunt's approach with my cousin, Ameri. She had taught her that magic was her birthright, and with it she could go far.

The result? My cousin Ameri is so skilled at using magic, she could rule the world if she wanted.

Chicago began to hand me his card. Before I could grab it, he pulled it back and gave me a stern look.

"This card has a lot of power, and I need you be responsible, okay? Don't go over a hundred," he said.

"A hundred what? A hundred dollars?" I asked, my face contorting into a grimace.

"A hundred thousand, shawty. Don't go over a hundred thousand. That should be enough for a whole new wardrobe."

Every molecule of air inside my lungs escaped in a whoosh, and I grasped the counter to steady myself.

Chicago turned back to his plate, while I ran to the restroom to change my underwear.

CHAPTER 14

After more than two hours of shopping, Cali and I collapsed into our chairs on the outdoor patio of a Mexican restaurant on Rodeo Drive. We had several bags which were so heavy, I was about to lose feeling in my pinky finger.

The waiter came over to greet us, and we ordered a bottle of champagne.

"Girl, I could really get used to this!" Cali said as she placed her bags on an empty chair. One fell over, and she quickly scooped it up before the contents fell out.

"Well, get used to it! We in the money now!" I squealed, beaming in my new luxury shades.

"I can't believe he gave you a hundred thousand dollars to spend! Thank you, girl, for bringing me along. I've been needing some new pieces. This new wardrobe is going to help me tap into some rich clientele."

A yellow Lamborghini rolled past, and we both eyed it, turning our heads as it sped by.

"Dang! If I had magic, I'd be in a car like that!" Cali said, her eyes glued to the car.

"In due time, my child," I reassured her.

The waiter came back with our bottle of champagne and poured us each a glass. We toasted to officially becoming part of the new money crew.

"I've never done anything like this with my magic before. I was so scared, but it's been a breeze. He's so easy. I honestly think it might not even be the magic. Maybe he's genuinely falling for me," I said, looking at Cali, hoping she would confirm my delusional beliefs.

She raised an eyebrow and took a sip of champagne.

"I don't know. The way he looks at me just makes me feel like the love is really there…that it's not artificial. Sometimes, I get the feeling that I could trust him and tell him that I'm a witch."

Cali twisted her brows and took another sip.

"Girl, what do you think? Say what's on your mind." My patience was wearing thin.

Cali let out a tired sigh and paused as she searched for words. "I definitely don't think it would be a good idea to tell him you're a witch. You don't know how he would react. What if he realizes that you used your magic on him?"

"But I think he would understand. Chicago is super sweet, and I know he really loves and cares for me. I don't think he would judge me like that."

I went over the scenario in my head trying to guess how Chicago would react. I wasn't completely sure what he would do. Maybe he would pull me in for hug and let me know that it didn't bother him, or maybe he would think it was cool and want me to teach him some spells. Then again, maybe he would look at me with disgust and assume I was some weird devil worshipper. He might even be scared enough to gather a village to stone me to death. I just didn't know.

The uncertainty of his reaction started to make me feel queasy. I was actually falling in love with him, and the thought that he might never love me in the same way unless magic was involved scared me. How on earth did my mom get so lucky that my dad had accepted her for who she was?

Cali placed her hand on her chin, her brow furrowing with concern. "Look, I understand if you're falling for Chicago. I mean, the man is a catch, so I totally get it. And it makes sense that you would want to share this part of yourself with the man you love but...in all honesty, I don't think it's the right time. There's no rush. I think it would be better to tell him once y'all are on your third year of marriage with two kids for security."

I took in what Cali was saying, and she was right. There was no rush. I was just getting started.

Besides, I didn't even have my hair salon yet.

CHAPTER 15

I stepped into that game looking like that bitch! Plenty of eyes were on me as I followed a staff member down to my courtside seats.

I was wearing a brown leather trench coat with a matching skirt, and a caramel-colored see-through top I bought when I went shopping with Cali. I hadn't bothered to check the price tag. I knew it would look good on me. I wanted it, so I got it.

Cali followed behind me with stars in her eyes. She was wearing a two-piece denim set that hugged her curves perfectly, the cropped jacket slightly off her shoulders to show just a bit of skin.

"Girl, I am so geeked!" Cali screamed in my ears.

I glanced over at her through my sunglasses. "I know right? This is cool as hell!"

We arrived fashionably late, so the game had already started.

The players took a time-out, and I saw Chicago walking over to his coach. He had his hands on his hips and determination in his eyes. He was already sweating and definitely putting in work. He caught me staring his way and let out a huge smile. I blew him a kiss, and he puckered his lips at me before turning back to his coach.

I couldn't believe I was in this position. It was amazing and better than I could have imagined. Just a few months ago, I had been in my small town, single, working at a job that I didn't care for, yet full of hope, dreams, and magic.

Now here I was in a great relationship with an absolute path to owning my own hair salon, sitting courtside with the rich and…was that Beyé sitting on the opposite side of the court? It was! Here I was sitting amongst the rich and famous.

Wow, so much can happen in such a short amount of time if you have faith and magic.

Cali and I chitchatted for the rest of the game, picking out players that she could be with. In the end, she wasn't interested in any of them.

"There is this guy I'm kinda talking to right now. We've actually been on three dates so far," Cali said shyly.

"What the hell, Cali? Why didn't you tell me? I'm supposed to be your friend and I'm the last one to know you're dating a new guy."

I was offended. Why would she keep that from me?

"Chill, you're not the last person to know! I haven't told anyone yet because I'm not sure if I want to even continue talking to him. He's nice, but he can be so annoying. Still, he's sweet and super fun to be around." Cali was twiddling her fingers, so I was sure she really liked this guy.

"How did you meet him?" I asked.

Cali took a deep breath "Well…see…that's the thing. You remember that guy I sat next to at the club the night you met Chicago?"

I replied that I somewhat remembered, although I couldn't picture his face. "Wait, didn't y'all talk about hot sauces or something?"

"Yep, that's him."

"Oh, so he's a friend of Chicago's. Do you need some advice? I can ask Chicago about him for you."

"No, it's okay. He seems genuine. I think I can have some faith in him."

"Okay, that's fine. Let me know if you want me to use some magic on him," I teased, nudging her shoulder with mine.

"Nah girl, I think I'll be fine. It's just so crazy how everything has been working out for us. There's you and Chicago...Chyna and Chicago. C and C. CC! That's what I'm going to call y'all from now own, CC!" Cali clapped her hands as if she had really discovered something.

I rolled my eyes at the cute but corny nickname. "So, what's your man's name?"

Cali shook her hand. "No, he's not my man. At least, not yet. But his name is Frankie Sullivan."

"Oh! Frankie and Cali. That has a nice ring to it."

"I know, right. Not only do our names sound good together, but we also look good together."

Cali pulled out her phone to show me the picture they had taken on their most recent date. They did look good together. Surprisingly, his Neo Soul style meshed perfectly with the new elegant-chic style she was adopting to impress her richer clients.

We both giggled like kids over our blossoming love lives, until the buzzer snapped us back to reality.

The game was over.

Chicago had scored the final three points that had won them the game. Cali and I jumped up and grabbed each other as we hopped around in a circle.

Chicago had won, so that meant we were going out to celebrate with his team, and I couldn't wait.

CHAPTER 16

"You see that final shot, baby?" Chicago screamed as he burst through the elevator doors and ran into the living room.

I was sitting on the couch fully dressed watching a show and scrolling through Pic-Talk. As soon as I heard Chicago's voice, I jumped up and ran over to hug him.

"Yeah, I saw baby! You did that!" I squealed as he squeezed me and swung me around in his arms.

He put me down and settled his eyes on my lips, then my breast, then all of me, taking my whole gorgeous self in.

I wore a long, black, semi-sheer dress that hugged my body in all the right places. It looked scrumptious on me. I pinned my curly ponytail into messy bun, letting a few curls frame my face just right. To finish the look, I dusted a bit of glitter on my skin for that extra glow.

"Damn! You look good! This all mines?" he asked, holding my hand and spinning me around to get a full 360-degree look at me.

"You like?" I teased.

"I do."

He smacked my ass then headed toward the bedroom. "I'm about to get ready. We're meeting some of my boys at the restaurant in an hour."

Once Chicago was ready, we were out the door and on our way to the restaurant.

We were riding in his matte all black G-Wagon. We buzzed in and out of traffic toward West Hollywood.

This would be the first time I met Chicago's close friends and teammates as his official girlfriend, and I wanted to make a good impression.

"Are you nervous, Chy? Don't be nervous," he said as he placed his hand on my thigh and squeezed it gently.

"I'm a little nervous. Is it going to be the same people from the club the night we met?"

"Nah, those were friends of my friend. These are my close friends and some dudes I play with."

That didn't quell my anxiety at all. I decided to use a tiny amount of magic to calm my nerves. Seconds later, I felt more relaxed and confident.

What was there to be nervous about, really? Chicago was already my man, and none of his friends would have the authority to convince him otherwise. Everything was going to be fine.

Once we arrived, we were greeted by a valet who took our car and then we were led by the maître d' to our table. I walked through the restaurant with total confidence.

We approached a table of about twelve people, and Chicago let out a loud cheer as he slapped his friend's hand and gave him a hug.

"That's him! That's the champ!" his friend said.

"Man, you already know, we up!" Chicago said in response.

As we sat down, Chicago introduced me to his group of friends. I saw a few familiar faces who had been on the court with him a few hours earlier. Some of them had brought their girlfriends along and they were welcoming. In fact, I recognized two girls who had been sitting near Cali when we were at the game.

"I think I saw you at the game today. I loved your jacket," one of them said. She looked Hispanic and had long jet-black hair.

"Yes, you're so pretty, and I love your dress," the other girl said. She was a mixed girl with green eyes and medium-length straight brown hair with blond highlights.

Both girls were super pretty. We made small talk until the conversation sizzled out.

I even saw Frankie, Cali's potential boyfriend, sitting at the end of the table.

"Shit! I thought it was a boys' night. If I would had known we were bringing girls, I would have brought someone," Frankie said, shaking his head in disbelief.

"What? Frankie, you got a girl? That's rare. I can't imagine a girl who would want to put up with your stubborn ass," one of the friends joked.

"She's something special, that's for sure."

Frankie made eye contact with me, and I knew he was talking about Cali. I nodded my head in agreement. Cali was definitely special.

She would have loved to be here sampling the food. This place was on the list of restaurants we wanted to try, so I planned to make sure to bring her next week and give her my own personal recommendations on what to order.

We ordered our food and had a big feast. Budgets were, apparently, nonexistent. There were plenty of steaks, lobsters, caviar, and top shelf champagne to go around.

When we finally finished our meals and the men had finished debating, we took a group picture on Frankie's phone.

He went around the table getting everyone's social handle so he could tag them in the photo once he posted it. I gave him mine then turned to Chicago for approval. He looked at me, a little confused before gently pulling me to my feet and ushering me to the side of the table.

Now I was confused until he waved Frankie over and asked him to take a picture of us. The photo came out great. We looked like a beautiful couple.

"I realize I haven't posted anything about you yet. I know we official. You're my girl, but I know I need to let the world know too," Chicago said as he posted our picture on his Pic-Talk page.

Within one minute, the picture had gained over ten thousand likes and thirty thousand comments from women posting crying emojis and men posting fire emojis.

My Pic-Talk page began blowing up with followers, likes and comments too. And just like that, I was a known person: the girlfriend of the popular basketball star, Chicago Moon.

"That was fun. I liked your friends. They were super funny," I said as our car pulled away from the restaurant.

"Yeah, they're some good people. I know how to pick good people in my life," he said as he turned and gave me a heartwarming smile.

We stopped at a red light, and Chicago leaned over and gently placed his lips on my forehead.

"I need more than that, Cago," I murmured as I grabbed his face and moved his lips closer to mine, gently brushing my lips over his then pressing them tightly in a sweet passionate kiss. Our lips melted together before we were rudely interrupted by a loud beep from the car behind us. The light had turned green.

I guess getting honked at for kissing at red lights was becoming our thing.

Chicago just chuckled and leaned in for one more quick peck before driving off.

I soon realized that we weren't heading in the direction of his condo.

"Chicago, where are we going? Where are you taking me? I'm ready to go home and take this makeup off." It was starting to feel heavy after being on my face all day.

I could feel my oily skin penetrating the layers of foundation and powder.

"Don't worry about it. Just trust me real quick." He glanced over and gave me a wink.

He was lucky he was so fine. I leaned back and looked out the window, watching as the lights from nearby businesses and houses began to fade.

We drove for over thirty minutes until the car started bumping and bouncing as it climbed a dirt road. I held onto Chicago's arm until he pulled over in a remote area. He got out and opened the door for me. So, I got out too.

"Where the hell are we?" I snapped, my mood sour from the bumpy ride that was making me nauseous.

Chicago didn't respond but lifted me onto the hood of his car then jumped up to sit next to me. I narrowed my eyes at him, confused about why we were sitting on the hood of his car in the middle of nowhere.

When he noticed me glaring at him, he took my chin between his thumb and forefinger and turned it to face forward.

My jaw dropped to the ground as I gawked at the most amazing view of LA, in complete awe. It was lit up like an expensive Christmas tree, sparkling in every direction. The lines of red from the LA traffic jammed up the highways, looking like tinsel garland wrapped around the tree.

"Wow, Chicago! This is amazing!" I leaned over and wrapped my arms around his chest.

"I told you to trust me. I know some good spots out here," he said, wrapping his arms around my shoulders.

"How did you find this spot?"

"My coach took me hiking out here a while back. I come out here to hike every once in a while to catch the view, but it looks better at night."

"I'm impressed. This was really nice and romantic of you."

"I'm glad you think so. Chyna, I don't know what it is about you, but I just have a strong urge to be around you and love on you. It makes me feel good when you feel good and you're smiling. I really like what we have. I want this to work…I think you might be good for me."

"Really?" I asked, curious to hear more.

He turned to face me and brushed his fist over my cheek.

"Yeah, you remind me of my mom. Just a genuinely good woman who loves me and wants the best for me. I want a loving, supportive family and a long, successful career, just like my dad. He had all the brand deals, the fans, but when he came home, he had real love and support from my mom. I need that too."

I assured him that I could provide that for him, because I wanted it too.

"My dad has always had my mom's back and given her unconditional love. I really want that," I said, feeling the emotion in my chest as I spoke.

"I could love you unconditionally. You haven't ever given me a reason not to. I feel like I can trust you."

I gave him a shy smile, knowing the reason he trusted me implicitly was due to the spells I'd used on him. But there was a chance he might have true feelings for me.

"Tell me about your mom. She sounds like a great woman," Chicago said.

"She is. She's so strong and powerful. Her presence and aura are so captivating that everyone that's ever met her just loves her and is attracted to her light. She has such a calm and nurturing demeanor, but she is also assertive and won't let anyone push her around. She's a huge inspiration for me, even when we don't see eye to eye."

"Why don't y'all see eye to eye?"

"She can be…a little too stiff about certain things. She tends to be a know-it-all. And even though she really does know it all, I can't stand it when she insists on proving she's always right. Honestly, I just wish she'd be more supportive of my dreams." I dropped my head down, somewhat ashamed that I had even admitted that to him.

I truly treasured my mom. Based on the stories my dad would tell me, bragging about my mom in her younger days, she had been amazing.

She once used magic to control everyone on her college campus to speed up the graduation ceremony. She had even controlled a herd of lions and ridden atop the biggest while she traveled through Tanzania. She was wild but reasonable, according to my dad.

Yet, when I tried to have fun experiences with my magic, it became a huge problem for her.

"She sounds special, like you. I can't wait to meet her one day. And I mean, she's your mom. It sounds like she does know best and doesn't want you to make the same mistakes she made. At least, that's how I see it, because that's how my dad is. He's always trying to coach me on things because he's been through similar situations and doesn't want me to make his mistakes," Chicago said as he raised my chin.

"You're special, babe. And just like your dad is on your mom's side, I'm on your side too. I got you."

Chicago had a very gentle and beguiling look in his eyes that made me want to fall into him. In that moment, I felt I could trust him…that he could have my back, my side, and my front.

I felt a sense of relief as the anxiety I had been feeling melted away, replaced by a cozy security blanket named Chicago.

I really wanted to tell him I was a witch. I was almost sure he wouldn't judge me. He would love me and support me just like my dad supported my mom. I didn't want to have to hide this secret from him anymore.

"Chicago, my dad was super supportive and had my mom's back because he knew something about her and didn't judge her.

He loved her unconditionally, even when things were foreign to him."

"What do you mean?" he asked.

"Chicago, I'm a ..."

Buzz.

Chicago's phone began vibrating against the hood of the car. He looked down to see who was calling.

"Hold up, Chy, it's my mom."

He hopped off the car and answered the phone with a huge smile on his face. "What's up, Mama? You see the game tonight?" He sounded like a little kid who had just drawn a stick figure portrait for his parents to display on the fridge. I assumed she'd watched the game by the way he was cheesing.

"Not trying to sound cocky, but I knew I was going to win that game," he said, sounding every bit of cocky.

They continued to chat, then he mentioned he was out with me, his new girlfriend.

"Yeah, I can't wait for y'all to meet each other. I was just telling her that she reminds me of you."

He turned to face me while still smiling brightly. "My mom says hi. She can't wait to meet you."

"Tell her I said hi! Is she coming to town anytime soon?"

"Mm-hmm, both my parents are planning to make a visit soon," he replied.

"Great! Tell her, I would love to take her out for a mani-pedi."

"She'd like that."

I was getting excited just thinking about meeting her, getting our nails done, and talking about Chicago when he was a baby.

He wrapped up the conversation and came back over to me, placing his hands on my knees.

"My bad, Chy, what were you saying? Were you about to tell me something?"

I hesitated. Maybe it wasn't the right time to tell him I was a witch. Maybe I would feel more comfortable after I met his mom. Maybe then I could tell her too.

"I was just saying that I'm very grateful to have met you and to have you in my life," I said as I placed my hands on his checks and pulled him in for a kiss.

CHAPTER 17

Work was starting to become very mundane, and Richard wasn't getting any more tolerable either. Even with the small punishments I gave him for annoying me, he just continued to bounce back like an unfazed roach.

I felt I was ready to move on from this part of my life. It was time to finally achieve my dreams and open my salon.

I walked into the office a little more irritable than usual after having to deal with the downtown traffic that was heavier than it had been in a while.

I pushed through the revolving doors and saw my friend, Ms. Shelly, at the reception desk.

"Hey, Ms. Shelly. Good morning," I said, trying to inject some cheerfulness into my voice.

Ms. Shelly turned toward me and let out a sigh.

"Hey, Chyna girl. Good morning. Whew, it's been a morning, and I'm ready to go home already."

"Oh no, what happened?" I moved closer to her desk so I could get all the tea.

"Well, just this morning, a former employee from the real estate company on the seventh floor had to be escorted out by security.

The guy had been fired the day before, he had surrendered his badge and laptop, but it turns out he had a spare badge. So, he was able to get back onto his floor and cause a big scene, throwing documents around and even breaking a few computer monitors," she said, voice heavy with exhaustion.

The company on the seventh floor called down to Ms. Shelly, asking her to send up security. She did, but they were occupied with someone who had snuck into our parking lot because they thought it was public parking. Even though posted signs clearly showed it wasn't.

"Child, it took security almost twenty-five minutes to finally get up to the seventh floor to arrest that guy, and by that time, he was able to destroy four monitors and punch his boss in the face," Ms. Shelly said as she rubbed her temples.

"The firm on the seventh floor was yelling at me to send up security, I was yelling at security to go up, and security was yelling at the person who had snuck into our parking lot. It was a mess."

"That's insane! All that, and the day just started," I said, rubbing her shoulder in an attempt to console her and calm her nerves.

"Exactly, but hopefully that's all the mess we'll have today. Speaking of mess, how's that coworker of yours? What's his name again, Richard?"

I scrunched my nose at the sound of his name. This had become a reflex every time his name came up.

"He's still working my nerves every chance he gets. I don't know what that man's problem is," I said, exasperated.

"He's probably just jealous of you because you've been killing it lately with all the winning cases you've assisted on."

She was probably right. It had only been a few months since I'd been here, and I'd already assisted with two cases that had won at trial. Richard obviously had more experience than me, but he still saw me as competition, even when we were working on a case together.

I finished my morning chitchat with Ms. Shelly and hopped on the next elevator.

I was about ten minutes late and was planning to rush over to the coffee station to fill up my cup before heading to my desk. But, as soon as the elevator doors opened, Richard was standing there holding two large binders. I believed they were the same ones I had created the other day.

"You're really late, Chyna. I wasn't going to let the director know, but I was starting to get worried. He said to send you to his office when you got here. And here, these are the binders you made last night. Thankfully they turned out right. I guess you're finally getting the hang of things."

"Thanks, Richard," I said, trying to brush swiftly past him and head to the coffee station.

"That's not all. We're going to need another copy of these for the new attorney we're working on this case with," he said as he pushed the two binders into my hands. "Don't forget to make a stop at the director's office."

Richard gave me a petty wink and waltzed off toward the coffee station that I had been planning to go to.

I decided to just head to the director's office to avoid having to stand next to Richard at the coffee machine.

On my way to the director's office, Sasha stopped me and gave me an annoyed and weary look.

"Did Richard tell you that he ratted you out? It's only like ten minutes. I'm sure the director isn't going to be that upset, but he probably has to give you a small talk and a warning."

"Yep, he sure did tell me before I even stepped off the elevator. What is his problem?"

"I'm not sure why he's acting that way toward you. But good luck Chyna. Come see me afterwards so we can discuss the next steps on our case."

I gave her a nod and made my way to the director's office.

"Hi, did you want to see me?" I asked in a small innocent voice.

The director looked up from his computer and motioned for me to have a seat.

"Hi, Chyna. How's your morning going so far?" he asked.

"Oh, not too bad. Traffic was a little more hectic than usual, but I made it unscathed," I joked.

"Well yes, LA traffic can get pretty harsh at times, however, we were all able to make it here in a timely matter. And usually, I have no problem if anyone is running a little late from time to time, but Richard informed me that you have been late multiple times since you started working here."

"I don't think it's as frequent as Richard is making it seem. I'm only late probably every other week or so," I said, trying to tally up all the times I had been late.

I began to realize that I do tend to be five to ten minutes late repeatedly, but I'd never been late to trial nor had tardiness ever affected my work.

We continued to discuss how my being late wasn't a good look for the firm, and how unfair it was to my team to have to wait—

even if only for a minute—to collaborate on projects due to my tardiness.

I tried to defend my case; however, it fell on deaf ears. Richard had probably presented the director with a strong case featuring many examples of my tardiness, so the director wasn't even trying to hear my pleas. He gave me a verbal warning letting me know that the next time I was late, he would issue a written warning, and if I was late for a third time after our meeting, I would be written up which would prompt him to evaluate whether I was still a good fit for the company.

What the hell was this?

I'd been good to this company and had done phenomenal work, all for them to reconsider my position over a few tardies that Richard had exaggerated. My pot was boiling and was beginning to bubble over.

I thanked the director for his time and took my big ol' binders back to my desk. I could have used some magic to erase the director's mind, but I planned to use that before he even had a chance to give me a second warning. I was too drained to use any magic now.

However, tired as I was, I did have just a little to spare for Richard.

After dealing with the holes I'd made in his paper cups, he switched to ceramic mugs. But of course, I managed to come up with a spell for those too.

I recited the spell and pointed at Richard's cup. Just as he was leaving the coffee station with a full cup of coffee, the handle of his mug broke off, sending the cup crashing to the floor and splashing coffee everywhere.

His shoes and the bottom of his pants were soaked with scorching hot coffee. He jumped up and cursed, causing a big scene. He was still holding the handle, which he threw across the floor before storming off to the bathroom. I snickered and continued my work.

I finished my tasks for the day on time, gathered my belongings, and walked to the elevator, excited to head to Chicago's place for our scheduled movie night. I pressed the elevator button for the first floor and began daydreaming about being wrapped in his arms when I was rudely interrupted by Richard, who was yelling my name.

"Chyna! Where are you going?"

"I'm going home. I finished those stipulations, and they're printed off and sitting on your desk."

I turned to step into the elevator, but he placed his hands in front of the door, blocking it from closing.

"You can't leave yet. We still have more work to do for this new case. I need you to retype this document because it wasn't saved in the system."

He pushed a stack of paperwork toward me, but I backed away.

"Okay, I can start on it tomorrow morning," I said, pressing the button for the doors to close and hoping Richard moved his hands.

"No, we need these done for our morning call tomorrow. You're going to have to stay a little late tonight," he said as he positioned his whole body in front of the elevator doors.

"I can't do that. I have plans." It was getting harder to hold back my irritation

"You're salaried not hourly. You know that if we need you, then you're going to have to work later. We can confirm it with the director if you want," He said as he crossed his arms and stared me down.

I stared back, a fierce rage in my eyes. I was furious because I knew he had purposely waited until right when I was going to leave to try to give me more work with a tight deadline. I'd asked him multiple times today if there was any other work that he needed help with, and each time he'd said no. I'd even asked multiple people to ensure that I'd be able to leave on time to spend the night with Chicago before he was gone for almost two weeks with back-to-back away games.

Right then and there, I decided I didn't need this job anymore. I just needed to feed more magic to Chicago so he would fund my hair salon.

"I'm not staying tonight, Richard. I asked you multiple times if there was any work that urgently needed to be done, and you told me there wasn't. I did all my work, so I am done for the day. I can come in earlier tomorrow and help out, but that's all I can do. Please move, because I need to leave."

Richard was shocked. He tried to make a comeback response, but he was speechless.

After a few awkward moments of him fumbling his words, he again tried to use his body to prevent the elevator doors from closing, while repeating his threat to run to the director.

My pot was now boiling over. I was done.

I stepped toward him and began reeling off a spell out loud which forced the elevator doors to start closing.

He was baffled. He couldn't understand it. He kept trying to push the doors back open, but they weren't budging. They continued to inch closer and closer, on the verge of crushing his body before he finally stepped away from the elevator and watched the doors slam shut.

CHAPTER 18

When I walked into Chicago's condo a couple of hours later, I wasn't empty-handed. I was towing a wagon full of all the groceries I needed to prepare a special meal.

It was Chicago's last night before he left for almost two weeks for work, and I was going to make him some Marry Me Chicken with asparagus, mashed potatoes, and his favorite cake: German chocolate.

Chicago was still at the gym, so I planned to start now so it would be ready by the time he got home.

I found the recipe on Pic-Talk, strapped on my apron, turned on an R&B playlist, poured myself a tall glass of red wine, and found a nice comfy spot on the couch while my magic went to work in the kitchen. I had been crafting spells that would turn my magic into the culinary expertise of a professional fine dining chef.

I'm pretty sure this was a skill I'd inherited from my mom because I know for a fact she did not cook or clean without magic. Whenever it was her turn to cook, she never asked for help and preferred for everyone to "not be in the way." It was most likely because she was using magic to help her out, and she didn't want anyone to know. I made a mental note to confront her about it the next time I saw her.

By the time Chicago walked through the door, dinner was ready to be served. I ran into the kitchen and threw some drops of water and chicken sauce onto my apron, so Chicago would think I'd been slaving away in the kitchen.

"Damn baby, it smells good! What did you cook?" Chicago asked as he swung into the kitchen, immediately dropping his duffle bag and rubbing his hands together, ready to eat.

I broke off a piece of chicken with a fork, made sure it was sauced up, and walked over to give him a taste. He cleaned the fork then let out a holler of approval.

"That's delicious," he said, beaming at me before reaching down to give me a kiss.

I kissed him back and enjoyed the lingering taste of the chicken on his lips. It *was* good. I was impressed. My magic really did that!

Chicago went to the bathroom to freshen up while I prepared our plates, giving him a large portion so he would be nice and full after the meal. He devoured the plate in less than five minutes. Once again, I was impressed.

"Chicago, relax. The food's not going anywhere," I teased.

"I know, but I am. I'm trying to get as much as I can before I leave," he said, scraping the plate clean.

"I made dessert too."

I went over to the fridge and pulled out the German chocolate cake that was decorated as if it had come from a real bakery. It was a three-layer cake with coconut pecan frosting and beautiful piping on top. I didn't even know we had piping bags. How did the magic do that?

I cut Chicago a big slice, slid the plate over, and he dug right in. He closed his eyes, and I could tell he was savoring it because he kept emitting grunts of approval.

Then there was a crunch.

It was probably just the pecans. But then he reached into his mouth, pulled out a piece of eggshell, and my eyes went wide, like a platter of food, while the rest of me crumbled in a pit of embarrassment.

SHIT!

"Oh noooo! I'm sorry, I didn't know any shells got in there!" I was frozen with shame.

How on earth did that happen? My magic should have been perfect. There shouldn't have been any eggshells in that damn cake. But I was a fool. My magic did the job, but it still needed to be supervised to make sure there were no issues. I had taken a nap on the couch and didn't even realize my magic was struggling.

Chicago chuckled but continued to eat the cake.

"No, don't eat it! I don't know how many shells got in there!" I said, my voice rising as I tried to take his plate, but he held on tight.

"It's cool, Chy. It's just a piece of shell. My dad used to make me drink shakes with blended up eggshells back when I was in training camp. So, this ain't nothing," he said as he continued eating.

I relaxed and pulled myself up from the emotional pit I had dug myself into.

I walked up behind Chicago and wrapped my arms around him, pressing my face into his back. I was happy I'd chosen him as my partner. He was so kind and sweet, and having his support meant everything to me.

I let out a big sigh. After the day I'd had, it felt good to be with Chicago. He helped me feel so calm and relaxed.

"What's the matter?" he asked.

I took a moment to gather my thoughts then I let it all out. I told him about the rough day I'd had at work, and how Richard had always made my job hellish. I even told him about the incident that had happened just before I left work, leaving out the part where I almost crushed Richard like an empty soda can with the elevator doors.

"Damn, that dude sounds like a bitch. You told me he was bothering you, but I didn't know it was that bad," Chicago said as he turned to give me a bear hug.

He rested his chin on the top of my head and rubbed my back. I felt safe.

"Yeah, he's just getting worse, and it's hard to report him because they'll only see it as him trying to implement leadership and help delegate tasks. He's technically not harassing me. He knows how to not take it too far."

"I wish I could beat his ass for you."

Now that made me chuckle. The thought of Chicago punching Richard in the face was very satisfying.

"I wish you could, too," I joked then paused and realized the situation I was in wasn't funny.

"I don't know. I wish I could just open my hair salon and be done with this job. It's not where I want to be. Maybe I should just take a chance. I could get a loan or something. What do you think?" I pulled back to look into Chicago's bright eyes.

I dug the tips of my nails into his back and said a spell in my head that would induce persuasive thoughts into Chicago's head.

I was ready for this transition. I had already envisioned almost everything I wanted for my salon, I knew the theme and design I wanted. I could see myself pulling up to my salon in my cherry red sports car while wearing an expensive light pink suit. I would unlock the doors and walk into my salon like a boss, turning on all the lights and setting up shop to start the day. By two o'clock, business would be booming with other successful women sitting in my chairs getting their hair done while chitchatting with my amazing team of stylists. I would be watching Chicago's game on the salon's TV while styling hair and gushing to my clients about how sweet my man was.

"I think you should quit if you're unhappy," Chicago said in a monotone voice that was devoid of any emotion.

"Really, you think so?" I asked as my spell seeped further into Chicago.

This spell was perfect for the occasion. Not only did it brainwash someone into doing what you wanted them to do, but even after the spell stopped working, they would believe that everything they had said and done was what they had truly wanted to say and do. As if the spell represented their own natural thoughts and ideas.

"I do. Let me take care of you," Chicago's voice became more urgent as the spell took root inside him, turning into a decision he believed he'd thought of himself.

"I would love for you to take care of me," I said before pressing my lips against his.

Our lips moved together slowly, both of us savoring the other's taste. They glided against each other until a fire sparked.

We tightened our embrace, the passion warming to a feverish pitch. We were panting as we tried to consume each other. Every part of my body began to heat up, starting with my face, then my hands, and then my thighs.

Chicago stood, lifting me with him. My legs automatically straddled his waist and squeezed tight, demanding more pressure between my thighs. He carried me off to the bedroom, and we enjoyed our last night together with moans, screams, and spells.

CHAPTER 19

I could see her captivating eyes again, staring me down. It was the same lady who had been in my dreams the first night Chicago and I slept together. I couldn't really see her face that well this time. Everything around me was dark and blurry except her eyes that pierced through my body.

Her gaze was heavy and relentless. It weighed down on me, crushing my soul, making it hard for me to breath. I found myself taking long and deep breaths but still feeling like my lungs were empty.

The room I was in was pitch black, and all I could see were her huge light brown eyes engulfing me until I couldn't breathe anymore. I was drowning in her eyes.

I gasped for air and then woke up suddenly. My pajamas were damp because that dream had me sweating. I placed my face in my hands and squeezed as hard as I could without messing up my lash extensions. What a nightmare! Who the hell was that lady, and why were her eyes so terrifying? It was all so confusing.

"Hey, good morning," Chicago said, walking into the bedroom with a towel around his waist. A few droplets of water were slowly rolling down the crease of his six-pack. I tracked one as it rolled down to his towel. I'm pretty sure that same droplet somehow found its way into my underwear.

Chicago walked over to me and kissed my forehead, his brow furrowing when he noticed it was sweaty.

"You alright, baby? Why are you sweating? You hot?" he asked.

"Yeah, I'm okay. I just had a bad dream."

I rolled out of bed and got ready for the day.

By the time I was dressed and walked into the living room, Chicago had already started cooking breakfast. I decided to help him make some eggs while he took care of the pancakes.

"Are you heading out today?" he asked as he scanned my outfit.

I had on a black turtleneck tank top, flared black slacks, silver accessories, and I planned to wear my black and white plaid trench coat once I headed out. My hair was pulled back into a sleek bun with a few curly edges.

"I have work today," I said as I cracked an egg onto the hot skillet and tossed the shell into the trash. "How do you want your eggs? Scrambled?"

"Mm-hmm, scrambled and add this." He passed me a pack of mozzarella cheese.

Leaning on the counter, he watched as I stirred the eggs. "I thought we agreed that I would take care of you."

"We did, but I still have to make sure I have enough for the salon. I can't just drop my job when I don't have a clear plan yet."

He walked over and placed his hands on my shoulders.

"The plan is to let me handle that. I don't want you working somewhere you hate. I don't want you working with that asshole anymore either," he said, gently massaging my shoulders.

"I get that, but I can't just quit."

"Yes, you can. I got you."

I turned the heat down on the eggs and looked up at him.

"Are you serious? Do you really mean it when you say you 'got me'?"

I studied his face for even a hint that he wasn't being sincere. "Yes."

He was serious, and there wasn't any magic in play. His eyes didn't lie. I wrapped my arms around his back and stood on my tiptoes to give him a kiss.

I won.

I kissed Chicago one last time before he stepped into the elevator to head out. Although I was sad he was leaving me for a few days, I was as happy as hell that my plan was coming to fruition.

Before Chicago left, he sent me a large amount of money to help me get by since I was no longer working. It was more than I would make in a year, so I was relieved.

By the time noon rolled around, I already had fifteen missed calls from my coworkers: ten from Richard, three from my boss, and two from Sasha. I decided I would email them a formal resignation tomorrow.

A small wave of guilt washed over me at the thought of quitting, only because a trial was coming up and they did need the help. But that guilt was quickly replaced by Neli's cuddles as we watched a movie and ate takeout.

Besides, they had the pretentious Richard on their side, so I figured they should be just fine. Every time I felt even a little bit guilty for leaving my job, I would imagine how Richard was reacting to my absence. I'm sure he was in a total panic and that made me feel better.

Later that evening I had an urge to call my mom. She answered immediately as if she had been expecting my call. She had probably used a spell on me to push me to make that call.

"Hey Ma, how's it going back at home!"

I was so excited to hear her voice. She rambled for almost an hour giving me updates on her clients, the new neighbors on the block that she'd taken a liking to, the mischievous activities my cousin Ameri had been involved in, and that my dad was entering a BBQ contest for our town fair.

The news and gossip were exciting to hear. It made me miss being home, back in my old bedroom. But I was now in my dream high-rise condo.

After my mom finished her ramblings, she wanted to know how I was doing. How was work? How was my apartment? Was I making more friends? How was my new friend Cali doing? Was I eating good food? Was Neli being good company?

I answered all her questions briefly, trying not to divulge too much. I especially didn't want her to know about the recent change in my career path. She would have been so mad and gotten my dad riled up.

I could tell she was starting to sense that something was off with me based on my short answers, so in order to distract her from investigating what was really going on, I told her I was in a relationship.

"Excuse me, WHAT?" she yelled.

I figured she'd be excited, but also confused and really curious. I'd only had one boyfriend in college, and that relationship had gone very south.

I had brought him home to meet my family for the holidays, and he had left with no memory of who I was. All thanks to my crazy witchy family.

It had all been Ameri's fault. She was constantly using magic, even in front of regular people.

On this occasion, she had used magic to set the table in front of my ex-boyfriend. So, candles, knives, a turkey, you name it, were flying around my aunt's dining room.

My ex was screaming like a mad man and almost passed out when Ameri floated a large knife toward him. In her defense, she was "just messing with him," but he didn't take it well.

We had to erase his memories of that night, and despite my pleas, they felt it would be best to erase his memories of dating me as well. My mom and my aunts both agreed it was for the best. They didn't believe he would be a good match for me because he hadn't accepted the fact that we were witches.

I told her how I met Chicago at a nightclub, and how we hit it off.

My mom was shocked when I mentioned he was an NBA player, and she couldn't wait to tell my dad when he got home from work.

She was worried about how the relationship would work, especially since Chicago didn't have magic. She feared his fame could expose our entire family if he found out. I reassured her that my skills were sharper now, and it would never come to that.

Of course, I had to leave out the part about using a love spell on him, but I did tell her that I had a feeling I would be able to trust him with our secret one day.

"I don't know, Chyna. I think you should play it very safe with this one. I'd love to meet him and feel him out. Especially before you tell him anything about us."

"Of course, Ma. I think you and Dad will like him a lot. He's a great guy. Super sweet and loving. He makes me feel so safe and seen. I just know I can trust him, but I'll hold off on telling him," I reassured her.

We talked for a few more minutes, and I told her that my skills were improving, but I still needed help. Especially when it came to using magic to cook.

I had even confronted her and asked her point blank if she used magic when she cooked, but she denied it, descending into an angry rant about how magic should be used responsibly. I tuned her out, watching the traffic start to build up on the freeway through the window. I was completely zoned out until her scream pierced my ear.

"Chyna! I know you heard me!"

She was upset about something, but I didn't know how she had gotten to that point.

"Sorry Ma, what did you say?"

"Don't try to act like you didn't hear me. I asked if you know what happened to my spell book. You took it, didn't you? Chyna, that book is important, and those spells are very dangerous. You know better! I know you remember what happened the last time you tried to use…"

"Sorry Ma, I've got to go. I've got to take Neli for a walk."

"Walk Neli? Since when have we ever walked Neli? She's a cat!"
Click.

I hung up.

I couldn't deal with that negativity at a time like this. Not when my dreams were about to come true. Instead, I looked out the window and began to plan. The next step was figuring out where I wanted my salon to be located.

CHAPTER 20

"This is it! I love it!" I squealed, tears welling up in my eyes. I turned to Chicago and gave him the best puppy dog eyes. "I want this place. It's perfect!" I said.

And it truly was perfect.

We had already toured two other locations, but neither had felt right. The first had been far too small, accommodating only half of what I envisioned. I wanted at least ten stylist stations, two private rooms for VIP clients, and twelve wash bowls. The second location was spacious enough but needed extensive renovations. The previous tenant's bright blue popcorn walls looked tacky, the tiles were chipped and outdated, and the neighborhood wasn't ideal for the luxurious atmosphere I wanted for my clients.

But the third location was everything I had dreamed of and more.

Situated on La Cienega Boulevard, the salon was spacious and beautifully lit, with huge front windows flooding the room with sunlight and high-quality LED fixtures brightening every corner. The lobby was wide enough for a chic waiting area that I would later furnish with oversized, plush round sofas.

A long hostess station with shelves behind the counter would perfectly double as a champagne bar, displaying bottles we would use to serve complimentary champaign glasses alongside premium human-hair wigs available for purchase.

Just beyond the hostess bar were the ten stylist stations, each offering ample storage space. Further back to the right stood twelve plush-seated wash stations, opposite twelve sleek hair dryers. At the very rear were two bathrooms, a break room for stylists, and a VIP room for exclusive clientele. There was a huge modern chandelier that hung elegantly in the center and marble flooring all throughout the salon.

Walking through the salon, I could vividly envision every detail from decor to paint colors. Chicago patiently listened to all my interior design ideas. Since the space had previously functioned as a salon, it required minimal renovations. The existing countertops, dryers, and wash bowls were already to my liking. All we needed were new, larger mirrors, fresh paint, and comfortable, cream-colored chairs.

Initially, the salon's prime location and minimal renovation needs made the price higher than Chicago had intended to spend. But with a little magical persuasion, he soon obliged, and the very next day, we purchased the property. I couldn't have been happier.

I was now officially the owner of a new hair salon on La Cienega Boulevard.

Immediately, I threw myself into preparations. New mirrors and chairs were ordered, and decorations chosen to enhance the ambiance.

Everything was happening so fast, and it had all started the day Chicago promised he would take care of me. From that moment, my daily routine shifted dramatically. No longer working my nine-to-five job, I had gotten very comfortable being a pre-housewife which involved cooking, grocery shopping, occasionally tidying up since we had a weekly cleaner, and reorganizing Chicago's condo to make it more functional.

In my spare time, I had worked diligently on my business. I created my business plan, defined my target audience, scouted salon locations with our realtor, and I had finally settled on a name for my salon.

I had come up with the name while hanging out with Cali and Neli during our girls' night, while Chicago was at an away game.

"I definitely think you should have something in relation to magic in the name. I know its cheesy, but it just makes sense. This is all happening thanks to your magical gift," Cali said as she assembled some meat, cheese and crackers from the charcuterie board.

I stared out the window at the view of downtown LA, biting on the end of my pencil. She had a point. But nothing catchy was coming to mind.

"Chyna's Magical Hair Experience? The Magical Hair Salon?" I rattled off a few names but none of them rolled off the tongue easily.

Neli was lying, eyeing Cali with intense focus as she devoured a cube of cheese. Cali noticed Neli gawking, so she decided to tease her by dragging the cheese back and forth as if she was going to toss it to Neli. Neli sat up in anticipation, not blinking once. Cali threw the cheese up into the air, then caught it in her mouth as she laughed.

In response, Neli placed her paw on my thigh and looked up at me as if she was recruiting me in her revenge plot. I looked down at Neli's paw and that's when the name came to me. Touch. Magical Touch. That was it! I thanked Neli with a small cheese offering.

"Magical Touch Hair Salon. How does that sound?" I asked Cali, unable to hide my wide grin as the name lit up inside of me.

"Oooh, I like that a lot. I think that's perfect!" Cali raised her champagne glass, and we toasted to the name.

After months of preparation, it was now just two weeks until my soft launch. We were planning to invite clients to come and mingle, see the salon, get free consultations, and book appointments. Our actual opening was scheduled for the following week.

So far, I had been able to rent out seven of the ten stations. It was a good start. I was confident that after a few months of being open, more hairstylists would be drawn to join us.

The salon's renovations were nearing completion, significantly easing my stress and anxiety. Just last week, we hired a team to install our elegant new sign outside.

The previous owner recommended painters who gave me a sweet deal on repainting the salon walls in an elegant nude pink that complemented the new chairs.

I was in the salon sweeping up some of the mess the painting crew had left behind when Cali stopped by to visit. She brought me tacos from my favorite taco spot.

As I watched her walk over to me, my eyes filled with admiration as I realized just what a super supportive friend Cali had been throughout this whole experience. I definitely owed her a huge gift and even a shopping spree at my expense to show my appreciation.

"Come eat. You need a break." She traded me a paper bag filled with tacos for the broomstick and took over the sweeping.

"I don't know why you aren't just using your magic to clean this up."

"I could have but I just wanted to do it myself so it could feel real. I needed this to be more real for me," I said, ripping open the bag. The tacos smelled like heaven. She knew me too well. I was starving and hadn't eaten all day because I was too stressed to even think of food.

"A pinch could help it feel real too," Cali joked. "But girl, I'm so impressed. Look at this! Look at what you did!" Cali dropped the broom and spun around the room as if she were in a 90s teen movie. "You really did it! You got the man and your dream salon!"

I covered my face to hide the tears that were welling up in my eyes.

This was the first time I had sat back and really realized what was happening. It had all happened at lightning speed. My move to LA, meeting Cali and Chicago, and then getting my salon. Although, it had happened months ago, it felt like it was just yesterday that I was lying on my bed back at my parents' house, dreaming up my master plan. And it had actually worked out!

Cali walked up to me and wrapped her arms around me.

"Aw, my little witch bitch. I'm so happy for you," Cali said, rubbing my back like a proud mom.

Tears were streaming down my face. "Cali, thank you so much for your support and loyalty. You've been my sunshine the entire time I've been here. I'm so happy I met you, girl," I mumbled through my sobbing.

"Aw girl, I'm so happy I met you too. We've been having such a blast, and I can't wait to see what else is in store for us."

My heart was full. Just the other day, Chicago also praised me and let me know how proud of me he was for pushing through the stress of starting the business and seeing it through. He was so happy that I was achieving my dreams.

I had my best friend, my future husband, and my salon.

What more could I ask for? Oh, that's right, I needed clients!

CHAPTER 21

I only had one week to quickly create some hype around the salon. Chicago had posted about it a few times, but most of his followers were male fans, so it created some traction but not much.

My main target audience was women who didn't mind spending extra money for quality service and products to improve their looks. Whether it was bundles, wigs, silk presses, box braids, natural styles, or pixie cuts, my salon would have it all.

Of course, I wasn't too worried. Despite the panic of getting my salon up and running, I still found time to practice my spells because the one I was cooking up was very important. I was even able to bribe my Aunt Crystal to help me with this spell by giving her two of my beloved Chanel bags. It was a worthy investment, because this spell would help me to have clients lining up around the block.

My aunt helped me craft a new spell that intertwined magic with the internet and social media. The plan was to cast it on my target audience whenever they came across my paid ads online. The spell would latch onto them through the ad, filling them with an irresistible urge to visit my salon. My aunt called it an elevated brainwashing spell.

To reach a high amount of engagement and interactions on my Pic-Talk post, I had to focus more of my attention and magic on this spell. It meant I had less magic to use on Chicago, but so far, everything with him had been great.

In fact, I'd already started to slowly ease up on the magic I was using on him since his real feelings for me had already taken root. The love spell had rewritten his memories so that he genuinely believed he had always been in love with me, never realizing the magic had planted that feeling in the first place.

I stared down at my phone for about three whole minutes, analyzing the content before I shared it. It was a ten second video promoting the launch of my salon by showcasing all the glitz and glam of the renovations, my new team of hairstylists, my receptionist pouring a glass of champagne and toasting the viewers, and finally me spinning around to greet the viewers with a big smile. The video ended with the name and location of the salon along with details of the soft opening.

I was beyond excited, but nerves crept in as my finger hovered over the 'post' button, ready to share my video with thousands of people. I rewatched it over and over, second-guessing myself, wondering if I should even go through with it. But I realized that was just my nerves trying to trip me up, pushing me toward self-sabotage. There was no way I could let that happen.

Not when I had magic on my side.

I closed my eyes and took a long deep breath before speaking my spell into existence.

Tap. Ding.

And just like the that, it was up. The video had been uploaded to my business page.

Posted ten seconds ago.

Refresh.

Posted twenty seconds ago.

Refresh.

Posted forty seconds ago.

I held my breath until it finally displayed *posted one minute ago.*

The deed was done. I threw my phone across the couch and laid back to stare up at the ceiling. This was all happening way too fast, but in the best way of course. I leaned back a little more until I could see the sky from the balcony window. There was a huge fluffy cloud slowly floating by.

Ping. Ping. Ping. Ping.

My phone started buzzing and pinging repeatedly. I slowly sat up and reached for it to see what the commotion was. My eyes nearly burst out of my skull when I saw that in less than five minutes, my post was blowing up. There were over ten thousand likes and hundreds of comments. Even the followers on my page had multiplied by the hundreds. And each time I refreshed the page, the likes and follower count doubled.

I clicked the comment section to see what the people were saying.

"Oh shit, this place looks so nice!"

"I'm loving the vibe!"

"Do y'all take walk-ins?"

"I'm coming to get that Brazilian wavy bussdown!"

"I'm gonna need about three glasses of champagne when I come through!"

My hands were shaking as I read through all the supportive comments. There were loads of potential clients and they were all more excited than I was!

One comment in particular stood out to me.

"Yasss! I've been looking for a new Black-owned hair salon in LA. I'll be there!"

It had been posted by one of my favorite beauty and fashion influencers who I followed on Pic-Talk, Cia Don. She had over seven hundred thousand followers. In other words, a vital amount of influencing power.

One time, she had posted about her favorite foundation and within minutes, it had sold out. I had been lucky enough to snag two bottles of my shade before it ran out. Not only did her endorsement lead to cosmetic products selling out, but clothes and wigs met the same fate too.

I sat there with the widest grin on my face imagining how fast my schedule would get booked out if I could get her in my chair.

I knew instantly that she would make the perfect brand ambassador. So, I sent her a private message from my business page to let her know I would love to have her in my salon. Complimentary service in exchange for more promotion.

The night before the soft opening I was barely able to sleep. I was way too excited and nervous.

After a few hours of tossing and turning in bed, I remembered the spell my mom used on me whenever I had a hard time falling asleep. So, I used it and fell asleep fast.

It didn't last for long, though, because I had another one of those weird dreams with the older lady wearing the blue dress.

This time, she was standing inside the house I believed would be my and Chicago's future home. She was right in the middle of the foyer, beneath a grand chandelier.

She wore a look of disdain and turned to leave. As she was walking away, the chandelier began to fall apart. Each crystal prism and light bulb crashing onto the marble floor like a shower of rain.

Once she exited the doors, the entire canopy of the chandelier came crashing down along with pieces of the ceiling which began to crumble, falling on top of me until I was no longer able to see or breathe. I was completely covered in the rubble, desperately gasping for air until I awoke and sat up in bed, panting.

Chicago was rubbing my back and calling out to me.

"Baby! Chyna! What's wrong?" His eyes were struggling to stay open. I looked over at the clock on the side of the bed and saw it was three o'clock on the dot.

"I'm fine. I just had a bad dream," I said, holding my face in my hands, trying to erase my memory of the dream.

Chicago got up and stumbled toward the door.

"It's probably just your nerves. I'll get you some water," he mumbled.

I stared into the corner of our dark room.

What the hell were these dreams about, and who the hell was that older lady? What did she want from me? Why was she so upset? Was she trying to kill me?

So many questions rushed through my mind that I couldn't process them all. I needed to rest.

Chicago handed me a bottle of room temperature water, just how I liked it. I took a few sips and laid back down, clinging to him and laying my head on his chest.

The motion of his chest rising and falling was soothing. After another hour or two of trying to decode my dream, I was able to fall asleep again.

I got a total of four hours of sleep, but I still woke up with high energy. The excitement I felt at bringing my dream to fruition was fueling me like two large cups of coffee.

I took my time getting ready since I still had a few hours before the opening. While Chicago made breakfast, I used a little magic to beat my face to the heavens. My hair didn't take long since I had prepped it the night before. I took out my curl set and pinned it into a cute curly bun.

As much as I wanted to arrive early to help with the preparations at the salon, I also wanted to experience my girl boss moment: confidently walking into my salon to give my nod of approval that the party was ready to start. Besides, I needed a few more hours of sleep after my horrid nightmare.

In order to make sure everything went according to plan, I had to use a heaping amount of magic.

When I met with my event crew, I explained the vision I had in mind, but I also used a spell to help them visualize my ideas. It enabled them to see images of the exact decor I wanted along with the layout that indicated precisely where everything should go.

I used the same spell on my hairstylist, Leslie, who became my right-hand woman, keeping everyone in check.

Leslie was arriving at the salon early to help the crew set up. She sent me photos of the balloon stands that were being built to decorate the entrance and interior of the salon. It was exactly as I had envisioned.

The DJ, who was a friend of Cali's, texted to confirm his arrival, as did the caterer. I had used a little bit of magic on them as well to ensure they would arrive on time.

Everything was going like clockwork.

I slipped into the outfit I had laid out the night before. It was a scrunched gold top paired with cream slacks that were trimmed with feathers just above the hem, and a matching cream suit jacket with feathers on the cuffs.

I added a pearl necklace and matching earrings. The golden shimmer in my makeup matched the top perfectly. I admired my look in the mirror, snapping a few selfies before heading out.

I walked into the kitchen, drawn by the mouthwatering scent of the breakfast Chicago had prepared for me. The aroma had filled the air while I was getting ready, and it was irresistible. The smell of crispy bacon made my empty stomach feel like it was pressed against my back.

On the kitchen island, he had laid out a whole spread, and it looked as delicious as it smelled. There was fried chicken, waffles, eggs, bacon, grits, and fruit. A whole feast. A champion's breakfast.

However, there was no Chicago in the kitchen.

I walked into the living room and saw him on the balcony talking on the phone. I wasn't trying to be nosy or pry into his business, but I was curious about why he was talking on the balcony and not in the kitchen. It was as if he was trying to have a private conversation that he didn't want me to hear.

He was pacing back and forth in front of the open balcony door, so I couldn't hear much, but I did hear him speaking about my salon opening today. I crept closer to the balcony and hid behind the couch.

"Yeah, I wish you were here too. I think you would enjoy it. You have to visit when you come to town. Chyna will hook you up," Chicago said on the phone, cheesing like a big kid.

Who on earth was he speaking to?

Neli found me behind the couch and assumed this was play time. She let out a big *MEOW* before jumping onto the couch and swatting at me.

"Stop. Not now, Neli," I said, trying to swat her back so she'd leave me alone.

She was not giving up, though. She was living in her delusion that I was trying to play with her and I ended up with two small scratches on the back of my hand.

When I tried to back away, I bumped into something firm and hairy.

What the hell?

I reached my hand back and felt Chicago's legs. Throwing my head back, I saw him staring down at me with a cocky grin while still holding his phone to his face.

"Alright, Mama. I have to get ready. I'll talk to you tomorrow. Love you, bye."

He hung up and glanced back down at me before walking off.

"What are you doing? Trying to spy on my conversations with my mom?"

"No, I wasn't trying to do that." I got up and dusted my ass to remove some of Neli's cat hair. "But if you were talking to your mom, then why did you go out on the balcony?"

He turned around to face me as he walked backwards toward the kitchen.

"I just wanted some fresh air. I can't have fresh air and talk to my mom? You need to be present during every conversation? That's my mom. I'm always going to talk to her and that doesn't always have to include you."

I tilted my head, beyond puzzled. Who the hell did he think he talking to? Where the hell was this energy coming from?

"Excuse me? What are you talking about? I didn't have a problem with you speaking with your mom. I didn't even care that you needed to speak with her privately. I was just curious about why you wanted to be private all of a sudden. Usually, you put her on speakerphone."

"Don't worry about it. You need to be focused on this event. This shit is about to be huge. Your dreams are coming true, babe!" He shot a half-smile my way before turning and continuing to walk toward the kitchen.

Babe?

When had Chicago ever called me babe? It had always been Chy or Baby. I wasn't sure where this energy or sass was coming from, but he was right, I didn't have time to focus on it.

Not now, at least.

But, once we got home tonight, he would get his next dose of the spellwork.

CHAPTER 22

We pulled up to the salon in Chicago's Corvette. He hopped out to open my door, and I saw that there was already a nice little crowd of about fifty people waiting outside for the event to start.

The nerves were starting to build up, but I didn't allow it.

Chicago held my door open while I said a little spell in my head to ease my mind and boost my confidence.

I stepped out of the car feeling like that bitch, that boss bitch. My dream moment was finally here.

I slid on my gold shades and walked up to the door. Leslie opened it for me with a big bright smile on her face.

"Hello, hello! Today is the big day!" Leslie said, unable to hide her excitement.

She looked cute in her short cream pleated dress. She had beautiful dark skin and freshly dyed burgundy hair that showcased a perfect twist out.

I looked around the salon and my eyes welled up with tears.

It was perfect.

There were fresh flowers everywhere, a beautiful balloon arch in front of the reception bar area, and the DJ was set up and searching for the right song to kick off the event. The caterers were installed beside the reception bar with an array of finger foods and desserts.

There were mini chicken wings, small lamb chops, fried shrimp on top of deviled eggs, as well as mini chicken sandwiches, mini egg rolls, a fruit platter, charcuterie board, and dessert platter with cupcakes and cookies.

Plus, the entire salon team was there, dressed to impress. We looked like Black luxury personified.

"Wow! This is so amazing! Thank you all so much for helping to pull this off!" I was truly grateful and amazed at the teamwork that had made this happen.

"Thank you for this opportunity! I'm so ready to start working! I love it here already," my fabulous hairstylist, Gee, said, lifting a glass of champagne in a toast.

His blond hair was styled in a fresh fade, and he was wearing a pale pink suit with flared bottoms. The color made his bronze skin glow.

Cali swanned in from the back of the salon with a beautiful bouquet of flowers that she presented to me. She was also wearing a pink suit with a white floral silk top.

"Congratulations, Chyna! I'm so happy for you and this beautiful salon!" Her voice was cracking, and I could see she was trying to hold back her tears.

I took a long deep breath, admiring my salon, my crew, and my man, all of which were nothing but blessings for me.

"Alright y'all, let's get this shit started!" I screamed.

The DJ threw on the first track, and we opened the doors and let our guests and future clients pour in.

A few of my hair stylists began to do simple hairstyles, and some were giving free consultations. I stood in the corner, sipping on my champagne and enjoying the environment I had created. Everyone was having a great time, chatting and mingling throughout the salon.

Chicago walked over with a red velvet cupcake that he handed to me. I ripped the wrapping off and stuffed the entire cupcake into my mouth.

"Damn, that cupcake ain't going nowhere, babe," he said.

There he went again with that "babe" instead of "baby." When did we regress to that? I decided to deal with that later, because right now, I needed to demolish this delicious cupcake.

"You deserve it, though. I'm very proud of you, Chyna. I'm excited to see what comes of this. Maybe we can get you another shop in Houston," he said before taking a sip of his champagne.

"Thank you, baby," I said as I crumpled the cupcake wrapper. "Thank you for investing in me and believing in me. Couldn't have done this without you."

I turned to embrace him. Chicago placed his hand on my back and kissed the top of my head.

"Of course. I got you. Always."

I looked over and noticed Cali speaking to a man who looked familiar. It didn't take me long to realize it was her potential boo, Frankie. I hadn't even seen when he arrived.

I could tell Cali was trying to suppress her smiles and laughter around him, but she was failing, gracefully. I liked them together. They looked good.

Cali glanced over at me, raising one brow to make sure I was good. I nodded and gave her an "I know that's right, girl" look, to which she made a shooing motion and gave me a "chill out" look.

We both chuckled, and she continued her conversation with Frankie. I wondered what they were discussing this time. Maybe ranch dressing or ketchup brands.

The DJ began playing another song, which had people either bopping their heads or rapping along. I let go of Chicago and moved toward the center of the salon to do my little dance and saw Leslie and Gee engaged in a rap off.

I was about to walk over and join in when I felt someone tap me on my shoulder.

I turned and saw two familiar faces, two stunning women I instantly recognized. One was Hispanic with long black hair and flawless lashes, while the other was mixed race with brown hair and striking green eyes. Both wore bodycon mini dresses, one pink and the other white. I recognized them from the dinner Chicago and I had attended with his friends after his team's big win.

"Hi, gorgeous. Congratulations on your new salon!" the mixed girl said as she handed me a small Dior bag.

"Yes, this is absolutely gorgeous. I need to schedule an appointment ASAP," the Hispanic woman said, chiming in while she admired the salon.

"Thank y'all so much for coming! I'm so sorry, but I don't remember if we properly introduced ourselves. I'm Chyna. Welcome to my new salon," I said.

"No, we didn't get the chance. I'm Brianna and this is Cynthia. Our boyfriends all play on the same team," the mixed girl said as she pointed over to all three of our boyfriends who were talking with each other.

"Chicago extended an invitation to us," Cynthia added. "I just want to say, damn, I'm so impressed. How long did it take for you to find this place? I've been wanting to open a lash salon, but it's so hard to find locations at a good price."

"Right? Especially for a place like this. It looks very expensive. How did you afford it?" Brianna asked.

I paused, my expression shifting to one of confusion from their questions.

We were all dating successful men who all had a few million to their name. I know because I had checked out their boyfriends when I did my initial search for a target.

"Well, Chicago helped me out with everything," I said proudly.

They were frozen with confusion.

"Wait. He paid for all this? Girl, how did you get him to do that?" Cynthia asked, flashing her man a dirty look.

"Cago has always been willing to help me achieve my dreams, so it wasn't that difficult. I just asked him."

Of course, I may have left out one little detail: I used magic on him. But I couldn't let them know that. I didn't trust them yet.

I realized, though, that the answer I had given them probably wasn't sufficient. Cynthia confessed that she had tried to gently push the idea of starting a lash salon, but her boyfriend would brush it off.

"Ladies, we are all with rich and very successful men. If these men aren't willing to help us become successful as well, then what are we doing with them? My advice would be to really open up about why you want to start your own business. Allow yourself to be vulnerable. Sweet talk him and make him feel obliged to help, as if it were the investment of a lifetime. Then make his favorite dinner, give him a nice massage, and present him with your business plan. Have your business plan mapped out so all he has to do is provide the funds," I said rubbing my fingers against my thumb.

"I have a good feeling that if you do this in the next few days while this event is fresh in their minds, you'll have a better outcome. They've seen what Chicago did for me and will probably want to compete and show off their women's new businesses. Trust me," I said, giving them a wink.

We continued to discuss more techniques for them to sway their men before we parted ways so I could mingle with the other guests.

As soon as we parted ways, I cast a few spells on their men to help the girls achieve their goals more easily. These spells would make it easier for their men to be willing to provide them with businesses, cars, clothes—anything they wanted.

Throughout the event, we had multiple clients coming and going, sharing content about the shop with their friends and followers. Near the end, I was able to book out my schedule for a whole month with clients I had met throughout the day. My hairstylists were able to accumulate a good number of bookings as well.

The soft opening had been a success.

I went over to the dessert platter and was lucky enough to snag the last red velvet cupcake. Just as I took a huge bite, I felt someone tap my shoulder.

I tried to gulp the mouthful down before turning around but it was too late. The person who had tapped my shoulder walked around to face me.

"Hi, you're the owner, Chyna, right?" she asked.

I instantly knew who she was. This girl was gorgeous with big dark brown eyes, and an extremely curly wig that fit her face perfectly.

I held up my pointer finger for her to give me a second while I tried to gather as much saliva as I could to swallow a bite of cupcake down. After it went down, I cleared my throat.

"Yes, I'm the owner, Chyna Cole. Welcome to my salon. Please help yourself to the remaining refreshments," I said, waving my hand in that direction so I could have a moment to finish my cupcake in peace.

"Don't mind if I do," she said as she grabbed a chocolate chip cookie. "By the way, you have some icing on your nose."

"Thanks," I said as I quickly patted my nose, hoping I was only removing the icing and not my makeup.

"My name is Ciana, but people know me as Cia Don on Pic-Talk," she said in a matter-of-fact tone.

"I knew it was you. I didn't want to be weird and fangirl out, but I really love your content. Are you looking for a new hairstylist? I would love the chance to work with you."

"Yes, I'm looking for a new salon. You don't have much recent work on your page, but I might be willing to let you touch my hair. You do have a license to do hair, right?"

I froze.

That was a major detail I'd completely overlooked. It was something that should have been sorted before I even opened the salon. I couldn't believe I had missed it. But I didn't panic. It would be fine. I could breeze through beauty school in no time. After all, I was a fast learner.

"Mm-hmm," I nodded, taking another bite of my cupcake.

I hadn't lied. Technically, I *would* have a license soon... hopefully.

"Great! Then can you schedule me in for a sew in? I'm hoping to get one next week. Do you have any kinky straight bundles for sale?"

I swallowed my last bite of cupcake and went through the types of hair bundles we had. After I booked her appointment for the following Thursday, we were all smiles.

Once the event was over and all the clients had left, my staff and I cleaned up the mess and said our goodbyes for the night. The official opening of the salon was next week, and everyone already had a fair number of clients booked. So, we were all set.

I gave Cali a long hug for all the support she had given me and made a promise to call her tomorrow. She insisted that she would call me because she might be busy, motioning her eyes over at Frankie. I raised my brow.

"Okay now, Cali. Be safe and have fun, girl," I teased before stepping into Chicago's car.

We drove out of the parking lot and headed to Santa Monica. I wasn't sure where we were going, but I didn't question it. I just sat back and enjoyed the ride to wherever he was taking me.

We arrived at a very fancy Italian restaurant. Chicago pulled up to the valet station and hopped out of the car before coming around to open my door.

I was starting to feel a little drained after the long day and knew I needed to save some energy for tonight's spell. I was about to suggest calling it a night when he gave me a fiery look.

"Come on. I have a surprise for you," he said, holding out his hand to help me from the car.

I obliged and gave him my hand.

As soon as we walked into the restaurant, Chicago had me wait by the door while he spoke with the host. When they came back, they escorted us to a private dining room.

My eyes almost fell out of my head at the scene that greeted me.

There had to be over a thousand red roses scattered around the room interspersed with small candles. Along one wall, big red balloons spelled out CONGRATULATIONS, and beneath that was a huge pink teddy bear made of roses. It was holding a small jewelry box in its hands.

My knees went weak.

Was he about to propose to me? Is that why he had been acting so strange this morning, and taking his phone calls in private?

Damn! That spell was really powerful. Here I was thinking I needed to up it, but it had been working all along.

Chicago walked over to the bear and retrieved the jewelry box. He came back to stand in front of me with a huge smile on his face.

"Chyna, I'm so proud of you for going after your dreams. Being with you has been like a dream. I don't know what you do to me, but I'm addicted to you. I love being in your space and in your mind. I just…I really love you, Chyna."

"Aw, I love you too," I said, sweetening my voice to match the moment, just in case he had a hidden camera to capture this for our families later on.

Chicago lowered his head and inhaled sharply before opening the box.

Inside was a beautiful heart-shaped…necklace. It was gorgeous, but it was a necklace, nonetheless. I quickly scanned his hands to double-check that he wasn't trying to trick me and follow up with a surprise ring, but nope.

"Wow…it's a necklace," I said, trying to keep the letdown from slipping into my voice.

"You like it? I thought it would look good on you. It's twenty-four karat gold," he said, sounding pleased with himself.

I finally closed my mouth which had been hanging open this whole time from being bamboozled.

"Yes, it's beautiful. I really love it," I said, managing to muster up some enthusiasm to spare his feelings.

I could tell he really thought he did his big one with this. And not to say it wasn't a big one, because I'm sure the necklace cost a great amount of money. My hopes had just been too high thinking he was ready to propose. But that just meant, I would need to work even harder to make him ready.

Once we arrived home, it was on.

The sexual tension had been mounting the higher we rose in the elevator. We tore our clothes off before we even made it out of the living room. I desperately needed this sexual release just as I desperately needed to up my spell, so it was win-win. We went at it for hours before we were stretched out on the bed, spent and gasping for air.

My body was limp and tired, and I didn't want to move. I needed a few minutes to catch my breath and reconfigure my brain.

Chicago's breathing slowed to a consistent rhythm, signaling that he was asleep.

Now was my chance.

I desperately wanted to close my eyes and fall asleep next to him, but I had work to do. So, I fought the drowsiness for a few minutes before finally dragging myself closer to him.

He was lying on his back with his mouth wide open.

Perfect.

I started off by placing a few soft pecks on his warm lips. I deepened my kiss while building up my intentions. Then I said the spell aloud and bit down on my tongue as hard as I could until I tasted blood.

I kept kissing Chicago, allowing the blood to seep into his mouth to finalize the spell.

CHAPTER 23

"So, was it like a pre-proposal necklace?" Cali asked as she drank more of her orange juice.

"No. I highly doubt it was. I think it was just him being romantic and nothing more."

I gazed out over the patio at the cars and people passing by.

It was the day after the launch and Cali and I were out for brunch, because we both had things we needed to catch each other up on. She had let me go first, and I had shared what had happened at the restaurant.

"I have to step my magic up. It's been working really good so far, but I have to take it to the next level in order for me to get a ring. I need to lock this man in."

"I feel you, Chyna. But I hope you don't plan to drink any more of that man's blood. That's just too much."

I bowed my head to hide some of the shame I felt.

"Girl, you did it again? You drank his blood again?" She was demanding answers.

"No! I didn't drink his blood. He just...umm..." I popped two mini pancakes into my mouth to prevent me from finishing my sentence.

But Cali was not done with the conversation yet. She sat there with her arms crossed, ready to hear my confession.

"I really don't understand the blood drinking. Ain't that what vampires do?" She tensed up and eyed me up and down. "You a vampire, Chyna?"

"Girl, shut up before people hear you! No, I am not a damn vampire. Witches use blood magic to make a spell stronger. It's not required but it's recommended for better results."

Cali looked off to the side as she pondered her next question.

"So, who did the drinking?"

I clasped my hands together and explained what had happened while ignoring the concerned face she was making.

"Cali, it is what it is. I'm getting a ring by next year even if I have to drain all his blood out to get it," I joked.

Cali did not laugh but squinted her eyes at me and shook her head.

"Anyways, enough about me. Tell me what's going on with you and Frankie. What happened after you guys left?"

Cali picked up her orange juice and gulped the rest of it down, choking a little before finishing the glass. She paused then smiled.

"Everything is good. No, it's great, actually."

I eyed her up and down, slowly raising my brow as I sat and waited for her to divulge more. After a few minutes of her not saying a word, I cleared my throat.

"Cali! Is that all you're going to give me?"

"Of course not, girl! I just wanted you to beg a little," she teased.

"Girl…" I said while playfully rolling my eyes.

"So, after your soft opening, we went to dinner at Nobu."

"The one in Malibu?" I asked, perking up.

"Yes, right by the water. It was so nice and romantic. Then afterwards we went back to his place which wasn't that far from there, and..." She paused and took a bite of her omelet. "And then we made cookies."

"Cookies?"

"Yes, cookies."

"That's it? What kind of cookies?"

"Chocolate chip. I had the munchies. Before we went to his spot, we also stopped at a dispensary. We went to his place, made cookies, watched a movie, and then I was out before it even finished. He was really sweet about it. He brought me some covers and laid down with me."

"That sounds nice. He does seem like a respectable man."

"And then...after we woke up, we made breakfast and fucked on the kitchen counter."

We both screamed, earning us stares from the people at the tables around us.

"You didn't!"

"I did! I had to! I needed to! It's been way too long, and I needed that."

I gave Cali a high five.

"I know that's right."

Cali had already told me that she'd been celibate for about two years after her last relationship. So, I knew that if she had decided to sleep with Frankie, then that meant he was special. I was happy for her.

"So...when are you going to squeeze me into your bookings? I've been wanting a sew in so I can put my hair up for a while," Cali said, pulling on her curly hair.

I let out a sigh followed by a grunt as I slouched over the table.

"Girl…in the midst of getting this salon up and running, I forgot about one very important thing."

"What? You forgot to buy some hair tools? We can run to the beauty supply store after this."

"No." I lifted my head and pouted. "I don't have a license to do hair."

Cali's jaw dropped, and she cocked her head to the side in disbelief. She tried to speak several times, but the words seemed to keep getting stuck in her throat. After several pauses, she gathered her composure and found her voice.

"Chyna, first off, what the fuck? How did you completely leave off getting your cosmetology license? I don't know why, but I just assumed you had one because you were so adamant about starting a salon."

"I don't know. I just…" I shook my head trying to understand how I had dropped the ball on that. "I knew it was something I needed to do, but the business process was moving too fast, and I didn't have time to sit and process everything."

Cali lifted her hands and clasped them together. "Welp, you have one week before your first client. I guess you just schedule a quick test and get the license, right?"

I buried my face in my hands. "No, unfortunately, it's not going to be that easy. The state of California requires you to complete one thousand hours at a licensed school. Then, once you've completed that, you fill out an application for a license and schedule your test. It can take up to eight to twelve weeks to receive a testing date. After that, you take your test which involves a written and practical exam."

"Damn!" Cali threw her hands up and began to shake her head back and forth. I joined her. We looked like two bobble heads.

"What are you going to do?"

"I don't know," I said, sounding defeated. "I have Cia Don's appointment next week. I told her I was licensed and I'm sure she's going to want proof."

"Don't give me that 'I don't know' shit, Chyna. You do know. Bitch, you have magic! Make that shit shake."

I sat there puzzled. Yes, I did know magic. But how the hell was I going to use magic to obtain a thousand hours of schooling and expedite a test in less than a week? That type of magic is advanced. That type of magic...was probably going to cost me a few designer purses. Maybe even a car.

Instead of heading home after my brunch with Cali, I stopped at the beach for a moment to myself.

Luckily, I was wearing a sundress, so all I had to do was roll up my dress a little to avoid getting sand on it. I always kept a towel in the car, so I brought it out and laid it on the beach. There weren't too many people about because the weather was a little chilly.

I sat there for about ten minutes, allowing the cold wind to blow against me as I began to meditate. I inhaled deeply, held my breath, then released it through my mouth. All I could feel was the wind pushing against my head and dancing through my hair. I focused on the goosebumps growing on my arm as the cool air brushed against my skin.

I fell deeper into my meditation until I began to notice strong vibrations coming from the ground. My mind drifted, wondering what could possibly be happening. My ears twitched as another cold gust of wind blew against them. Then off in the distance, I heard bells jingling softly. They grew louder as they got closer, developing into a melody.

My eyes flew open, and I realized my phone was ringing, which was strange because I usually didn't get good service when I was at the beach. I dug into my bag and pulled out my phone. It was an unknown number. I hesitated at first but decided to answer.

"Hello, who is this?"

"Hey, cousin. About time you answered. Didn't mean to interrupt your meditation. It looked so peaceful."

I could recognize the voice anywhere. It was airy and captivating, with every word she spoke. I always loved how it sounded, like she was reciting a spell with every sentence. It was my cousin, Ameri.

"Ameri! Hey girl, how have you been? Wait, how did you know I was meditating?"

"Oh, I can see you I'm watching you right now through my pocket mirror. Damn, that beach is nice!"

I looked around at my surroundings frantically.

"You can see me in your mirror? Are you using a spell?"

"Yep, I learned this trick a while back."

I widen my eyes in disbelief.

Ameri was only three years younger than me, but her magic was much more advanced than mine. It would take me months to master a spell that she was able to master in a day. I'd always been a little jealous of her magical abilities and the freedom she had. Her mom never tried to stifle her curiosity about spells.

"Oh, you have to teach me that spell!" I said.

"I got you. So, how have you been? I saw your post about your salon. Congratulations! That's so fucking dope, Chyna!"

"You have to come check it out one day! I'll hook your hair up like I used to."

"Bet! I've been managing my hair with magic, but it isn't the same as when you do it. But I am happy for you. Really. You moved to LA and scored an NBA boyfriend and a salon! You're doing the damn thing!"

I felt like I had won first place at a spelling bee; I was over the moon to hear her praising me, especially when I was so stressed.

"Thank you, Ameri. I really needed to hear that. Everything has been great, but it's also been moving so fast. I was just going to call your mom later today for some magic lessons. I have this little issue, and I don't know how exactly to tackle it. It's going to take some strong magic."

"Oh no. Well, if you're calling my mom for help, I hope you know you're going to have to provide some really expensive items or something. She's been extra greedy lately because of this stupid trip she's going on."

"Shit, I figured. I have a few Chanel bags I could give her." I bowed my head, dreading the thought of giving her more of my precious bags.

Ameri let out a chuckle. "She has plenty of those now. So, you might have to come harder. But I'm always here for you if you need help. What's the issue?"

I sighed then poured out my world of issues to my cousin. I told her that I'd used a love spell to get Chicago to fall in love with me and then buy me a salon. I also told her about the pressing issue of the cosmetology license that I had to have within a week.

She was silent, momentarily. It was a lot to take in.

"Damn. You used a love spell and got a man to buy you a hair salon? Brand new and fully furnished? That must be some spell. If you're magic is strong enough to do that, then you should be able to use it to get that license, right?"

"Wrong. I used a love spell in a book I grabbed from my mom's lair. That was the only one I could understand and easily learn. The issue I have now requires way more than manipulating one person."

She went silent again.

"Hello? Ameri?"

"I'm here! I was just thinking. I think I know what book you're talking about. I always wanted to know what spells were in that book. Your mom had that thing locked up for a while. How the hell did you get it?"

"It was pretty easy. My mom would never think that I would take it. She would assume I was too brainwashed by her to even attempt to steal her powerful book of spells."

"Shit, I did too," she said, chuckling. "I wouldn't have thought anyone could get that book from her. Dang, Chyna. You're kind of sneaky. I really thought you'd turn out to be holier-than-thou like your mom."

"As if! Magic is too precious to let it just rot away!"

"I agree. So is that spell book. It has some really good spells in it."

"I know. I'm keeping it safe and sound. No one's going to find it."

Ameri cleared her throat then went silent again.

"Thanks for calling me. It was good to hear your voice. Hopefully, I'll see your face in my salon soon. Especially since you can see mine now." I waved my hand up at the sky.

"I'll be there soon. Especially after you get your license."

"Yeah, I'm going to call your mom right after this so we can get started on—"

"Seriously, I can help with this issue if you want. It seems easy enough. I'm positive I could have your license to you today."

I perked up at the offer. "Really? If you could, it would mean so much to me! And I have the perfect handbag to thank you with."

"Yeah, I absolutely can, and you don't have to worry about the bag. I don't really care about those things."

"Then what else can I give you? I know you said it's an easy task, but still. I want to look out for you just like you're looking out for me."

"Well, now that you mention it, that spell book you took from your mom has the perfect spell to help with this. It's an alteration spell that can alter time and the memories of many people in order to change things in the present. It's actually a really cool spell. It pulls from other dimensions to alter our current dimension. We could use that spell to find a dimension where you already completed the cosmetology requirements and morph that into our current world. Basically, the spell could pull your license from another dimension into our dimension, so you wouldn't have to take the test, but the state would have your license, and it would be in their database as certified."

I was now the silent one. I was puzzled. Her explanation sort of made sense, but at the same time, it was extremely confusing. Pulling dimensions into other dimensions. Even for someone like me who had magic, that still sounded insane.

"I don't know. Is that really possible? It sounds kinda wild. Is it safe?"

She laughed. "Is that love spell you're using safe? Of course, it is. I've traveled to different dimensions before. It's a difficult task, but that spell book has all the tips and tricks to perfect it. With the spell book, nothing in this dimension will change other than you being a licensed cosmetologist. Trust me, Chyna."

"The spells in that book are kinda difficult to learn. I only managed to master like two or three of them including the love spell. Most of the others were written in some other language."

Ameri used that airy voice of hers to speak to me in another language. "I know that language very well. Look, if you want to wait on my mom that's fine. I have to go now." She sounded annoyed.

This was too good of an opportunity to pass up. Yes, I could wait for my aunt, but Ameri definitely seemed to know what she was talking about, and she made it sound so easy. What did I have to lose?

"No, wait! Okay, I trust you. Let's do it."

CHAPTER 24

As soon as I got home, I did what Ameri had instructed. I retrieved the spell book from the closet where I had been hiding it and got to work.

She gave me a spell that could create a physical copy of the book, and thanks to her being such a great spell coach, I pulled it off seamlessly. I laid the original spell book on a white piece of cloth and the copy on a black piece of cloth, so I wouldn't mix them up. They looked completely identical.

Once the copy was made, Ameri created a portal through our bathroom mirrors, and I passed the copied spell book to her. She winked and assured me that in just a few hours, I would have my cosmetology license.

The whole process was very quick. One minute I was sitting on the couch eating some chocolate chips cookies and watching Chicago's game on TV. Then, I blinked, and I was still watching the game but sitting on the opposite side of the couch as a strange feeling washed over me.

Suddenly, I remembered the day I had taken my cosmetology exam for the state of California. I remember it was a super windy day, and I was almost late showing up for some reason. During the exam, I had been nervous but super confident. I had passed just a few points shy of 100%.

It was an amazing yet strange feeling. I could remember all the things I had learned in class, but the faces of my instructors and classmates were blurry. I sensed that I had made a good friend during that time, but I couldn't remember her face or name. All I could remember was her short pixie cut.

All my memories from that period were very hazy. The only things I remembered clearly were the lessons. Things I had learned in class and on my exam. I didn't even know what I had done after I passed my exam. Had I celebrated? Was I even dating Chicago at the time? Trying to think about it made my head hurt, so I gave up.

I got up from the couch to grab another cookie, and that's when I saw it: my cosmetology license framed and sitting on the kitchen counter.

I couldn't believe it had actually worked. I was officially a licensed cosmetologist, and I hadn't even had to go to school or take an exam.

I immediately called my cousin.

"Thank you so much, Ameri, you're the fucking best!" I yelled through the phone.

"No problem. Like I said, I'm so happy for you, and I'm psyched about all your accomplishments. Let me know if you need help with anything else. I got you!"

I could tell she was just as excited as I was that the spell had worked.

"Are you sure there isn't anything else I can do for you? This is such a huge relief. You really came through for me!"

"Not at all. This book is all I need because it has so many cool spells. Thanks for lending me a copy. Just do me a favor and don't tell your mom I have this, okay?"

"You don't have to worry about that. I'm not even supposed to have it in the first place."

She chucked. "You're so sneaky. And if you do want to do something else for me, just squeeze me into your chair whenever I come visit."

"Duh, I got you!"

We talked a bit longer, discussing a petty drama that was unfolding in our family circle, and I promised to save Ameri a seat in my chair whenever she came to visit.

Easy peasy.

I took a picture of my license and sent it to Cali with a winky face emoji. She texted back right away demanding to know how I had pulled that off in only a few hours. She questioned whether it was legit, and I was happy to let her know it was.

I reminded her that I came from a family of witches, and we had made it happen. She joked, like she always does, asking if my family could magically insert a million dollars into her bank account? I wondered if Ameri could do that? Maybe that was a task for another day.

On the day of my first appointment, I walked into the salon bright and early. My hostess had already arrived and made sure the lights were on and all the equipment was ready for use.

"Good morning, Chelsea. How's your morning going so far?" I asked as I walked through the front doors.

"Morning, Chyna. Everything is going smoothly so far. Ready for your first client today? I believe she arrives in another hour, right?" Chelsea asked.

Chelsea was a very pretty girl with a bubbly, vibrant attitude—perfect for being the first person clients saw when they walked in. She had a sharply cut bob that framed her round face perfectly, and she wore a white sun dress with a white cardigan, following the employee dress code.

I had requested that everyone wear either white, cream, or tan colors so we could compliment the salon's décor. Thankfully, everyone had been on board with the idea.

I had even provided each hairstylist with two white T-shirts they could wear at work. On the front, their name and social media handles, while the back displayed the salon's name and logo.

"Yeah, my client will be here in an hour. I'm kind of nervous to do her hair. She's a huge influencer," I said.

"Don't stress. You got this," Chelsea said, giving me an encouraging smile.

I took in her encouraging words then went over to my station. I noticed Gee was prepping bundles by one of the wash bowls in the back, and another hair stylist, Stacy, was already working on a client's hair. She was taking down her client's old wig braids. I greeted them both.

"Hey Chyna, good morning. How many clients you got today?" Stacy asked.

"I think I only have three today, all sew-ins. So, I'll probably be here until four or five. What about y'all?"

"I just have this one for today, but I have to prep some hair for the clients I have tomorrow," Stacy said.

"I have three today too. One quick weave and two silk presses. I know Leslie will be in today for a client, and Tamara is coming in today too," Gee informed me.

"Perfect. Let's make some magic happen today," I said, giving them a quick smile.

I pulled out my cosmetology license and placed it on a shelf along the wall near my station. Then I laid out the bundles I had washed the other day as well as all the tools I needed and began to thread my needles.

Cia Don arrived right on time. Chelsea walked her over to my station and I got her settled in.

She was wearing a simple graphic T-shirt, sweatpants, and a bucket hat that hid her tired, month-old braids. She had her complimentary champagne in hand along with her phone which had been recording from the minute she'd entered the salon. She waved at the camera before turning it on me, momentarily catching me off guard before I quickly recovered and waved back.

I was so glad I had decided to look presentable today. I had my curls out and was wearing a cozy cream sweatsuit with layered gold necklaces, including Chicago's heart-shaped necklace, of course. And needless to say, my makeup was flawless thanks to my magic spells.

Basically, I was camera-ready.

I presented Cia with the bundles she had requested, and she shrieked as she recorded herself running her fingers through the hair.

"Oh, Chyna, this is it! This is going to match my real hair perfectly!"

"Yeah, it's going to be everything! You're going to look fabulous!"

We began the process by taking down her old braids and detangling her hair. I then walked her over to our lush wash bowls and shampooed her hair.

She was recording snippets of the process to make a video for her social media page that would highlight her experience with me. This was definitely what I needed, and I didn't even have to use a spell on her.

We chatted while I was washing her hair, in particular about her social media success and how she had blown up so fast.

"I won't say it happened overnight, but my followers grew quickly. They really appreciate what my page has to offer. I love giving them fashion and beauty advice that they can apply to themselves to boost their confidence. That's why I felt this collab with you would be perfect. It's a win-win."

"It definitely is. Thank you for taking a chance with me. I know I'm a new salon owner, but I believe my team and I are going to make a name for ourselves and become one of the best salons in LA."

"I can see that. I mean, including a hair take down and a wash & blow dry into each service is one of the biggest pluses a salon can offer."

"Exactly!"

After I blow dried her hair, I trimmed her ends. Her hair was very healthy for the most part, and she didn't have much breakage. I braided her up and began to sew the bundles in.

As she recorded her reflection in the mirror, her excitement was clear as day. She gushed about how amazing her hair looked to her future viewers. She displayed just the right amount of theatrics that would definitely keep viewers entertained and influenced.

I let her choose whether she wanted to keep the hair in its natural state, straighten it, or curl it to add some volume. She wanted to straighten it, so I did as she requested.

It came out looking perfect. She took many videos and pictures during the entire process so I couldn't wait to see the final video when she posted it. I planned to use a spell to give it three times its normal push.

"Ooh, I can't wait to come back!" Cia said, giving me a hug and a nice tip before she left.

My first client of the day had been a success!

The next client, unfortunately, not so much. She walked into the salon with the biggest attitude. As Chelsea led her over, she sniffed the champagne flute in her hand and turned up her nose.

"It smells cheap. I don't drink champagne that costs less than $200 a bottle," she said as she shoved the glass back into Chelsea's hands.

Chelsea's eyes grew wide with shock before she turned and walked back to her desk. I knew she would let me know exactly what she thought the minute the client left.

I had met this client briefly at my soft opening. Her name was Maya, and she had been a lot more pleasant then. She had been very curious about the sew-in process because she usually got quick weaves. I explained the difference and the benefits, and she had agreed to give it a try.

That very day, I sold her three of my Brazilian straight bundles, explaining how well they would match her hair texture once it was straightened.

Maya plopped into my seat and tore her hat off to reveal old, matted hair that still had globs of hair glue in it. Whoever had done her hair previously had absolutely no training on how to do a proper quick weave to ensure the glue did not directly touch the client's hair, let alone become matted within the hair.

I may have just gained in-depth hairstyling knowledge myself, but even I knew this. Whenever I performed a quick weave on myself, I always made sure to use a cap and protector to create a barrier so the glue wouldn't directly touch my hair.

Luckily for her, I had some hair glue remover.

The process was taking some time as I had to unbraid her hair, work the remover through it, and gently comb out the pieces of glue. I could tell that the longer it was taking, the more annoyed she was growing. She kept shifting in her seat and sucking her teeth. I even caught her using her phone camera to see how far I had gotten.

"I thought this process was only going to take two hours. You haven't even washed my hair yet. I mean how long does it take to unbraid a few little braids? I could have done that myself!"

"Yes ma'am, it usually doesn't take long for me to do a sew-in, but I have to get this glue out of your hair before I wash it, so you don't experience any breakage or fallout. I care about each of my client's natural hair and do my best to protect it," I said as professionally as I could.

I glanced up to catch Gee shooting daggers at my client. I pursed my lips to the side and shook my head. He chuckled and mouthed, 'Good luck.'

She continued to grunt as I spent only five more minutes working the remover through her hair until all the braids were undone and all the glue was out.

Fortunately, she only lost a small amount of hair due to natural shedding. I showed her a bundle the size of a quarter, proudly boasting that she had lost much less hair than most people would have.

"Like I said, I could have done that myself and saved half the time," she said, giving me mega attitude.

I wondered how much hair she would have lost had she done it herself.

"Who did your hair previously?"

"My niece. I would have gone back to her but she's away at school."

I hoped her niece would come back soon to save me from her annoying aunt.

I guided her over to the wash bowl, and after selecting the pre-cleanse wash, I began to pour it into her hair when she reached up and grabbed my arm.

"Um, excuse me! What is that? What are you putting in my hair?"

I pulled my arm free and took a deep breath to calm myself. I explained that I was using a pre-wash cleanser to ensure all the glue was out before washing her hair.

She insisted on reading the label because her scalp was sensitive, so I handed her the bottle. She could probably sense I was becoming slightly annoyed, as she became defensive, saying she couldn't put just anything in her hair. I smiled and assured her that she was in great hands.

Minutes later, she was still turning the bottle front to back, obviously intent on reading every single word. My patience was wearing thin, so I reached out for the bottle.

"Ma'am, is everything okay? If you don't want to use the pre-wash, then that's fine, I won't use it," I said through my teeth, trying to keep a smile on my face.

She narrowed her eyes then slowly handed the bottle back to me.

"Fine. It should be fine to use."

Once the pre-wash was done, I moved on to the shampoo. I planned to use three different bottles. One to thoroughly cleanse. One to promote hair growth. And one to add moisture and promote healthy hair. I handed her the bottles for her inspection, explaining what they were for.

"My niece never uses so many shampoos! I mean what is the point of all of this! This is going to take way too long. Does one bottle not do the job? This stuff must be cheap if you need multiple bottles!"

It took everything in me not to suck my teeth loud enough for the whole salon to hear.

All of these bottles were, in fact, expensive and would be beneficial, but if she didn't want to use them, then that was on her.

At this point, I was sure she was trying to piss me off on purpose. Maybe she was hoping for a discount or a free service if she was able to get me to go off on her.

"I guess that means they're cheap products if you're just going to put them away. Do you even know what you're doing? How long have you had your cosmetology license? A day?"

How the hell did she know that!

By now, I was very annoyed. I know this may not have been the best decision, but I couldn't help it. I used a spell to put her in a trance to keep her mouth shut until I had finished with the wash process. I also used another spell to ease her mind so that she could remove that stick up her ass for the remainder of the appointment.

The waters calmed, and I could finally breathe and think again now that I didn't have to deal with such a nagging client.

While I washed her hair, I worried whether I had made the right career choice. I could have put all this magic toward my paralegal career and became a lawyer by now.

Yes, I was thankful that I was standing in my very own salon at someone else's expense, but the thought of dealing with another client like this one made my skin itch.

After casting my spell, finishing the appointment was a breeze. Once I was done, I snapped my fingers to wake my client from her trance and encouraged her to check herself out in the mirror.

"Wow!" she said, looking dazed as she tried to collect herself. "I think I must have fell asleep. You got this done pretty quick, and it looks great!"

She ran her hands through her hair and gave it a shake. The style fit her face well. It featured marvelous curls and volume just like the picture she had shown me for reference at the beginning of the appointment. She turned and gave me a big hug, which I returned with a soft pat on her back, still bothered by her behavior earlier.

She paid and went about her day as happy as ever.

I guess all she needed was a fresh do to mend her attitude.

I realized doing hair could really change lives. But was this all I wanted? I wasn't sure how much longer I would be able to keep this momentum going.

CHAPTER 25

I was exhausted trying to keep up with Chicago. He was making it look so easy as he casually jogged up the side of a hill, while I huffed and puffed trying to follow.

"You got it, baby! We're only halfway there," he said, encouraging me to keep going.

He was an athlete for sure. Every time I paused to take a break, he would jog in place to keep his heart rate going.

I had never been a hiker, but I would occasionally hike with Cali for fun. We would select a simple easy walking trail to show off our stylish matching workout sets.

But hiking with Chicago was on a different level. He didn't want to do a simple walk. He wanted to jog on an advanced trail that would make my leave-out sweat and revert.

I knew I should have just stayed in bed when he asked me to go on a hike with him, but I wanted to spend more time with him. Chicago's games had been picking up, and I'd also been busier at the shop, so we hadn't had much time together lately.

Luckily, the long distance wasn't interfering with the magic because I could tell he was still in love with me. I just needed to take it to the next level so I could get my ring as soon as possible.

"Sorry Cago, but can we take another break. I can barely breathe."

I sat down on a rock and gulped down some water. I wish I had taken the time to learn a spell that would let me exercise with ease.

Chicago had promised me a spectacular view, but I was already liking what I was seeing, so far.

From where we were, I was able to steal a peek at the coastline below. Occasionally, a soft breeze carried a faint scent of the salty ocean. I was in a relaxed state of mind, and honestly, I would have been satisfied to stop right here.

"At least it's not too hot today. Last time I came up here, it was so hot, I almost passed out," Chicago said, stopping to take a couple of sips of water.

"Why do you do that to yourself? I get that you have to stay active, but you always go to the extreme when you exercise."

"I have to push myself. The more I push myself every day, the easier it will be to push myself in the game. I've always got to be in it to win it," he said in a matter-of-fact tone.

"Just a few more minutes, and it will all be worth it," Chicago said, as continued out walk.

And he was right.

It was still early when we reached the summit, and the sun was just starting to peek above the horizon. We took a seat and watched Mother Nature's show. The view of the ocean below was second to none.

"This was really worth it," I said as I laid my head on Chicago's shoulder and took in the vista below.

"I told you."

Chicago took out his phone and began to record the gorgeous view before turning it on us for a selfie.

I quickly touched up my hair, threw on some gloss, and had him redo the video. He grunted but obliged. We looked good with the golden rays of the sun beaming down on our skin.

"I love us. We look so good!" I said.

"The perfect couple. Not only do we look good, but our work ethic is good too. I'm proud of you. You've been in the salon every day, and your social media has been growing too. Are you enjoying your work?"

I bit my lip to ponder how work had been lately.

"I mean...it has its challenges, but it's been a great journey. I've been building good relationships with my hairstylists. They're all so dope. Each of them brings something valuable to the shop.

"I've also built real trust with my clients, so they know they can always come back and get taken care of right. They realize that I'm not just giving them a style but I'm giving them an experience they'll want to keep coming back for. My favorite client so far has been Cia Don, she's been coming to the salon consistently and so have her followers."

I was proud of the progress we were making at the salon. Every single one of my hairstylists was booked out. Even though I still had the odd difficult client at times, my magic had helped keep them in line.

We even had a client that tried to run out on paying Gee, but I had discreetly used my magic to make sure she came back with the cash and a nice tip. We don't play that over here. Not while I'm around and my magic is still sharp.

Cia Don had been a huge benefit to my salon as well. She was becoming the second face of Magical Touch Hair Salon with our multiple Pic-Talk videos going viral. We even made it onto some of the big social media blogs, showing off the bold colors I used to dye Cia's wig.

Chicago wrapped his arm around me and squeezed.

"That's amazing, baby! Just keep on going and it's only up from here."

"For sure! And you're going all the way to the championship to get that ring, right?" I asked.

"You already know it! I've been dreaming of winning a ring since I started taking basketball seriously, and right now, we're on the right track to make it happen."

"You'll get it. I've been watching your games and hearing people talk. You deserve it, and everyone knows."

I hadn't been able to attend Chicago's games lately, but I was keeping tabs on them and watching highlights. Although the finals were still a few months away, the sportscasters were already taking bets that Chicago would take his team to the championship game.

Chicago looked down, visualizing the championship ring on his finger. I mimicked him, stretching out my ring finger and imagining my wedding ring on it.

"Hopefully, we'll both have our rings next year. That would be nice," I said in a teasing tone, but I wasn't joking.

I felt Chicago glance over at me. Then he leaned down and kissed my temple.

"That would be nice, right? Two rings for me, and a big fat one for you."

I turned to face him trying to hide my smile, but I don't think it was working. Chicago let out a soft chuckle and kissed my lips.

Once we made it back down the to the city, we stopped to get some brunch. I noticed that some workers were starting to put up Christmas lights and decorations along the street. The holidays were coming up, which had me thinking about all the holiday specials I could run for the salon to increase our clientele.

"I forgot to tell you that my parents are planning to come up for Thanksgiving. My place is too small, so they're going to rent out a house and host a dinner. Do you want to invite your parents too?" Chicago asked before biting into his breakfast sandwich.

"Oh really? So, I'll finally get to meet your mom?"

My stomach flipped at the thought of meeting Chicago's mom. She did know of me, but we had never had the chance to speak to each other yet. It was strange, though, because lately, she always called when I wasn't around. She used to call when I was there, but now it felt like it was a pattern. Chicago said it was a coincidence, and I didn't really have a choice but to believe him. I didn't push the subject because he hadn't spoken with my family either.

"I told her about your salon and everything about you. I rave about you, and she's been way too excited to meet you. She said she's happy she might have a future daughter-in-law," Chicago said.

"I'm really happy to hear that. I'd love to bring her to the salon and give her a style. I haven't talked to my mom or dad yet to see what their plans are for the holiday, but my mom has been saying she wants to visit, so it would be the best time, I guess."

I had been trying to keep my mom from visiting because I still hadn't found the nerve to tell her about the spell I'd put on Chicago. I was paranoid she'd easily pick up on it the second she met him—

or even spoke to him—and I couldn't risk her interfering. Especially now, when I was so close to getting that ring. But with my dad around to keep her calm, maybe she wouldn't have the chance to ruin everything.

I did want to see her, though. I wanted her to see how much I had grown and accomplished since moving here. I still hadn't told her that I had quit my job and opened a salon. I knew the yelling she would give me would have been too much for my delicate ears.

But now that I was established and my business was successful, maybe this would be the best time to tell my parents. It would be too late for them to suggest I backtrack, and once they actually saw the salon, that would solidify that this was official, and it was where I chose to be.

CHAPTER 26

Within seconds of sending the text to my mom inviting her and my dad to visit for the holidays, she called me.

I was excited to finally tell her my news. I figured it would be better to tell her about the salon now rather than her getting here and making a big scene about it.

"Hey, Chyna, I just got your text. Yes! Your dad and I already purchased our tickets. I was going to surprise you and just show up, but I'm happy you sent an invite."

I should have known she'd pull a surprise visit on me eventually. She'd been begging to come ever since I moved here, but I kept giving her excuses that I wasn't ready—because I truly wasn't. But now that my life was going perfectly, it seemed like the best possible time for her to visit.

"I figured you'd do that, but it's fine. You'll finally get to meet Chicago and his parents too."

"Yes, I want to get a feel for them all. Hopefully, his mom has some good sense and isn't one of those overbearing mothers."

"Also...you'll be able to see my new salon."

I squeezed that bit in quickly, almost hoping she didn't catch it. Even though I would rather she know now, I was still worried about her reaction.

"Salon? Oh, you found a new hair salon to go to? I might have to check it out. Do they do braids? I've been thinking about getting some ever since I saw Crystal's. She just got these cute burgundy box braids, and now I want some too."

"No, Ma. I own a salon now."

The phone went silent.

I took a deep breath and repeated myself to make sure she had heard me.

"What are you talking about? Owning a salon?"

"I own a hair salon. It's been doing really good too. I have hairstylists who work with me, but I'm the boss. I have a good number of clients too. I've been booked almost every day for the past few weeks."

I was speaking fast, trying to get all the pros out before she interrupted with her negativity.

The line went silent again, and then I heard my mom make a scoffing sound.

"Oh, so you saved up and finally got your dream salon? That's amazing. I'm not sure how you're going to run the salon and continue to work toward becoming an attorney, but I'm sure you'll manage. You'll probably have to go back to school, though. Your dad heard your news too. He wants to know if you got a big bonus at work. Is that how you got the salon?"

I was starting to get a little annoyed that they continued to bring up the law career that I had never wanted in the first place.

She recognized that the hair salon was my dream only because she thought it was a secondary path, a hobby.

"No, Ma, I'm not pursuing law anymore! I'm a full-time hair stylist with a cosmetology license. I own a booming hair salon and have been bringing in enough income to put down a deposit on a house if I want to. And this is only the beginning. By this time next year, I'll own other salons! I'm not going to be a lawyer anymore. I'm going to be a big-time celebrity hairstylist and the wife of an NBA player!"

The more I tried to stick up for myself and my dreams, the more I could feel my blood boiling. I was finally living my dream life. Not my parents dream life, but mine. And they were not going to mess that up for me.

"Wife? Don't tell me you're married already too! You quit your career to slave away doing hair and now you're going to be a housewife too? Where is all this coming from? Don't tell me you slipped up and got pregnant!"

I could hear my dad yelling in the background.

"Pregnant! No! Please don't tell me my baby girl is pregnant already!" he screamed, his voice muffled but unmistakably clear.

"No, I'm not pregnant! This has always been my dream, but you and dad never wanted to listen to me. I finally made it happen without you, without letting you know about the process or relying on you just to avoid your criticism and judgment. I made it happen on my own, and I will flourish on my own. If you're not going to support me and my dreams, then don't bother coming!"

I hung up and tossed my phone across the living room, casting a spell at the last minute so that it fell gently to the floor, sliding across the marble tiles before coming to a stop in front of a pair of feet.

It was Chicago coming out of the bedroom, he had been taking a nap earlier and must have heard me yelling at my parents. He bent down and picked up the phone, inspecting it.

"Wow! It didn't break! You're alright, Chy? I heard you yelling."

I grabbed the pillow next to me and buried my face in it, letting all my tears and frustrations out.

Chicago rubbed my arm and kissed the back of my head. It was comforting, but my heart was still heavy after having it out with my parents.

I couldn't believe that after all this, after moving away to grow and spread my wings and pursuing my dreams, they still didn't hear me. They still didn't support me or my dreams.

Being a hairstylist didn't affect them in the slightest. I could understand that they wanted the best for me and wanted me to succeed, but even after I had achieved success in my own way and on my own terms, they still didn't support me.

"Talk to me, Chy. You alright?" Chicago asked again as he pulled me into a hug.

I squeezed the pillow tighter and leaned into Chicago's warm embrace, allowing myself to release the tension in my heart. I let out a few more sobs before the words spilled out.

I told Chicago how annoyed and disappointed I was with my parents. How, even though I had achieved a dream that had been important to me since I was a child, they didn't care. They weren't even a little happy for me.

It hurt because I was already doubting if I made the right career choice. I kept questioning myself, wondering if I really wanted to keep pursuing this. And instead of support and encouragement from my parents, all I received was backlash and negativity.

It was a heavy feeling, and I could feel a panic attack coming on. I felt like my throat was closing, and sticking to itself, causing my airway to become slim. I began to gasp for air, pushing through the growing pain in my chest.

Suddenly, I felt a hand on my back and a kiss on my temple. My throat relaxed, parted ways, and I took a deep breath.

"I know how you feel Chyna. It hurts when your parents, the people who you expect to be your biggest supporters, don't meet your expectations. It's painful. But you'll get through it because this is your journey. You just gotta show them versus telling them. They have to see for themselves what you already believed in and chased after before they can finally see you."

I could tell Chicago was remembering the trials he had faced with his own parents. Issues that I wasn't aware of. I wanted to know what those trials were, maybe it would help me to distract myself from my own, or hopefully it would lead me to the right advice.

"What happened? I thought your parents had been supportive of your career ever since you were a child?"

"They were supportive of me playing basketball, because they'd always wanted me to play in the NBA like my dad. But my dad was pissed that I signed with LA instead of Houston."

"Why did you? Was it a better offer?"

Chicago stretched out his legs and shifted on the couch.

"No, it was actually less than what Houston was offering, but I wanted the change of scenery. I finally had the chance to experience living somewhere new. Plus, it was the team all my favorites had played for. I kind of wanted to follow in their footsteps a little. But my dad thought that was stupid. He wanted me to stay in Houston to become a legend in my own right instead of following after other legends. He also never understood the need for me to want to move out and live somewhere else on my own."

I wiped some of the tears from my face. I felt a connection with Chicago. I had also been desperate to move out of my small town and live somewhere else. Not just anywhere, but far away from my parents so I could have the room to grow on my own.

"I understand where you're coming from."

"Hell yeah, especially since you're from the middle of nowhere," Chicago joked as he nudged my shoulder.

I chuckled, knowing he was stating facts.

"I wanted to escape from the grips of my controlling ass parents. But even when I'm thousands of miles away, they still find a way to try to control me and my dreams. I just can't understand it. Why won't they just let me live my life and be happy for me!" I exclaimed.

"They always act like they know best. They may have more knowledge than us, but they don't have all the answers."

"Exactly! Well, I'm glad you took a chance and came to LA. Otherwise we never would have met." I looked up at him and smiled.

Chicago had helped me calm down and made me feel happier, seen, and understood. This man was perfect for me in ways I hadn't even realized. I had made the perfect choice choosing him.

Chicago leaned down and planted a sweet kiss on my lips, pulling me even closer as our kiss deepened.

"I think I may really be falling in love with you," Chicago whispered to me while his eyes were still closed.

I couldn't help but to curl my lips into a joyous smile. My smile stretched so wide, you'd think I just won a beauty pageant. I was so happy that the spell had worked.

"I love you too, Chicago Moon."

CHAPTER 27

"She's perfect!" I squealed, sitting behind the driver's seat of a brand new, baby blue Porsche Macan. The car had been on my vision board for almost two years. We'd just finished test driving it, and she drove smoother than room temperature butter.

"I want her, Chicago!"

"It's a her?" Chicago raised one eyebrow and glanced at me from the passenger seat.

"Doesn't she look like one?"

After the heated conversation with my parents, I had been down for a few days. I would go to work, but when I returned home, I would go right back to my bed. My energy and spirit were depleted. Beyond drained. And I was having a hard time coping.

I'd had heated conversations with my parents before, but this time was different. This time hit a little harder. It wasn't like I could just walk downstairs to the kitchen and bump past my mom, trying to ignore her as she made a funny face. This would lead to me rolling my eyes and my mom throwing a balled-up paper napkin at me, which would put an end to the silent treatment and return us to our normal routine. I wasn't sure how we would fix things this time, and a part of me didn't want to.

I didn't want to have to deal with my mom finding out that I had used a magic spell or two, or three, or a bunch to finesse my current lifestyle. I didn't want to hear more of her mouth. Even though not being in a good space with her made my heart ache, for now it was the best option. But I still felt like shit.

Chicago must have grown tired of my sad girl shit because he was on a mission to lift my spirits. He started treating me to more romantic date nights, amazing massages, great sex, and little gifts here and there.

But this gift right here was going to top it all. My dream car. I'm glad that by constantly pointing it out whenever I saw one on the road, he'd gotten the hint without me actually having to ask for it.

"If this is the one you want, then let's get it. I want my baby pulling up to her salon in style," he said as he leaned over and stroked my thigh.

"I do! I want it!" I leaned closer and planted a deep kiss onto Chicago's freshly licked lips.

The car salesman came over to the window and let out a gasp when he saw us.

"Oh, sorry. I was just checking to see if you liked how it drove?"

Chicago and I pulled apart and turned to face the salesman, whose face had turned red. He was a young white guy who had probably just started working at the dealership a few months ago. Chicago tilted his face toward the man and nodded his head.

"Yep, we'll take it."

"Awesome. I'll get the paperwork started," he said as he sprinted off to his cubicle.

I leaned my head back against the headrest and gripped the steering wheel tighter, envisioning myself rolling everywhere in this car. I was too excited and couldn't wait to roll out of the dealership.

The process went pretty quickly since Chicago was paying with cash. I got a warranty, and they even included a full tank of gas that I planned to burn through before the week was over.

We pulled off and headed to collect Chicago's suit for his team's charity event tomorrow. He had already had an initial fitting but had to go back for a second.

For myself, I had purchased a stunning dress the other day. It would be my first time being professionally photographed and covered by bloggers as Chicago Moon's girlfriend, and I had to make sure I looked the part.

We arrived at the store after closing hours so we could have some privacy while Chicago had his fitting. It felt surreal to be back at this location and actually walking around with confidence knowing I could buy whatever I wanted without having to use magic to acquire it.

While Chicago was changing, I picked up a few items and had the employee hold them at the register for me. I was trying on a pair of heels when Chicago came out in his gray sharkskin-patterned suit. Underneath was a black shirt unbuttoned at the neck to show off his diamond chain necklace. He was also wearing a new pair of shiny black snakeskin loafers. He looked good. I couldn't help but pause while adjusting my shoes like a deer caught in the headlights.

"What you think?" he asked confidently.

He knew exactly what I thought.

I closed my jaw, which had fallen to the ground, swallowed my drool, and smirked.

"You know you look good, Chicago. I don't even know why you asked me."

He chuckled and took one last look in the mirror before nodding to the sales rep that he was ready to pay.

After changing back into his clothes, he purchased the suit, shoes, and the few things I had selected, and we headed out to a late dinner.

The next day, I was up bright and early to make a delicious breakfast for Chicago. Nothing too heavy, just some French toast, eggs, grits, and turkey bacon. I used my magic to steam our clothes so they would be ready for later, while Chicago took the opportunity to go down to the gym and get in a workout session.

He wanted me to join him, but I hated working out with Chicago. Although, I loved seeing sweat drip down his six-pack, the view didn't erase the pain I felt after one of his workouts. He was a harsh trainer. He allowed few to no breaks, and he constantly planned workouts that make me want to throw up and pass out. No matter how much I pleaded with him that his workouts were too intense for me, he didn't understand. He thought that less intense meant one less burpee rep.

By the time he finished his two-hour workout or what I call training for the doomsday apocalypse, the food was cold. He didn't mind though.

He ate quickly and then we got ready together. It was always fun getting ready with Chicago. Usually, I would share tales of all the clients I had dealt with the day before, but today I was too focused on the charity event we were going to.

His team was sponsoring the event to raise funds for local school districts, pledging a five-million-dollar donation to support after-school programs. These programs provided students with tutoring and fitness activities. All his teammates would be attending, along with the local press and the mayor of LA.

I could tell Chicago was excited because he was getting ready faster than he usually did for anything else. He loved events like these that helped kids to have more opportunities. He said it reminded him of the opportunities he had as a child that had set him on the path to where he was today.

"Did you finish your speech?" I asked, as I applied my setting spray to my face.

The players had been asked to say a few words during the event, and Chicago had been working diligently on his speech for weeks.

"I did. I don't know if I want to read it or just freestyle it."

"Freestyle? I think it would be better if you had a pre-written speech," I said with a laugh.

"Want to hear it?"

"Of course."

Chicago sprinted to the bedroom to grab the half sheet of paper he'd written the final draft of his speech on and came back into the bathroom to read it to me. He stood upright and adjusted his suit as if he was giving a class presentation. It was cute. With an air of confidence, he read his speech then looked at me for confirmation.

I was impressed with his speech. He had been stressing over it so much, putting all his time and effort into making sure it was perfect, and it was definitely going to pay off.

"Cago, that sounded really good. I think everyone's going to love it. I loved how you were vulnerable and shared your experiences with programs like this. That was really sweet, and I think it'll stick with people and have an impact on the students."

Chicago cheesed like he'd won a first-place medal.

"Thank you, baby. You inspired part of my speech too. The part where I mentioned always going after your dreams, even when your own family is against it. Just like you did."

He leaned over and kissed my cheek before heading back to the room to finish getting ready.

I caught my reflection in the mirror and saw my cheeks were lit up. He had me flustered.

We arrived at the event, which was taking place at the basketball arena where the team held their games. Rows of chairs occupied the middle of the court along with a stage, and the press and teachers from the local school district were sitting courtside.

Chicago escorted me to the second row where I had a reserved seat, but before I could take my seat, we were accosted by the press.

"Chicago, is this your girlfriend?"

"What's her name?"

"How long have you two been dating?"

We were bombarded with questions, and that combined with the flashing lights from their cameras made me freeze. But Chicago handled it like a professional. He confirmed that I was his girlfriend, and he even shouted out my hair salon.

I stood there smiling for the cameras with my arm resting on his. I felt like I was exactly where I was meant to be.

They didn't spend too much time on us once the team's star player arrived, though. They ditched us and ran over to him and his wife. It was their turn to be questioned and photographed.

Chicago kissed my forehead and headed to the stage to take his seat, shaking hands with some of the teachers and board members on his way there.

The event began with a joint speech by the team owner and team coach describing how beneficial the donations would be to the community. The directors of the school district also spoke, describing how much this meant to them, even calling a few students who would benefit from the opportunities up to the stage. The students then addressed the audience and took photos with their favorite players, Chicago being one of them.

When it was the players' turn, Chicago was the third to speak, and he delivered his speech with confidence and poise, just like he had when we were at home. Everyone was touched by his words, especially when he showed his relatability to the students and expressed his hope that the donations would afford them opportunities that would shape them just as he had been shaped.

I'm sure I was clapping the loudest.

Once the check had been presented and the official photos had been taken, people began to mingle. Servers carrying trays laden with glasses of champagne began circulating, and Chicago introduced me to his coaches and teammates.

"She looks like a keeper," his head coach said.

"He's our rising star. You got him at a good time," the assistant coach joked.

I raised my eyebrow in disapproval even though I knew what he said was true.

We decided to sleep in the next morning, but the universe had other plans as I woke to the sound of my phone pinging. I unlocked my phone to see that I'd been tagged on Pic-Talk by a plethora of blogs whose owners were posting photos and video clips from last night's event. We were going viral as a couple.

I wasn't bothered at all as I figured this was bound to happened. I scrolled through a few of the comments to read what people were saying. I was happy to hear that they thought I was gorgeous and that we made a cute couple. I checked both my personal and business pages, and they had both gained a significant following. My personal page was now up to eighty thousand followers. I felt like a mini celebrity. I squealed to myself then tossed my phone aside to get ready for the day.

CHAPTER 28

A few of the other basketball wives and girlfriends invited me to the team's practice at the arena before the game tonight. I was excited because this would be my first time seeing Chicago practice, and I couldn't wait. Plus, I was finally going to meet the WAGs. I was looking forward to being around women who understood what it was like to date a pro baller. It also felt like the perfect chance to turn a few of them into clients.

Most of all, I couldn't wait to meet Serena, the star player's wife. She was in her early forties but didn't look a day over twenty-five. She even owned a clothing boutique that was very popular and was raking in millions of dollars yearly. I had a few of her pieces and they were of great quality.

She was everything I aspired to be. From the way she carried herself with so much confidence during interviews, to the way she dressed and presented herself.

"You finally ready?" Chicago asked, not even trying to hide the impatience in his tone.

I couldn't really blame him for being moody. I'd been getting ready for two hours because I wanted to make the best impression on Serena.

"Yes, I am," I sang as I gathered my water bottle and phone.

I decided to wear a high-end, light pink two-piece lounge set that hugged my body in all the right places. I put my hair up into a high sleek ponytail and added a pink bow.

I embodied the soft life.

I snapped a selfie of Chicago and me as we waited on the elevator and then posted it to my Pic-Talk story. I had to give the people want they wanted: a peek into my amazing life.

As soon as we arrived at the arena, Chicago jumped into the practice game that had already started. I found the WAGs sitting in the courtside seats, so I joined them.

"Oh, wow Chyna! You look so cute! I love that set. I have one in purple," Cynthia said as I sat down beside her.

"Yeah, it's cute. I love that jacket," another girl said.

I returned the compliments and took a moment to introduce myself to a few of the WAGs I hadn't met yet.

"So, I see you're going viral for being Chicago's girlfriend," said one of the wives, whose name escaped me almost instantly.

"I know. It's so wild. My Pic-Talk has been going crazy with follows and tags. I'm trying to get used to all this new exposure," I said.

"That's nice. Just don't let it get to your head. You're not married yet so what you have now can end as quickly as it started," she said, her grin full of petty satisfaction.

I cut my eyes at her.

She had a short stiff blond bob with a bitter look on her face. She wasn't wearing any makeup and obviously hadn't had much sleep, going by the dark circles around her eyes. I wasn't sure what that comment was about, but I wasn't accepting it. She didn't know me, Chicago, or our relationship to make that kind of statement.

"Don't worry about that. Chicago and I will be just fine," I said, flashing a petty smile of my own.

"Yes, y'all will. You and Chicago are such a beautiful couple, and you're both young. You have time still," Serena, the wife of the star player said.

Serena was sitting pretty, wearing an outfit from her brand. She pushed her silk-pressed hair behind her ears and gave me a wink, while showcasing a large diamond ring that glittered on her finger.

"I saw your salon's Pic-Talk, you're really good at doing hair. Hopefully, you can squeeze me in one day," she said.

"I would love to. Your hair is already beautiful, but I would take great care of it."

"You own a hair salon? How long have you been doing hair?" the bitter wife asked.

"Yes, I do. It's located on La Cienega if you'd like to—"

"How long have you been doing hair?" she repeated in an aggressive tone.

I frowned and responded that I had been styling hair for a few years now. Sure, I'd only recently started taking on real clients, but I'd had years of hands-on practice, so it wasn't exactly a lie. Plus, with my magic helping me out, every hairstyle I created turned out bomb. So, who was she to question me?

Before I could clap back at her some more, my phone started ringing—it was my mom. I still wasn't in the mood to talk to her, especially since I knew she had seen the blogs by now. I declined the call and tuned back into the conversation with the girls.

But she called right back. So, I dismissed myself from the group and walked to a corner of the court, debating whether I should answer the phone and try to hear her out or not.

Out of the corner of my eye, I saw Chicago make a slam dunk. His teammates began letting out victory cries.

That settled it. I let the call go to voicemail, again. If I did decide to speak to her, it would be at a later date, when I was ready and in a good head space. Right now, I just wanted to watch Chicago play the sport that he loved. It made me feel warm inside seeing him light up with a smile each time he shot and scored.

That pleasant moment ended abruptly when I heard my mom's voice yelling at me. I looked down to see her face on my phone screen, waving at the camera and calling my name.

"Chyna Cole! I know you hear me, child!"

How the hell had she gotten on my phone? I hadn't even heard my phone ring again, but here she was on my phone, though video call.

"Mom? How come you're on my phone? I didn't answer your phone call."

"I know you didn't. That's why I had to do what I had to do. You know I don't like using my magic like this, but I had no choice because you didn't answer! Why weren't you answering your phone? Where are you?" she asked berating me through the phone.

"I didn't answer for a reason. I'm busy! I'm at Chicago's practice right now before the game starts. I'll call you back later."

"No! We need to talk now! You've been ignoring me for days. Look, I know you're upset about the conversation about your little store, but that's no reason for you to—"

"Little store?" I cut her off. "It's not a little store, Ma. It's my salon! My dream salon!"

I could feel my blood starting to simmer. I walked through the tunnel that led to the changing rooms, looking for a private place to talk. I didn't want anyone to hear me raging at my mom.

"Store, salon, whatever. I'm calling you because I'm seeing you all over TV with this man—"

"This man? His name is Chicago. I already told you about him!"

"What's up with this tone, little girl? I'm not sure why you're being so hostile and aggressive with me, but let's not forget that I'm your mother. You are not to take that tone with me or that snappy attitude. What on earth is going on with you?"

"It's you! You're still trying to control me and treat me like a little girl, but I'm not a little girl anymore. I'm a grown ass woman. I won't let you continue to belittle me, my salon, or any other dreams I have!"

She went silent on the line for a few seconds before letting out a heavy sigh.

"Look, Chyna," she said, rubbing the side of her temple. "Let's just discuss this when I get into town."

"No! I just decided that I don't want you to come anymore. Just stay home and leave me alone!"

From the forced video call, to her belittling my salon and calling it a mere little store, to her still calling me a little girl, I was not in the right space to deal with my mom in person. Especially when I was going to meet Chicago's mom and needed to make a good impression on her.

I was beyond furious, and I didn't want to deal with my mom and her judgmental, condescending, arrogant ass any longer. I needed a break.

I could still hear her yelling at me, but her voice began to sound muffled and warped. The next thing I knew, her image on the screen became distorted as the phone was engulfed by fire. My phone, which was on fire in the palm of my hand, soon became a pile of ashes, and it was all my doing.

I didn't recall reciting the spell, but I knew I did it because I recognized it. It was a spell I had been practicing for a while that turned any object or person into a ball of fire before turning it into ashes, leaving everything else around the object—like my hand— safe from burns.

I brushed the ashes from my hands and returned to the court as if nothing had happened.

Chicago, whose eyes had tracked me from the minute I walked back into the arena, raised his eyebrows and gave me a curious look. I nodded to let him know I was fine. Then I rejoined the girls and pushed the last few minutes from my mind.

CHAPTER 29

I hopped into the passenger seat of my car as Chicago took the wheel, and we headed to the airport to pick up his parents. My nerves were overflowing, and Chicago could tell. He reached over and grabbed my hand to stop me from sliding my bracelet on and off.

"Don't be nervous, baby," Chicago said softly.

"I can't help it. I want your parents to like me."

"They will."

Once we arrived at the airport, I watched as Chicago got out of the car and walked over to a man who looked like his twin, except he was several years older. That had to be his dad.

I silently said a spell to boost my confidence, then I stepped out of the car and walked over to them.

"Hi, it's so nice to meet you! I'm Chyna!" I said as I reached forward to shake Chicago's dad's hand.

His dad looked at my hand and shook his head then spread his arms wide.

"I'm a hugger. Nice to finally meet you, Chyna," he said with a deep and raspy voice.

"Where's Mama? The restroom?" Chicago asked.

"You already know, man."

I stood awkwardly to the side, watching them load the trunk of the car with suitcases.

"You must be Chyna?" a warm and tender voice behind me said.

I turned around to see an older woman in her mid to late fifties with light brown skin and hazel eyes. Her honey brown hair was styled in shoulder-length finger coils with copper and blond highlights throughout. She was wearing a cute denim dress with white sneakers and had the sweetest smile and a calm and gentle aura.

"I'm Jackie, Chicago's mom. It's so nice to finally meet you."

She gave me a warm hug and rubbed my back.

"Hi, Jackie. I'm so happy to finally meet you too. You're so beautiful."

"Aw, thank you, baby. You're very beautiful, and I love your hair. Hopefully, you can make some time for me this weekend to do something with this," she said fluffing up her curls.

"Yes, of course. I can get you in tomorrow. What do you want done? Your hair already looks good, and I can tell it's very healthy."

"I don't know. Maybe a silk press. I haven't worn my hair straight in a while."

"I can do that for you," I said, giving her a friendly wink before walking her over to the car.

When Chicago saw his mom, he lit up, hugging her tightly, rocking her back and forth. It was obvious he had missed his mom a lot, and it made me realize how much I was missing *my* mom.

I hadn't talked to her since our conversation last week at Chicago's practice. I had ended our conversation abruptly by setting my phone ablaze.

I told Chicago I had accidentally dropped it down a sewer grate while I was outside taking photos. I had to wait until the next day to get a new phone, and when I did, I decided to change my number to make it a little harder for her to contact me again. Even though I knew that she could still easily get a hold of me by using her magic. In fact, I was a bit surprised she hadn't already. Maybe she was just as bitter and salty as I still was.

I couldn't tell what Jackie thought of me, because during the ride to their hotel, she was pretty reserved. Chicago would ask her simple questions like how the flight was and what she wanted to do while she was here. But she remained mostly tight-lipped, so I couldn't get a good read on her. I wish I had taken the time to learn a mind reading spell.

We all decided that tomorrow, Chicago and his dad would spend some time together, and Jackie and I would hang out and get better acquainted. However, so far, all I had planned was a trip to the salon to do her hair. We could maybe go shopping and then visit some museums afterward, but that would depend on how she felt about the idea.

After arranging to meet up later for dinner, Chicago and I headed home where I spent over thirty minutes trying to find the perfect dinner dress that was fashionable yet somewhat conservative. I needed to look like the perfect candidate to be Chicago's wife. I needed his mom to accept me, because that would help everything work out so much better.

I settled on a long black, sleeveless dress with a mock turtleneck. I wore the necklace Chicago had gifted me, a pair of black and silver heels, and a small silver clutch bag. It was a simple yet elegant look, and I figured it would be perfect for a dinner out with my future in-laws.

We were just heading to the elevator when Chicago got a call from his dad.

"Hey, Dad. We're about to head out to get y'all now. What? For real? Damn. Alright, I understand." He let out a hiss and then hung up.

"What is it?" I asked, with a tube of lipstick suspended millimeters from my lips.

"It's going to be just us two for dinner," he said, disappointment in his eyes.

"What? Why?"

"My mom wasn't really in the mood to go out tonight. She said she's tired from the flight and just wants to order room service and call it a night."

"Damn." I shook my head.

I had really been looking forward to trying my best to impress her tonight at dinner.

"It's cool. Y'all will have all day tomorrow to hang out," Chicago said.

He must have been reading my mind, but he was right, I had tomorrow.

We got home pretty late after topping up on tequila shots. I could tell he had been drinking to calm his nerves about his parents being in town. He admitted he was anxious about how his dad would react at the upcoming game and wasn't sure if he was still upset about him playing for LA. He even believed they might've skipped dinner because of it, but I reassured him that wasn't true.

He was also pissed that he had to leave his car at the restaurant since he was too drunk to drive. He spent the whole Uber ride stressing, hoping nobody would mess with his sports car. I suggested we wake up early to retrieve it, even though I was pretty sure we would end up sleeping in late. Luckily, I only had to do his mom's hair in the afternoon, followed by our day out in the city.

As soon as we got back to the condo, we quickly undressed and let the tequila take control. Chicago released his frustration inside me multiple times until he was finally at ease and fell asleep. My head resting on his chest, I followed shortly after.

That night, I had another unsettling dream. In it, I was walking from the kitchen to our gorgeous back yard, carrying a tray with four glasses. Each glass contained freshly made lemonade with round ice cubes, thinly sliced lemons, and mint garnish on top. I had just made the lemonade, and I was eager to have Chicago try it.

I walked through our large back yard until I arrived at the pool where Chicago was sitting near two women. I walked over and placed the tray on the table in between everyone, passing the glasses out individually.

Setting a glass aside for myself, I placed one in front of Chicago, another in front of Jackie, and the last glass in front of the lady with the blue dress from my previous dreams. I sat next to Chicago and looked up at both of the women. They looked eerily alike, the woman in blue looking like a slightly older version of Jackie.

"Who are you?" I asked as she pierced me with her dagger-like eyes.

She continued to stare at me with a disturbing intensity until her face broke into a grin. She mouthed a response, but I wasn't able to hear it. Then out of nowhere, the world began to shake while she was speaking, yet I was still unable to hear her.

"What are you saying? I can't hear you."

The only word I heard her speak was "karma" before I was jolted awake by Chicago who was shaking me.

"Baby, you alright? Were you having another bad dream?" he asked with a concerned look on his face.

"Yeah, I was."

I massaged my temples to try and erase the negative feelings the dream had left me with.

Who the hell was that woman? Why did she look like Chicago's mom? Why was Jackie in my dreams now? And what the hell had she meant by karma?

I shook the dream from my head and rolled out of bed. I noticed Chicago was already dressed and putting on his cologne.

"You're heading out?" I asked.

"I have to go get my car then I'm going to take my dad around. Let him see the arena."

I suddenly remembered that I had to be somewhere too.

"Oh, shit! I need to get ready too so I can pick up your mom," I said as I headed to the bathroom.

CHAPTER 30

My plan had been to pick Jackie up from the hotel, but she had insisted that she would take an Uber instead.

I wasn't sure why, but it felt like she was trying to avoid me. From missing the dinner we had planned last night to not wanting me to pick her up, I was becoming worried that she wouldn't show up at the appointment at all.

And I had even more questions as to what connections she had with the lady in my dreams. She could have just been some random woman, and her presence in my dream might have been purely coincidental, but I wasn't entirely convinced. They had to be related, right? I was determined to find out, so Jackie had to show up at our appointment, even if I had to use my magic to make it happen.

I arrived at the salon just as Jackie stepped out of her Uber. She took a good look at the building's exterior and smiled. I parked then walked over to greet her.

"Hey, Jackie. How was the ride? Was everything okay?"

She turned to me, and I was taken aback by the intensity in her gaze. It felt as though she was searching for something in my eyes.

Then, as if she had found what she was looking for, her expression softened, and she gave me a faint smile.

"Yes, the driver was great. Very friendly. We did a little sightseeing on the way here."

"That's good. But you know I could have swung by and got you."

She waved her hand and started walking toward the entrance. "No, don't worry about that. I didn't want to burden you and make you go out of your way. You're already doing my hair."

I sprinted toward the door to hold it open for her. Once we walked in, we were greeted by Chelsea who handed us each a glass of champagne. I declined, but Jackie happily took hers.

"Hi, you must be Chicago's mom. You two look so much alike. Welcome to Magical Touch Hair Salon," Chelsea said cheerfully.

"Thank you, darling. How fancy! My son sure outdid himself with this place," Jackie said, looking around the shop.

I cleared my throat. "Thank you. I decorated everything. I picked out the colors and all the equipment. You think it looks nice?"

Jackie whipped around to face me as she took a gulp of champagne, placing her hand on her chest as she swallowed.

"But he paid for all of it, didn't he? The building, the decorations *you* selected, even the equipment, right? That's why I said *he* outdid himself," she said raising her left eyebrow.

Was she trying to throw shade? How did she even know any of this? Was Chicago telling her every damn thing?

As tension hung in the air, Chelsea stepped back, excusing herself to check on the clients in the waiting area, ensuring they were alright.

"But if you picked out the pretty colors then yes, you did well," Jackie said.

She then guzzled the rest of her champagne and placed the empty glass on the hostess's desk before spinning around and gracing me with a delighted smile.

"Alright! Let's get started on this hair. I can't wait to see how well you do."

I nodded stiffly, trying to collect myself and get hold of my emotions as I directed her to my chair.

Once she sat down, I draped a cape around her neck and began to gently comb out her curls to prep her for her wash.

It was time to start digging, not just into her hair, but into the family affair. I needed to find out who that creepy lady in my dream was and what she was after.

"So, Jackie, Chicago hasn't told me much about his family. Do you have any siblings?"

"Yes, I have an older sister."

Aha! So, was she the lady in blue?

"We have a really small family back in Houston. It was just me and my sister growing up. She took care of me after our parents passed away."

"Oh, it's only you and your sister? No other family?"

"Nope. My parents moved from Louisiana, away from our whole family when we were children. So, I didn't get a chance to connect with the rest of my family until later in life. But Stephen's family welcomed me when I married him. They were all the family I needed. Other than my sister."

"So, are you and your sister still close?" I asked, guiding her toward the wash bowl.

She followed me, waving at some of the stylists as we walked by.

"My sister and I aren't the closest anymore. We never really were that close because we always had different views of the world, different beliefs, and…we were just different," she said, sighing.

"I think it was because of her relationship with my mom. I was very young when my mom passed away, so I don't remember her that well, but my sister does, and she remembers the relationship they had. That's why I think she's so different." Her eyes became glassy, and she looked somewhat sad. Something heavy was on her, and I felt bad for making her reminisce about the past.

"I'm sorry. I can't imagine how that must have felt."

"How about you? Chicago mentioned that you come from a two-parent household like him. No siblings?" she asked, shaking her head as if trying to free herself from her memories.

I gladly took up the conversation to give her a break.

"No siblings, but I was really close to my cousins growing up. We're still cool, but we're also going on different paths, so it's hard to keep up with each other."

"How's your relationship with your mom?"

I sat with my thoughts for a second before answering her question, allowing the water to penetrate her hair, then applying the cleansing shampoo.

"Our relationship? It's…good. It's been a little rocky lately because she isn't too happy with me and my choice to open a salon."

"Why is that? You seem pretty good at it, so it seems like a good investment."

"She always wanted me to be a lawyer. Something serious, moral, and straight."

I began to suds up her hair and work the shampoo through, giving her scalp a good scratch. She nodded then directed my hand to scratch a spot in the middle of her head.

"I mean, I can understand that to a point. But parents have to trust their children to make the right decisions for themselves."

"Exactly! I'm grown now, and I want to follow my own dreams and passions."

She let out a faint chuckle that sounded like a huff. "But...children sometimes don't know what's best for them. They sometimes dabble in the wrong thing and get caught up in the wrong situation. So, maybe she was trying to direct you and keep you on a safe path. Keep you from getting mixed up with certain people."

As I began rinsing her scalp, she opened her eyes and stared into mine. She wore an eerie grin that reminded me of the lady from my dreams. I felt my heart sink to the pit of my stomach as we silently read each other's eyes.

She broke the stare first, closing her eyes and then clearing her throat.

"But that's just my opinion. Mothers always want the best for their children. Give your mom some grace, Chyna."

I felt off but couldn't clearly understand where this feeling was coming from. The air in the salon grew thick, making it hard for me to breathe properly. I felt pressure building from the back of my neck to the front of my throat.

I quickly lathered her hair with conditioner then excused myself and dashed to the restroom, where I collapsed against the door gasping for air.

What the hell was up with this woman? She was creeping me out. I wasn't sure how I was going to last the rest of the day with her.

I recited a confidence-boosting spell then made my way back to the wash station. Soon as she saw me, she gave me her usual warm smile.

"You okay, Chyna? Did I say anything to offend you?"

"No, I'm okay. I'm feeling a little lightheaded for some reason. I know we were supposed to hang out afterwards, but I think I need to rest after I finish your hair."

"Yes, of course! I don't mind. I'll hang out with Chicago and my husband today. It's been a while since the three of us have hung out."

Even with the tension still hanging in the air, I managed to finish her hair quickly.

"I love it, Chyna! You did amazing, girl!" she said as she ran her fingers through her now silky straight hair in disbelief, shaking it back and forth as she admired her reflection in the mirror.

"Jackie got her groove back!" I joked.

"I sure did! Now, I'm ready to take on LA."

"You need me to drop you back off at the hotel?"

"No, my Uber is only three minutes away," she said, gathering her things.

"Oh, I didn't know you'd ordered one," I replied, feeling a little disappointed.

I was ready to break away from her energy, but I wanted us to end our day on a good note.

"I didn't want to burden you after you said you weren't feeling too good. I really hope you feel better soon, so we can all hang out and do something fun. I'm confident you will feel better soon, though."

She gave me another one of those intense stares as she said her last few words, then walked out the door. I stood frozen at my station for a moment, unable to move, trying to gather my thoughts.

CHAPTER 31

I nstead of going home, I decided to hit the beach and invited my girl, Cali, to join me. I got there early with a small charcuterie board.

Not long after I arrived, I heard footsteps crunching in the sand behind me and turned to see Cali walking toward me. Her calm smile and positive energy were like a soothing balm.

I waved her over as I munched down on a cracker.

"Hey, girlie!" Cali said as she sat down beside me.

We leaned over and hugged each other.

"It's been days since I saw you. I've missed you."

Cali let out a tired sigh. "I know, girl. Between work picking up and hooking up with my man after work, I've been busy. I know you have too, Miss NBA Girlfriend slash Salon Owner."

I was happy Cali had found some time to spend with me. She was right, we had both been pretty busy and caught up in our own lives. With both of us having careers and love lives waiting for us at home, it meant more days apart from each other. Back when I lived in my old apartment, I could just step outside and knock on Cali's door to see her. I missed those days.

She was now officially dating Chicago's friend, Frankie, and she couldn't have been happier. I truly loved that for her. It was nice seeing her loved like that.

"I don't know, girl. I'm not trying to be a super-lover-girl, but I really think this man is the one," Cali had said, showing every single one of her teeth as she gave me the biggest smile.

I had clasped my hand over my mouth, hoping to mute the squeal that escaped, but it didn't work.

"Cali, I'm so happy about this! I think y'all are really cute together, and from the things Frankie tells Chicago that Chicago tells me, he really likes you too."

Cali squeezed her cheeks, probably to stop them from hurting since she had been smiling during the entire conversation.

"Aw, I'm so happy to hear that," she said.

Cali and I chatted for another hour, discussing our love lives and our next steps.

She was planning to move into Frankie's house in Culver City. I approved of Frankie, so I was all for it.

"I just don't know if I'm ready to take that step. It's been so long since I was in a relationship let alone lived with a guy. I lived with my ex back when I was in Houston, and it ended so badly. He was such a dick. He kicked me out and I had to stay at a hotel to regroup."

"Damn, Cali. I didn't know that. Your parents couldn't take you back in?"

"They eventually did. I was just stalling because I didn't want to tell them. I knew my dad would have his 'I told you so' moment, and I didn't want to hear it. He hated my ex. I hate my ex now too, but back then I was so in love. I was way too stupid, and I don't want to end up in that situation again."

"First off, I don't know why parents love to have that moment. Like, yes, I know you lived a long life, but you ain't got all the answers," I said, and we both laughed.

"But seriously, I think Frankie's solid. I get the vibe that he wouldn't do any shady shit, especially since Chicago vouched for him. So, I don't think you have to worry about any of that kind of mess like that with him. Besides if anything does happen, I got you, girl. I'll never let you go homeless out here."

Cali leaned over and nudged my shoulder with hers.

"Okay, I think I'll take the leap then. Might as well. I'm tired of that small ass apartment anyways. Girl, they moved this nasty neighbor into your old place and he's always leaving piles of trash bags outside his door, attracting all kinds of bugs. Not to mention that someone with a baby just moved in above me, and that baby cries all night," she said before eating a cracker.

"I know my parents wouldn't approve so I won't tell them yet. But if I see myself getting married to Frankie in the future, I have to know what it's like living with him first. You can't marry before living with a person. I need to know how he really is on a day-to-day basis."

"Exactly. It gives you a better idea of who you're with. I was so surprised to learn that Chicago is a clean freak. I thought since he was a sports guy he would be so messy and dirty, but he's the opposite. He cleans up after himself all the time. Like if he's brushing his teeth and washing his face in the morning, he'll immediately wipe down the counter, wash the clumps of toothpaste from the sink, and wipe the mirror. It was such a turn on to learn that about him."

"Chicago gives that. He always seemed like a humble and disciplined guy. Good to know he was raised right."

I let out a huff and shifted my body so I could stare out at the ocean. There was a cruise ship in the distance. I'm sure it was huge, but from here it looked extremely small.

"Uh-oh. What is it?" Cali asked before popping a cheese cube into her mouth.

I shook my head not breaking my gaze on the ship.

"Oh, that's right. You said his parents were coming to town this week. They're here, right? What are they like?"

I tilted my head in her direction and gave her a bothered look, signaling that things were not going right.

I threw a cube of cheese into my mouth before spilling all the tea on his mom. I told her about my first interaction with Jackie and how well I thought it went. How sweet she seemed at first. Then the dinner cancelation, which I had thought was a mere fluke, but after her actions today, it was clear to me now that she had canceled on purpose. She was sneaky and I didn't know what her intentions were.

"Hell nah. I ain't even met the lady and she's giving me bad vibes. And the way you couldn't breathe around her…something is off."

"Right! And the fact that she mentioned confidence, after I had just used that spell while I was in the bathroom. It's weird right?"

"Very. Do you think she heard you? Did you say the spell out loud?"

"I did, but I wasn't yelling. I was whispering, and no one else acted like they heard anything."

I was happy I had Cali on my side, confirming my suspicions. I wasn't sure if I should tell her about the woman in the blue dress from my dreams and how she looked like Jackie. I figured it was too weird, and the thought of those two being connected was already making my stomach turn.

Cali shook her head and gave me a sympathetic look.

"I say ignore it unless she confronts you. She might be a little jealous her son has a girlfriend or something. You know how some boy moms can be."

I nodded in agreement, trying to convince myself that her statement was true, but I had my doubts.

She reached over and grabbed my hand.

"Don't stress, Chyna. Let's go do something fun to take your mind off things."

We decided to have a "Cheer Chyna Up" day, complete with two of my favorite things: shopping and sushi. It was the perfect remedy for forgetting my worries.

I didn't realize how late we were out, but by the time I got home, Chicago was there waiting for me. He was sitting in the middle of the living room with the lights dimmed like a wife who just found out her husband had spent the evening with some other woman.

"Chyna, where have you been?" he asked, his eyes filled with frustration.

"I was out with Cali. Just hanging out."

"Shopping?" His gaze fell to the bags of clothes I had picked up from the boutiques Cali and I had visited.

"Yeah, just to take my mind off things," I said heading toward our bedroom to put away my new clothes.

He got up and blocked my way to the bedroom.

"You were supposed to hang out with my mom today, and you blew her off to hang out with Cali? That's not cool." His nostrils were flaring, and his arms were folded tightly across his chest.

"What? I didn't blow off your mom. I don't even think she wanted to be around me in the first place."

"What the hell are you talking about? She was worried about you. She said you weren't feeling well and headed back home. I thought you would be here in bed when I came home, but you weren't. So, I figured you went out to get medicine or something, but instead you were out shopping. I brought back soup and medicine for you."

Chicago pointed to the bags of food and medicine sitting out on the kitchen island.

"I wasn't feeling that well, but I started to feel better after hanging out with Cali. I wasn't sick, it was more of a mood thing. I got a strong feeling that your mom didn't like me, so I went to get some space to ease my mind."

"That's not true. She was looking forward to hanging out with you!"

"I couldn't tell! She was shading my salon the entire time I was doing her hair. That woman doesn't like me, and I know it for a fact!" I blurted then bit my lip, wondering if I should take it back. But I didn't, because I meant it.

Chicago walked toward me and bumped my chest as he glared down at me, exhaling loudly.

"'That woman' is my mom, Chyna."

I dropped my bags and wrapped my arms around Chicago in defeat.

"I'm sorry, Cago. I really think your mom doesn't like me. Maybe we got off on the wrong foot or something. Did she say anything to you?" I looked up at him, letting a few tears slip out on cue.

I tightened my embrace and began to pour my spell into him to calm him down and gain his trust and love again.

Chicago closed his eyes then opened them, blinking multiple times as if he had just woken from a nap. He placed his hands onto my lower back, caressing me.

"Sorry baby, I didn't mean to come at you like that. My mom means a lot to me. You do too, and I don't want no issues between you two. You're wrong. She likes you. I can tell."

"How can you tell?"

"You're still here. If she didn't like you, she would have ran your ass off," he said, laughing.

She almost had.

But I was in this for the long haul—I'd already invested too much.

It was at this moment that I realized I had no choice but to make Jackie like me. If I was in good with her, then I would be in a better position with Chicago. There would be no resistance to my magic if his mom was on my side.

Though I had gotten pretty good at using the love spell for dealing with romantic partners, I needed to master something that would make people, Jackie specifically, like me.

Once Chicago was asleep, I went to the closet and dug out the book of spells to begin my research. It wasn't long before I found the perfect spell. It was similar to the love spell, but was purposely designed to make people admire you. I realized this would also be a perfect spell to get celebrities to befriend me for future clientele.

The spell was more complicated and required more items than I had with me, so I wouldn't be able to perform it just yet. For now, I could use a simpler spell to prep the target by making them more compliant.

I stayed up until three o'clock in the morning trying to get the hang of it when an uneasy feeling washed over me. I looked down and saw the hairs on my forearms stand straight up, only to fall back down as if blown by an invisible breeze.

My eyelids felt heavy, and I figured my exhaustion was playing tricks on me. I decided to call it a night, realizing that practicing the spell had drained my energy, and I needed to rest.

CHAPTER 32

I was awakened just two hours after falling asleep. And despite feeling very tired, I had a strong urge to stay awake.

Every time I tried to close my eyes for longer than a second, they would sting. I laid in bed for a few minutes, wondering why I couldn't get back to sleep then I remembered I'd experienced this before.

On mornings when I hadn't felt like getting out of bed to go to school, my mom had used a spell on me that would wake me up and prevent me from falling back asleep. But why was I experiencing this now?

I sat up with a jolt when I heard soft murmuring and the sound of a glass being filled coming from outside the bedroom. I was fully awake now.

I jumped out of bed, grabbed my silk robe and threw it on. I stood by the door, trying to determine where the voices were coming from, but my heart was pounding too loudly to hear. I opened the door slowly and tiptoed down the dark hallway toward the living room. There was only one light on in the kitchen, and it was illuminating the hall.

As I crept up along the corridor, I could see the kitchen reflected in the floor to ceiling windows, and I craned my neck to see who was in my home.

There was my mom standing at the kitchen island, sipping a cup of tea and petting Neli, who was sitting on the counter. My dad was there too, sitting on a barstool.

My eyes began to water the moment I saw them. It had been months.

Part of me was ecstatic, and I wanted to run over and give them each a big hug. But another part of me was annoyed.

Why the hell were they in my home? And how the hell did they get in here? And why hadn't Neli sent me a warning or something?

It didn't take a genius to figure it out. My mom, who constantly forbade the use of magic for bad intentions had used it to break into my home.

How on earth did she even know where I lived?

My irritation grew.

I was still upset with my mom for the way she had behaved that day on the phone. I wanted to barge into the kitchen and tell her off. Cuss her out. I wanted to scream.

But I couldn't move. Part of me was frozen with shock that they were even here.

"How long are you going to stand there and glare at me, Chyna?" my mom snapped, arms crossed and foot tapping as she locked eyes with my reflection in the window.

My dad flinched and whipped around to see where I was at.

I stepped out of the hallway and walked to the end of the kitchen island, to keep some distance between us.

"What are you guys doing here?" I asked, not even trying to hide how angry I was.

"Is that how you talk to your parents?" my dad asked, turning to face me, his gaze sharp as his shoulders tensed.

"Oh, yeah! This is the new Chyna. The Chyna who thinks she's so grown. The Chyna who talks disrespectfully to her parents." My mom slammed her ceramic mug onto the counter, making Neli jump down and scamper off.

Surprisingly, it didn't break. She must have used a spell to prevent that from happening.

"The Chyna that steals from her parents!" My mom growled as she summoned the book of spells from my closet.

My eyes widened and I reached out to snatch the book as it sped through the air toward her outstretched hands.

"Oh, no you don't! You won't ever see this book again!" she said as the book disappeared into a ball of dark purple smoke.

"How could you steal this book from your own mother? This isn't some silly little book of magic spells that you use for fun. These are very dangerous for an inexperienced witch like yourself!"

"I wouldn't be so damned inexperienced if you had taught me! We're witches! Why are you trying to erase that from me? This is my life and I'm going to live it how I want. And I want to use my magic freely."

My mom took a step back and looked me up and down with disgust. "By any means necessary, huh? Even if that means using a love spell on someone who doesn't love you?"

I cocked my head at her comment, not exactly surprised that she had figured out that was the reason I had used the book.

"Chyna, that is a dangerous spell to use on people, and you're not skilled enough to use it properly without suffering any backlash," she said.

"Like I said, if you had been a better mom and taught me properly then we wouldn't be having this discussion in the first place."

"I didn't want to teach you because I knew you weren't to be trusted with certain spells. You're hardheaded and you don't think properly before jumping into things."

The atmosphere grew heavy as we stared each other down. My mom stood with her arms crossed tightly over her chest, her face etched with a mixture of frustration and concern. Her eyes, usually warm and soft, were guarded now—like she was holding back everything she really wanted to say.

I also crossed my arms, signaling I wasn't going to back down. I stood there with heavy feet and a hot head.

My eyes were once again welling up with tears. I had never wanted my relationship with my mom to turn out this way. I wished we could go back to the way things had been at home. We would have laughed it out. But I was a woman now, and I needed to stand my ground. It was hard, though. As much as I wanted to run over and hug her tightly, I needed her to hear me.

My dad let out a deep sigh, taking his glasses off and placing them on the island as he rubbed his temples.

"Never thought I would see the day that you two were this upset with each other. Chyna, we understand that you're not a child anymore, but you also have to understand that we want the best for you—"

"Obviously not!" I cut him off. "If you two had it your way, I would still be working at a job I hated, living in a tiny-ass apartment, and possibly five years of paychecks away from having my dream salon."

I'd never cursed in front of my parents like this, but this was the only time I could get away with it, so I was going to take full advantage. It felt freeing and exhilarating.

"Yes, you did it, Chyna. You left your job and your tiny-ass apartment and got your salon by using someone. Not just using them but taking full advantage of their mind and heart. That's malicious," my mom said.

"I did what I had to do," I said, my voice cracking.

My mom shook her head, disappointment written all over her face. "No, baby girl, you didn't have to do that. I don't know where you even got the idea that you had to do something like that." She dropped her head to avoid eye contact.

The room was silent for several moments.

"I think we should head back to our hotel. We all need to take some time," my dad said, walking over to hug my mom.

My mom nodded then called Neli, who came trotting into the kitchen.

"I'm taking Neli with me. Clearly you don't need her companionship anymore because you're too busy manipulating people." She picked Neli up and scratched under her chin. "Look at her. She's gotten so thin."

"No, you're not! Neli is fine here with me," I said in protest.

I moved toward her to snatch Neli away, but my mom quickly clasped my dad's hand as a cloud of purple smoke emerged from the floor and engulfed them all.

Within seconds they were gone.

One hot tear rolled down my face followed by another until they pooled together beneath my chin.

Just like that, my parents had busted into my life and turned it on its side.

What was she even talking about? Of course, I had to do what I had to do. Did they really think I should spend my life behind a desk before I'd truly had a chance to live? I had magic! The rules were different when magic was involved.

I was upset that she had taken the spell book, but it was fine. The spell wasn't really necessary anymore because I knew Chicago really loved me now. The spell had only helped him reach that decision.

"She can keep the damn spell book," I said to the empty room. "I don't need it anymore anyways."

CHAPTER 33

Chicago was up and moving around, making it very difficult for me to catch up on my lost sleep.

After a series of very loud bumps and bangs, I was pretty sure he wanted me to hear that he was up so I would get up too. But I didn't want to get up. I needed to rot in this bed today.

I was able to fall back asleep for another hour before I heard some more noises in the living room. But it didn't sound like Chicago's regular routine. It sounded like a bunch of people moving around and talking.

I figured it was Chicago's parents who had come over to see him, so I got out of bed and crept to the bathroom to make myself presentable.

As I left the bathroom and walked down the hall, I heard a couple of familiar voices that did not belong to Chicago's parents but to mine.

I dashed into the living room where I discovered Chicago and my parents having a cozy chat.

"Chy, you're finally up? Look who came to visit!" Chicago said, giving me a big grin.

"What are you two doing here?" I asked, killing the cheerful vibe.

I was not happy about them intruding into my home for a second time, never mind chatting it up with my man without even waiting for me to do the introductions.

"I didn't know they came over last night. You should have woke me up so I could meet them," Chicago said, breaking the silence.

"They weren't invited then, and they definitely aren't invited now. You two need to leave," I said, crossing my arms.

"Now Chyna, that's enough," my dad said, standing up and crossing his arms in a near-perfect imitation of me. "I understand things got a little heated last night, but you're still our daughter, and we love you. We're here to make amends, meet your new boyfriend, and become involved in your new life. Chicago seems like a nice guy, so I'd like to get to know him more."

Chicago and my dad nodded at each other, signaling that they were off to a good start and bonding well.

My mom sat on the couch, staring out the window, avoiding eye contact with me. My dad shot her a sharp look and cleared his throat. She sighed before turning to fix her eyes on me. We had a stare-down until she finally broke her silence.

"You've done some stuff, and I've done some stuff. Let's let bygones be bygones, okay? I understand that you're grown and have made your own choices in life, and that's something you'll have to deal with. It has nothing to do with me anymore because I've done my job. I did what I thought was best for you, whether you appreciated it or not. You're a big girl now, and you've proven that you'll do what you want. I just hope you can handle everything on your own.

"Now, I want to get to know this young man and have some time with you two before we leave." She sounded sincere even though her eyes betrayed some concern.

I knew that my mom was trying to put things behind us, so I closed my eyes and exhaled deeply, releasing all my pent-up anger and stress.

"Okay, I'll let bygones be bygones. We can be peaceful today."

My mom got up from her seat and came over to me, opening her arms for a hug. As we stood face-to-face, all that tension from a few minutes ago started to fade, and in its place was this deep feeling of relief—like we were finally letting our guards down. I ran into her arms and held on tight. Giving her the hug that I wished I could have given her earlier this morning.

My heart was overflowing, and I melted into my mom's embrace. That hug spoke volumes, conveying a depth of emotion that words alone could never capture. I had missed her, and I needed her now more than ever. A few tears slipped from my eyes as she rubbed my back.

Later that day, we made plans to go to a restaurant in Malibu so my mom could have dinner on the beach, since it was something on her list to do while in LA.

It was just going to be me, my parents, and Chicago for the night. We planned to get everyone together, including Chicago's parents, tomorrow. I figured it would be best to spend today dialing back the tension and giving my parents and Chicago time to bond.

When we arrived at the restaurant, the hostess seated us on the patio with a view of the beach. My mom was in complete tourist mode, taking pictures of the beach and even the little plants decorating the restaurant.

"Wow, I can't believe you have the option to see this every day, Chyna," my mom said, staring out at the orange sunset being reflected in the ocean. She shook her head in disbelief.

"I think this environment fits Chyna perfectly. You get the busy city, but you also get to escape to this peaceful beach when you need a break. It gives you a nice balance, right?" my dad asked before taking a sip of his wine.

I could tell he was trying to reel me back in and get me to be comfortable around them again.

I wasn't trying to hold a grudge, but it was hard to let go of the awkwardness and fully embrace my parents like I used to. Maybe it was my pride trying to sabotage me.

"It does. I think that's why I like it here so much. You get a little bit of everything: beach, city, mountains. I'm even a hiker now, thanks to Chicago," I said, allowing myself to be drawn into the conversation.

My mom's eyebrows shot up. "Hiking? I would never have expected that from Chyna."

"I've been taking her out with me once a week. We're working up to two days a week, but it's been a difficult process," Chicago said, laughing.

"I can imagine. When Chyna doesn't want to do something, she doesn't do it. She's true to whatever she wants." My mom took a sip of her wine and gazed out at the beach.

The table grew quiet for a moment, as we processed my mom's comment which I took as shade.

"That's true, but that's also what I love about Chyna. She has big dreams and won't stop chasing them. Y'all have to see the salon! She really outdid herself and created exactly what she had envisioned. Seeing her there while she's working...her smile is brighter than those LED mirror lights. You can see that she's truly happy when she's at the salon," Chicago said, glancing over at me with a proud smile on his face.

"Is that so? I'd love to see her in her true element. She's been wanting a salon since she was a little girl," my dad said.

"And surprisingly, Chyna always gets what she wants. This was with your help, right? Your funds? I'm sure she couldn't have saved up nearly enough money from her paralegal job," my mom said matter-of-factly, spoiling the mood again.

Chicago adjusted his seat before speaking. "I did. I helped her."

"Why? What do you get out of helping our daughter open a salon?" My mom was going in for the kill.

"Seeing her smile is enough for me. I have the funds, so why not? I don't know what the deciding factor was exactly, but I just knew it would be worth the investment," he assured her.

My mom let out a slight huff and broke into a grin. She wanted to laugh because she knew precisely what had pushed him to pay for my salon.

I glared at her.

What was the point of trying to make amends if she was just going to stir the pot again? Who does that?

"You know, I really appreciate Chicago. He was willing to believe in me and support me before my own parents. That's real love," I said looking to Chicago.

He smiled down at me, blushing slightly.

"Love?" my dad questioned. "Love already?"

"I love Chyna," Chicago said.

"And I love Chicago," I said, grabbing his hand.

My dad let out chuckle and glanced at my mom for backup before looking back at me and Chicago. "Don't you think it's a little too soon for you kids to throw out the 'love' word?"

"I'm not a kid," Chicago said, a hint of steel in his voice. "I know what love is because I've seen it with my parents, and I've both given it and received it before. This is love."

My mom stared at Chicago as she took a large gulp of wine. Her eyes darted toward me then she hastily shook her head as if trying to convince herself not to speak on it.

I'm glad she didn't.

The waiter brought out our food, and we ate in awkward silence.

I couldn't wait for them to go home. I hadn't wanted them here in the first place. Yet they had come with no invite and completely turned the happy life I had built upside down.

"Why weren't y'all sold on Chyna opening a salon?" Chicago asked my parents. "She's good at doing hair, and she's super passionate about it. Plus, the fact that the salon became really popular in such a short time should tell you this was meant to happen."

"I never said she wasn't good," my mom said, clearing her throat. "Not sure if you've seen this side of Chyna yet, but she can be very irrational and impulsive. Jumping into situations that she shouldn't. She tends to think she has all the answers when she's still learning just like everyone else. This has gotten her into problems before, and I just don't want that to happen again."

My mom shot me a look that said, 'you know what I am talking about.' I sulked, knowing exactly what she was referring to.

It was something that had happened in the past and should be left there.

"We just want Chyna to live an honest life. We're her parents and we just want to protect her. I would be more than happy to support her dream of owning a salon if she did the honest work of saving her hard-earned money to open it herself. That's way more rewarding," my dad shared his two cents.

Chicago slowly nodded his head, analyzing their concerns before responding.

"I can understand that. I haven't noticed Chyna being impulsive because I feel like I'm the same. I guess it's just a difference in age. As y'all know, I'm in the NBA. Playing basketball was a hobby of mine as a kid, but my dad didn't see it as a hobby, he saw the potential that I had. He invested in me so much as a kid that my 'hobby' became my lifestyle and got me to the place I'm at today. That's how I think parents should treat their children. Invest in them so they won't have to look to anyone else for support, whether it be from a partner or a friend. Maybe with the right guidance and encouragement, Chyna could have found other connections. But like I said, I don't regret helping. It felt good to do that for her."

I was caught off guard by Chicago's response to my parents. He respectfully ate them up like fresh, steamed crabs at a buffet.

I looked over at Chicago. Our eyes met, and in that moment, I saw his strength and conviction which filled me with admiration. He had told them something I'd always wanted to say to them. The way he stood up for me really showed how much he respected me and had my back.

My parents absorbed what he said, and their demeanor seemed to change a little. I was hoping they would recognize the difference in our upbringing. Hoping they would see how Chicago's parents had poured themselves into helping him make his dreams a reality, whereas they had chastised me about mine, even hindering my magical skills, which could have made my dreams come true sooner.

"You make a good point. No, we weren't perfect parents. There are things that we could have done differently. But I think we're still set in our beliefs, so we'll just have to agree to disagree," my dad said.

Then he turned to me, he added, "I'm not mad at you for owning a salon, Chyna. I'm actually proud that you own a business and you're achieving something you wanted. I just think you should have chosen a different path to get there. So, let's just let this conversation die at that."

"We'd love to visit it, right?" my dad asked my mom as he rubbed her thigh.

She seemed to have disconnected from our conversation.

"Mm-hmm, I'd love to see Chyna smile brighter than LED lights. How about tomorrow?"

Her eyes were as cold as glass. They made me feel uneasy, and a little guilty.

CHAPTER 34

"Wow, I'm really impressed," my mom said as she stood in the middle of the salon with a glass of champagne in her hand. Her eyes were wide as she caught every detail.

My dad stood beside her, nodding his head, declaring how impressed he was too.

"You really did it, Chyna. You have a salon," he said.

Leslie came over to introduce herself while her client was under the hair dryer. She had her beautiful burgundy twist out styled half up and half down with two strands in front.

"Hi, it's so nice to meet you. I'm Leslie," she said, shaking my mom's hand.

They chatted while I prepped my station for the wash and roller set my mom had unofficially booked me for.

I hadn't planned on working today. I had taken a few days off to spend with the family, but I made an exception to do my part in mending our relationship.

Instead of waiting in the salon for us, my dad and Chicago decided to head to a practice game with his teammates to get ready for tonight's game. Both sets of parents were attending, so I invited

Cali along for moral support. I couldn't deal with the parents alone while Chicago was working.

After conversing with Leslie, my mom grabbed another glass of champagne and sat down in my chair.

"The salon is absolutely beautiful, Chyna. It fits you very well," she said, making herself comfortable.

"Thanks, Ma, it's exactly what I always envisioned my salon would look like. Even when I was younger, I wanted a chandelier like that in my salon, and now I've got it."

My mom grew silent then let out a sigh.

"Your dad and I aren't against you. I don't want you to think that, and I don't want you to feel like we don't want you to win in life. But what you did was wrong. Using magic on that young man to get him to fall in love with you and buy you this salon is wrong. You shouldn't use magic to play with people like that. That's why I never taught you a lot of spells, because I didn't want you to go crazy and use them on innocent people like this. But I guess you found a way to do it anyway.

"I'm not disappointed in you for quitting your paralegal job as much as I'm disappointed that you used magic on someone."

She turned to me and searched my eyes.

"And I can see it in your eyes, that you really like this boy. I think you may even love him. But that love spell you used…any love spell will always backfire because it goes against fate. That's what I wanted to protect you from," she said.

"I can understand that you're upset I took your book and used it on Chicago, but I felt like I had no other choice. If I had taken the route you and dad had planned for me, I wouldn't have had this salon for another ten years, and I don't have that kind of time.

"I hated my job. My coworkers were assholes, the work was draining, and I wasn't happy. There was no way I was going to last there for over a year. This was the best way. Besides, I've barely been using that spell book since Chicago doesn't need the spells anymore. He cares for me. I know in my heart that that's true. The love spell may have drawn him to me, but what we have now is real. We've built a strong bond and a genuine relationship. We've shared so much and grown to love each other. It's not all because of the spell," I said.

My mom continued to stare into my eyes, and she must have found what she was looking for because her features softened, and her once furrowed brow smoothed into lines of acceptance, although her eyes were tinged with unease.

The tension that had etched itself onto her face gradually ebbed away, replaced by a gentle coolness. A faint smile tugged at the corners of her lips and her eyes grew blank.

I believe this was the moment she realized there was no more fighting it. What was done was done.

"Okay, Chyna," she said then turned around and readjusted herself in her seat. "Can you use the big flexi rods?"

"Yes, we can do that," I said, prepping her hair.

Throughout the rest of our session, she didn't say anything else about the salon or Chicago. Our conversation instead turned to her clients and the small petty dramas going on within our family.

It felt like old times.

Chicago was on fire tonight.

His determination radiated in every move he made, driven by a strong intention to connect every shot.

With each basket he made, the crowd erupted into cheers, the sound echoing through the arena as he racked up back-to-back points. He would occasionally glance over at his parents after he made a shot, clearly seeking approval. His dad would nod and clap loudly, fueling him even more.

My parents were also impressed.

It was my dad's first time sitting courtside, and he was ecstatic. Even though he was more of a football fan, tonight you would have thought his favorite sport was basketball.

"Wow did you see that throw? Look at that jump shot! That boy is good!" he said, cheering alongside Chicago's dad.

They both were jumping up, clapping each other's hands and sitting back down in sync, as if they had rehearsed it.

My mom was trying to enjoy herself, but she had never liked attending games. They were always too loud and rowdy for her. I could tell that being up close and feeling the rumble of the floor as the players ran and jumped around was making her nervous, but she still cheered when Chicago made a shot.

Cali sat next to me tuned into the game and jumping up and down with the proud fathers.

"Chicago is really showing out tonight!" Cali yelled.

"Mm-hmm, I think he really wants to impress his dad. This is the first time they've come to one of his games."

"Wow, really?" Cali asked, shocked. "His dad looks so proud and he's so into the game. I'm surprised he didn't come sooner."

"Well, his dad was upset with him for a while because he didn't want him to sign with LA. But I guess he's made peace with Chicago's decision."

"Dang, I'm glad he changed his mind and decided to come. I bet his coach is glad too," Cali said, pointing to the coach, who was smiling as if they had already won the game.

The game might as well have ended early because it was the third quarter and there was no way the opposing team could make a comeback. Chicago wasn't going to let them.

Not tonight.

Jackie was taking plenty of videos and photos of Chicago. She was super excited, jumping up and waving each time Chicago was positioned near us.

She even made it onto the Jumbotron, getting a shout-out from the announcers that she was Chicago's mom. The crowd cheered, and she turned bright red like a rose with a huge smile on her face.

It was a little awkward seeing her, as I hadn't seen or spoken to her since the day I had styled her hair at the salon.

Earlier when my mom and I had arrived at the game, Chicago's parents and my dad were already there and appeared well acquainted.

Jackie hugged Cali and my mom as she introduced herself then waved me a quick hello before sitting back down.

No hug for me.

It was definitely confirmation that she had a problem with me, but I wasn't sure if my mom had caught it or not.

The game ended with Chicago's team winning by a landslide. It was one of his best games.

His parents ran onto the court to take photos with him once the game was over. They were beyond proud, and it was good to see Chicago so happy.

Even though he and his dad had their differences, I knew he was thrilled that he had made his dad proud. It gave me hope for me and my mom.

After our talk at the salon, I hoped that she would eventually see that everything had worked out for the best.

The game had ended so we all headed to the family room in the arena and had some refreshments while we waited for Chicago to shower and change before going out to dinner together.

Chicago's parents were mingling with the other players' family members, while my parents were completely starstruck by the players and their wives.

I joked with Cali that they were gawking at one of the wives who happened to be a famous model. Cali then reminded me how I had acted the first time I met the players, which I didn't find funny.

My mom eventually broke free from her fangirl moment and made her way toward us.

"It's so nice to finally meet you. Chyna has been a ray of sunshine for me," Cali said to my mom.

"That's good to hear. I'm glad you two met. You seem like a genuine person. I hope some of that rubs off on Chyna," my mom replied, nudging her shoulder against mine.

"Ma, Cali's my best friend out here. My partner in crime. She helped me come up with the name for my salon," I said.

"Really? That's nice. You did good with that. So, what do you think of Chyna and Chicago's relationship? You've seen more than me. You think they're a good match?" my mom asked.

I wasn't sure where she was going with that question, but she had a look in her eyes that concerned me.

Cali glanced over at me looking slightly confused.

"I think they're great for each other. Chyna is always so happy around him. She lights up whenever someone says his name. And Chicago's always treated her well. I really think they're meant to be." She clasped her fingers together to seal in her answer with confidence.

My mom nodded. "Is that so? It's crazy how he 'helped' Chyna with her salon when they haven't even been dating for a whole year yet. Don't get me wrong, I'm proud of my daughter for achieving her dream, but I find his intentions a little questionable."

Cali shook her head. "His intentions seem pure to me."

"Are yours?" My mom asked, raising her eyebrow.

Cali placed her hand of her chest in shock and confusion.

"Why wouldn't they be? I want the best for Chyna. She's like a sister to me."

"You want the best for her? Well, I want the best for her too. After all, I'm her mother. But wanting the best for someone also includes calling them out when they're in the wrong. Don't you agree?"

Cali chuckled. "That's true. But at the same time, Chyna is a grown woman who has to explore life on her own terms. I didn't always agree with the choices she made, but those were her choices. And honestly, they've worked out pretty well for her so far."

"Mm-hmm, sure does seem like it." My mom turned her lips into a sly grin then walked back over to my dad without a backward glance.

I had never told my mom that I revealed to Cali I was a witch, but I think she just found out—and I also think she approved. She probably realized it was good for me to have someone by my side who knew exactly what I was capable of.

"Cali, you've got to come to dinner with me tonight. I can't be there alone with these parents," I pleaded.

She had told me earlier that she wouldn't be able to do anything after the game, but I was hoping I could persuade her to change her mind.

"I can't, girl. I have a date with my man tonight. Frankie wants to take me to the grand opening of his friend's restaurant. That's why he didn't come because he had to help his friend get everything set up. Besides, you won't be alone. Chicago will be right by your side," she said as she stuffed a mini jalapeño popper into her mouth.

She was right, I did have Chicago, but around his parents I felt alone. His mom obviously had a strong hold on him, but I wanted my own hold on him too. Especially since his mom was not too fond of me.

"Just relax and try to enjoy your time with your parents and future in-laws," Cali said before heading off to her date night.

"Okay, I'll try."

"Girl, I don't know why you're letting yourself get so stressed. You have the ability to use magic, right? Use that shit to your advantage," she said as she walked out the door.

CHAPTER 35

The air was thick with the tantalizing aroma of smoked brisket and barbeque sauce. Not only was my mouth watering, but I had to squeeze my stomach in an effort to suppress its loud rumbling.

Chicago's parents had rented out a home and flown in a chef from Houston to surprise us with a Texas barbeque dinner.

Chicago was over the moon that one of his favorite Houston chefs was preparing his favorite dishes. The small menus placed on each of our plates read: beef brisket, smoked beef sausage, four-cheese mac and cheese, meaty baked beans, creamy corn, green beans, boudin balls, and potato salad.

I had never had Texas barbeque, so I was excited to try it, as was my dad, who owned a barbeque restaurant back home.

He'd never been a fan of the Texan barbeque flavor, but he was willing to give the chef a chance.

"Too bad we didn't know you also cook BBQ. We could have had a good old-fashioned friendly BBQ cook-off. That would have been fun," Jackie said when my dad revealed that he owned a restaurant.

"I wonder who would win?" Chicago's dad teased.

"Oh man, I would have loved to feed you Texans some real BBQ. Juicy and full of flavor. Next time we meet up, I'll bring my sauces," my dad said.

He loved a competition, especially when it came to grilling.

"I actually just won second place at a BBQ competition back home. I'm that good!" my dad added, gloating.

"Yes, he did! And the mayor of our town is a regular at the restaurant," my mom said, joining in on the boasting.

"Sounds promising. I would love to try it one day," Chicago said with a smile.

The chef and his assistant carried the dishes into the dining room and laid the spread out on the table. He then described each dish and told us to dig in.

We didn't hesitate, and shortly after, the room fell silent.

I didn't want to admit it, but the food was very good and could go toe-to-toe with my dad's.

I glanced over at him picking at the ribs and sausage. I guess he disagreed. He later told me and my mom that Texan barbeque didn't hold a torch to his. My mom and I silently nodded indulging him in his ego trip.

I'm not saying the food was better than my dad's, but it was definitely a runner-up.

"This is so nice. It reminds me of when Chicago was younger, and we would have our family get-togethers. Stephen's brother would roll out this raggedy grill and cook us up something," Jackie said.

"Mm-hmm, that grill was raggedy, but Stanley would smoke the best damn brisket with it," Stephen said, chiming in.

"Man, I remember those briskets he made. He never wanted to share his recipe," Chicago said, shaking his head.

"Hell nah. Smoking a brisket is all he's good at, so he's not about to let anybody else steal the show," Stephen said as he chuckled.

"Chicago bought him a fancy new grill, so he's been experimenting with grilled kabobs, and they're pretty good," Jackie said.

"I have to get back down there to try them. I miss the family. I can't wait to see everybody again. And hopefully, I can introduce everyone to Chyna," Chicago said as he winked at me.

I could feel Jackie's eyes piercing me like daggers, but that didn't stop the smile on my face.

"I would love to meet the family. Jackie was telling me about them when I was doing her hair. They sound like they would be very welcoming."

"They're nice people. They have that southern hospitality, and I think they would love you," Chicago said, reassuring me.

My dad cleared his throat. "That's a pretty big step, meeting the whole family. You don't think it's too soon?" he asked.

I'm sure he figured that if I met Chicago's whole family, then Chicago would want to meet my mine—and they're witches. I couldn't imagine Chicago meeting Ameri and having to live through part two of her exposing magic to my boyfriend at dinner.

And I didn't need my family trying to erase Chicago's memories, especially after our relationship had progressed so far.

"I agree. I think it's too soon. We don't know how long this thing between you two is going to last, so we should wait it out and see," Jackie chimed in.

I let out a dry laugh at her statement. "I think our relationship is doing just fine. It's obviously not just some fling. This is real. We're serious about our relationship...about our love. Right, Chicago?" I looked at him for reassurance.

He nodded, then wiped the barbeque sauce from the side of his mouth with his napkin.

"This is serious. We have a real connection and future together. Chyna's going to be by my side for a long time. If she's going to be my future wife. Why not meet the whole family?" Chicago said proudly.

I turned my head and smirked at Jackie who looked like she had stopped breathing.

"Wife? I don't think so. No." Jackie snickered.

"And why don't you think so?" my mom asked, her voice growing defensive.

Jackie turned to my mom and looked her up and down. "My son isn't ready for marriage. He's fresh into his career and honestly doesn't need any distractions. I figured this was just a fun time for him and went along with it, but—"

"I agree that they're still young and shouldn't be rushing to jump into marriage. But when the time comes, I would allow it," my mom interrupted.

It warmed my soul to know my mom would support me once Chicago popped the question.

She wasn't happy with how I'd gotten here, but it appeared that she finally had my back. Even if it was just her being defensive and jumping to the rescue because her cub was being attacked, I would take it.

"I wouldn't allow it. Look, I know you think highly of your daughter just like I think highly of my son. We both want the best for our children. And if I'm being honest, I don't like these two together. I just don't," Jackie said, throwing her hands up in the air.

She was finally admitting what I'd known all along—that she did not like me.

"Mama…" Chicago said before I interrupted.

"I knew it! I knew you didn't like me, Jackie. I'm not sure why, though, because I've been nothing but kind and loving to you," I said in my own defense.

The mood had shifted fast. I could feel the tension creeping in as the conversation headed into dangerous waters.

Jackie's eyes narrowed, and her lips pressed into a thin line of disapproval.

"I'm his mom," she shot back, her voice tinged with icy resolve. "I only want what's best for him, and it's not you, Chyna."

The words hit me like a slap in the face, igniting a firestorm of anger within me.

I clenched my fist and took a deep breath before responding. But before I could say anything, my mom fired back at Jackie first.

"Now hold on just a minute," she said; her voice started out steady but was beginning to become sharp and annoyed. "I know my daughter, and she may not be perfect, but neither is your son. No one is. But I do know that she loves your son, and I can tell he loves her too. They're grown and can figure this out themselves without us interfering."

Jackie flicked her gaze between me and my mom. "I don't care how much they love each other. It doesn't seem that sincere to me," she said, her voice dripping with disdain. "I don't trust your daughter and I barely trust you. I know something is off here. And I want my son far away from it."

The words hung in the air, a heavy silence descending upon the room as our conflicting emotions swirled like a tempestuous storm. In that moment, the divide between us felt insurmountable.

"Mama, what are you talking about?" Chicago asked, a worried look on his face.

Jackie was silent for a moment, studying Chicago before speaking. "Son, I'm not sure how to explain it, but I've felt this way since the moment I met this girl. Whenever you talk about her, I feel itchy and get this strange feeling."

My mom and dad both looked over to me, concern in their eyes.

"I don't know what you're talking about, Mama. Dad said he's never seen me as happy with anyone as I am with Chyna."

"You say that with your mouth, but your eyes say something else, Chicago." Jackie leaned in as if she were reading Chicago's eyes like a book. "What has she done to you, son?"

I slammed my hands down on the table, beyond infuriated.

"That's enough, Jackie!" I screamed, causing everyone to jump in their seat.

"Chyna, don't yell at my mama like that!" Chicago said, snapping his head toward me with a scowl etched across his face.

"Oh, but you have no problem with her saying the things she said about me? Really?" I yelled.

My mom got up from her seat. "Chyna, calm down."

"No, I will not calm down! This woman is trying to ruin me, and I won't allow it! Not after everything I've been through!"

Anger and fear surged through me. I was pissed that all my hard work was going to shit, and deep down, I was scared my whole scheme was about to blow up.

"Chyna! Calm down now!" my mom yelled.

"No!" I screamed, causing every piece of glass in the room to shatter.

Everyone gasped.

"What the fuck!" Chicago jumped back from the table.

"Chyna, stop it! You can't keep doing this!" my dad said, jumping up.

My blood was burning, but I couldn't calm myself down. I felt hopeless and desperate…like I was losing control and couldn't recover anything.

The tension in the room had reached boiling point, and I was gasping for air.

Apparently, the sound of glass shattering sent the chef rushing into the dining room.

"Are y'all alright? What happened?" he asked, his voice frantic.

As adrenaline coursed through my veins, a tingling sensation rose inside as my magic stirred within me. On a reckless impulse, I raised my hand, channeling raw intense power. Aloud, I recited a familiar spell that I was forbidden to use.

With a swift flick of my wrist, I unleashed a wave of energy in the form of a dense ball of purple smoke that sent the unsuspecting chef hurtling across the room. His body collided with the wall with a sickening thud, knocking him unconscious.

The room erupted into chaos, and there were gasps of shock as everyone recoiled in horror at the sudden display of magic.

Jackie's eyes widened in disbelief, her features contorted with fear and alarm as she took in the scene before her.

"I knew it," she said in a whisper.

"Chyna! No!" My mom cried out.

I fell to my knees. My chest heaving with exertion as my heart pounded in my ears. Regret washed over me in a wave instantly, mingled with the lingering anger and frustration.

I met Chicago's shocked, frightened gaze, and my stomach twisted with guilt and shame.

"I'm so sorry. I know how…I just…" I fumbled for the right words, but nothing came out.

I turned to my mom, but my eyes were filled with tears.

"Ma…I'm sorry," I cried.

I heard my mom let out an exasperated sigh. Then the chaos in the room dissipated.

I blinked a few times to disperse the tears that were preventing me from seeing properly.

I turned toward Chicago, and he was completely still, not even blinking, yet his horrified gaze remained fixed on me. That look made my stomach turn.

Jackie was also frozen to the spot, and I could see that she was about to raise her hands to her mouth. My mom must have used a spell to pause time.

She stormed over to me, slamming each heel into the floor with intense force. With her thumb and forefinger, she tilted my chin up before her hand connected with my cheek in a firm, resounding slap.

The sound reverberated in the tense silence, echoing the weight of disappointment and frustration that was now present.

As I recoiled from the force of the slap, my eyes widened in surprise before understanding dawned. It was justified punishment.

A wake-up call.

"What? You're sorry? Sorry that I have to clean up your mess again?" My mom stood up and stomped her feet. "You can't keep doing this!"

My dad came over to console my mom, massaging her shoulders.

My mom looked around and shook her head before her eyes settled on mine

"This is going to take a few hours to clean up, and you're going to help me."

CHAPTER 36

The crisp, cool air filled my lungs as I stepped into the chaos of the schoolyard. Each crunch of fallen leaves beneath my feet matched the rhythm of my racing heart. My curls bounced with every stride, and a small smile tugged at my lips. I was ready for whatever the day had in store.

It was the middle of fall, during my first year of middle school. I reveled in the freedom of youth, caught up in the joy of the moment, without a care in the world. Middle school was my sanctuary, a place where I could shed the weight of the world and bask in the simple joys of adolescence.

I had two good friends I loved spending time with, Tiera and Drew. We always met up at Tiera's locker after our classes to talk about our crushes.

"So…did he look at you today?" Tiera asked my other friend Drew, who had just had first period with her crush.

Drew looked down with a huge smile on her face.

"Well! Did he?" I was too excited to wait for her to act out a dramatic pause.

"Not only did he look, he smiled at me!" she screamed, jumping up and down.

We grabbed each other's hands and jumped up and down in a circle, beyond ecstatic that she'd made progress with her crush.

We were super innocent back then and thought just talking to our crushes was the biggest thing. None of us had gotten to that point yet, so Drew getting a smile from hers was sending us over the edge.

We quickly quieted our squeals and closed in on Drew to hear all the details of what had led up to the smile. I glanced around and noticed a dark cloud of evil hovering over a chubby-cheeked girl with a braided ponytail called Amanda.

She glared at me, flaring her nostrils, then sliced her hand through the air in a swift, decisive motion, her fingers forming a chilling silhouette against the backdrop of her clenched jaw. With a sharp jerk of her thumb across her throat, she delivered the message loud and clear—a silent but unmistakable threat that hung heavy in the air like a guillotine poised to strike. The gesture sent a shiver down my spine and left no room for misunderstanding.

What I didn't understand was, why me? Why did Amanda hate me?

Since my first day at this school, I had made it my mission to try to befriend everyone. I wanted to have the type of friendships that I saw in the movies. I wanted to be the popular girl.

Even though my mom had drilled into my head that I needed to distance myself from people because of my powers, I wanted the opposite. I needed to find my tribe.

It took some trial and error, but I finally found my people in Tiera and Drew. With them I felt heard and seen. Those two were my main friends, but I still tried to branch out to expand our posse.

I even tried with Amanda, who from day one didn't like me. And it wasn't the simple "I don't like you so I'm going to ignore you" vibes that I received from others. It was a "I don't like you so I'm going to make your life a living hell" vibe.

Our first interaction occurred in the cafeteria when I overheard Amanda complaining that she didn't have enough quarters to get a cookie from the snack bar. I turned around, tapped her on the shoulder, and offered her my sugar cookie with a big smile. In return, she rolled her eyes at me, snatched the cookie from my hand and threw it on the ground. Her friends laughed as she turned back to them and kept on complaining. I sat there dumbfounded.

"Forget her, Chyna. Amanda is a complete witch," Drew whispered.

I spun around in my seat, my eyes wide. "Wait, what? She's a witch? Really?"

"Mm-hmm, an ugly witch too! She's mean for no reason," Drew said.

Completely naïve at the time, this information made me want to be friends with her even more. If she was a witch and everyone knew and accepted her, maybe we could become friends and be witches in public together.

After our class, I ran over to Amanda.

"Hey, Amanda. So, I heard you're a witch. Maybe we could practice some spells together," I said, my face lighting up with a smile.

"What the hell did you call me? Did you just call me a witch? Oh, I'll show you a witch!" Amanda said at the top of her lungs.

She pushed me up against a row of lockers before grabbing my backpack and emptying it all over the hallway.

"Don't you ever call me a witch! I'll whoop your ass!" she yelled as a crowd began to surround us.

I heard a teacher shout, "Hey, what's going on?"

Everyone, including Amanda, scattered.

I stood there dumbfounded and embarrassed, once again, as hot tears rolled down my cheeks.

I didn't know what to do. I'd never had a bully before. I'd tried to be friendly and cordial, but nothing had worked.

I had to seek outside advice.

The first person I went to was my mom, but the advice she gave me could have stayed to herself. Instead of actually helping me, she lectured me about morals and being the bigger person.

It was a conversation that someone should have had with Amanda, the bully. Not me, the victim seeking help.

"Chyna, at the end of the day, don't let anyone get you out of character. She's only picking on you because she's jealous of you. All that won't matter in a few years, and you won't even remember who she is."

Solid advice from a therapist.

Sure, it might be good advice for an adult dealing with an asshole they may never have to deal with again. But for a young teenager in need of acceptance and friendship who had to see this person daily, the advice wasn't the best.

"We have magic, Ma, why can't you just use a little of it to make her stop?" my voice breaking as I pleaded with her.

"We don't use magic on people like that in this house. An eye for an eye is not the answer. You have to ignore this girl and understand that she's just desperate for attention."

"What is the magic for, then?" I yelled, storming off to my room.

I couldn't stand that she wanted me to just forget I had magic…to act like it didn't exist unless it benefited her.

My dad, on the other hand, was a little more helpful. He wanted to be more involved with the school, making sure the teachers and principal were aware of the issue and could prevent any further bullying from happening.

This did have a positive impact, but only when the teachers and principal were around, which they weren't majority of the time.

Of course, during class, Amanda was as sweet and fake as she could be. But outside of the classroom when no adults were around, the real Amanda would rampage through the halls.

I was beginning to lose myself. With each passing insult, each mocking laugh, each shove into the lockers, my patience was wearing thinner and thinner until I could barely contain the simmering rage that boiled within me. I didn't deserve this, and I was no longer willing to accept the role of victim.

The next time I saw Amanda, I automatically moved out of her way to avoid the habitual shove into the lockers. But instead, she walked right past me with a sneer of disgust as if she was walking past a dumpster on a hot summer day.

I exhaled, relieved that I had been saved from today's encounter, until I heard a mischievous laugh coming from behind me.

"Oh no, I'm so clumsy!" Amanda said as she "tripped" and crashed into me.

She purposely pushed her full body weight into me, crushing me against the lockers and making me gasp for air. When she pulled herself off me, I dropped to the floor.

"My bad, Chyna, I didn't even see you there, let me help you up," she said grabbing my backpack instead of my hand.

She took off with it, her giggling friends running along behind her.

I jumped up and chased after her.

Once I caught up to her, I rammed my shoulder into her back sending her tumbling to the ground. She quickly rolled over and gave me a death stare.

"Give me back my bag, Amanda! I'm not gonna play these games with you anymore!" I said.

A surge of heat washed over me. My heart pounded in my chest, each beat echoing in my ears like a war drum as I stared down at Amanda.

Amanda rose to her feet, her face red and just as fiery as mine. I stood my ground, staring Amanda down as the tension ratcheted up several notches.

With a savage swing of her arm, Amanda's fist connected with my face, the force of the blow sending me reeling backwards. Sharp pain erupted along my lip, and the taste of blood, metallic and acrid, flooded my mouth as I lay sprawled on the hallway floor, dazed and disoriented.

Amanda grabbed my backpack, and in what was now a familiar move, emptied its contents on the floor beside me before stomping on them.

I laid there on the cold hallway floor with a throbbing lip, watching through tear-blurred eyes as Tiera and Drew came over to help me up.

I wanted to cry out loud, but I didn't.

Beneath the pain and humiliation, I was determined to seek revenge.

After the day I had just had, I wanted to go home and bury myself in my bed. Unfortunately, I had made a promise to do Ameri's hair after school. As much as I wanted to put on a happy façade, I couldn't hide my defeated mood or my bruised lip.

My Aunt Crystal soon noticed.

"Uh, what happened to your face, Chyna?" she asked, pausing her TV show as soon as she saw me.

"It's nothing. I just fell at school," I said, too ashamed to admit what had actually happened.

She studied my face for a moment then huffed.

"If someone at that school is messing with you then you need to tell me or your mom. You need to talk to someone. Don't let no one bully you."

I nodded then scurried down the hallway to Ameri's room.

"Damn Chyna, what happened to your lip?"

"Shh, don't worry about it. Now sit down so I can do your hair and go home."

Ameri only wanted a simple style today. Some braids in the front and her natural curls in the back. For about two hours, I worked on her hair in silence while we watched a movie.

We were both satisfied with the finished look, so much so that my cousin proudly posed as my aunt took some pictures on her phone to show her coworkers.

"You're getting better and better, Chyna!" my aunt said, clearly impressed.

"Thanks. Well, I'm going to head home," I said, gathering my things.

"What? You're not going to have dinner with us tonight?"

"No, not tonight. I'm tired," I said, heading for the door.

"Hold on, Chyna." My aunt stopped me to pass me a nice little tip for doing my cousins hair and also a note.

I opened the note and saw a spell written inside of it.

"I know something's going on with you, and I know your mom acts real silly about you using magic, but we know how to use it, so why not?

"Now, this is a simple spell that will give someone a little zap. Don't use this spell directly to their face, otherwise they'll know you're using a spell on them. It's best to do it as a little kick back once they have their back turned. It's nothing too crazy. Just enough to get someone off your back and make them a little scared," she said.

"Thanks, but I think I may need something a little stronger."

"For what? You trying to fight a bear?" she asked then chuckled at her own joke. "I don't have anything stronger for you. Your mom might in her lair, but this should be good enough to make a difference. If it doesn't work, then let me know and I'll take matters into my own hands."

"Do you have something for this?" I asked pointing toward my busted lip.

I knew there was a spell for healing because I'd seen my mom use it when she cut herself cleaning up a broken dish I'd accidentally dropped. But I couldn't remember the words.

My aunt nodded then recited the spell, pointing her finger at my lip to instantly heal it.

"It's done," she said, smiling as she opened the door to lead me outside.

"Thank you, Aunt Crystal."

"No problem, honey. I'll watch you walk home."

As I walked down the street, thinking about everything she had said, I looked over the spell and tried to memorize it.

A little zap? Amanda needed more than a little zap, for all the torment she had inflicted upon me.

I got home and pretended that everything was fine so my parents wouldn't question anything.

"Is that little girl still bothering you?" my mom asked while we were eating dinner.

"Nope. I took your advice Ma, so she left me alone," I said, lying through my teeth.

I wasn't completely lying, though, because after tomorrow, Amanda would leave me alone.

Once my parents were asleep, I made my way to my mom's lair. I had trained Neli to stand by and meow really loudly if my parents woke up.

My mom had shown me around her lair before, back when she used to train me and teach me simple "good spells" like removing acne, gaining confidence, or a motivational boost to help with studying. And I remembered exactly where she had hidden the "dangerous spell books." Luckily for me, my mom underestimated me and didn't think she needed to put much effort into binding them or hiding them away.

I grabbed the book and flipped through its pages until I found what I was looking for. The spell that completed the one my aunt had given me.

I took out her note, wrote out the rest of the spell, then returned the book to its original spot and ran back to my room to memorize the words.

The next day at school, I walked through the familiar halls with a newfound sense of confidence coursing through my veins like a warm current.

With each step, I held my head a little higher, a radiant smile playing at the corners of my lips. I no longer felt the weight of Amanda's torment hanging heavy on my shoulders.

Today would be the day everything changed.

Drew and Tiera ran over to me.

"Chyna, what are you smiling so much for? Girl you should be ducking and dodging after what happened yesterday," Tiera said.

"Wait, your lip isn't busted anymore. How come?" Drew asked, staring at my mouth in confusion.

"Don't even worry about it. I'm doing great. That's why I'm smiling so much," I said, cocky with pride.

"Chyna, are you okay? Maybe you should have gone to the doctor after Amanda knocked you down yesterday," Tiera said, placing her hand on my forehead to check my temperature.

I shook off her hand and reassured them both that I was doing just fine.

"I'm telling you, I'm okay. Today's going to be great. Amanda isn't going to bother me anymore."

"Really? How do you know that?" Drew asked.

"Just trust me!" I said as I walked off.

This day felt different.

Probably because I knew I was going to finally end the bullying and not have to worry about Amanda anymore. I was very eager to get the action started. I was ready and waiting for Amanda to carry out her usual tactics. I felt trigger-happy.

During our first and second period, though, Amanda didn't acknowledge my existence at all. It bothered me and made me itch to use my spell even more, but I waited patiently.

After my second period I went to my locker to switch out my books. That's when I heard a familiar annoying voice huffing behind me. I turned and there she was, Amanda, standing with her arms crossed and a smug smile on her face.

I crossed my arms too and tilted my head to the side. She didn't even realize the cat had now become the mouse, and the ball was finally in my court.

"So, it's true. That's weird. What the hell happened to the busted lip I gave you yesterday?" Amanda asked.

"It's gone. Just like your days of bullying me. Now leave me the hell alone!"

"Screw you! I'm not a bully. You're just a little bitch!" She said, her friends snickering behind her, clearly agreeing that I was soft.

She knew exactly what to say to trigger me and get under my skin.

A few students who were walking past stopped. I heard them whisper that this was going to be part two of yesterday's smackdown, which made me even more upset and slightly embarrassed.

"She must wanna be thrown to the floor again!" Amanda said at the top of her voice, ensuring that the kids who had stopped overheard.

"Fuck you!" I said.

Amanda whipped her head in my direction, then stormed up to me. She was inches from my face, staring me down with a look of disgust.

"What the hell did you just say to me? Don't play with me 'cause I'm ready to go again!"

"So am I!" I shot back, standing my ground.

She shoved me into the lockers, the sudden impact making me gasp.

Without even thinking twice, I clenched my fist and swung. I realized I wasn't a good fighter as soon as my fist connected with her shoulder and not her face as I had intended.

Amanda raised an eyebrow, her head tilting in disbelief. She hadn't expected me to really fight back. She took it as an invitation to release all of her rage and proceeded to pummel me with punches to the head, face, and chest.

I tried to throw my fist around, but nothing was connecting, and I was becoming too disoriented. I could barely keep myself from falling to the ground and curling up.

A teacher, who had noticed the students gathered around us, parted the crowd and made her way over. She screamed when she saw us, which made Amanda jump back and throw her hands up.

"Why are you girls fighting? That's it! Both of you to the principal's office, now! And everyone else needs to the clear the halls!"

Amanda pleaded with her, saying she hadn't started the fight and claimed that I had thrown the first punch, and she was just defending herself.

"I don't care who started it. I saw you punching too, so you're both getting in trouble! Let's go!" the teacher said, grabbing Amanda by the arm and motioning for me to follow them.

"No! I'm tired of Amanda's shit! I'm not going to keep letting her bully me! And I'm not going to get in trouble for finally standing up for myself!" I said, tears streaming down my hot and bruised cheeks.

"Shut up, Chyna. I was not bullying you," Amanda said, along with a bunch of other words, but I could no longer hear them.

I began reciting the spell I had practiced all night.

I could feel a tingling sensation as the magic flowed through my entire body. I raised both hands and held them out in front of me, unleashing a powerful force of energy in the form of purple smoke that threw Amanda against the lockers and held her there.

I slowly curled my fingers toward me causing Amanda to cry out as the bones in her arm began to break.

The teacher ran over to Amanda to try to pull her down, but it was useless.

"Oh, my God! No! What's happening?" the teacher cried.

"It's Chyna!" some of the bystanders said. "Chyna's doing it!"

"Chyna! Are you doing that? What are you doing?" Drew asked.

I didn't know if she had been there the entire time, but she was there now, and she was yelling at me. She brought me back to the present, and when I looked around, everyone's face displayed the same emotion.

Fear.

They were fearful of me, which made me fearful of them.

My mom had always warned me that if people knew I had magic, they would chase me down and burn me. I knew that she was talking about the old days, but the thought of it happening now, after what I had just done to Amanda, didn't seem too far-fetched.

I released the spell and let Amanda fall to the ground.

Slowly, the purple smoke began to disperse.

"I'm sorry," I said, my voice barely a whisper before I turned and ran off.

As I fled the school, fear gripped my heart like a vise, tightening with each step I took as I realized the magnitude of what I had done.

Guilt gnawed at my insides, twisting my stomach into knots as I grappled with the consequences of my actions. I couldn't fathom what my mom would say when she found out what I had done. I didn't even want to think about it. I just wanted to hide away and die in a hole.

I sought refuge in a secluded spot nestled deep within the dense woods bordering my neighborhood—a place known to my family as a sanctuary. It was where we practiced magic spells without anyone bothering us. Usually, my aunt would cast a spell to keep us hidden from anyone or anything else that was out in the woods.

Amidst the whispering trees and dappled sunlight, I found solace in the quiet embrace of nature. I sought comfort in the familiar rustle of leaves and the soothing chorus of birdsong.

I tried desperately to erase my memories, but unfortunately, I hadn't learned that spell yet.

After a few hours, I heard the sound of branches cracking. Footsteps were heading in my direction. I quickly buried myself under a pile of leaves, unbothered by the dirt and bugs.

"Chyna? Where are you hiding at?"

It was my dad, calling out to me.

I didn't move.

I couldn't move.

I couldn't bear to face him after what I had just done.

I had broken the arms of my classmate in front of a majority of my fellow students. By now this event should have reached the news outlets. Soon choppers, the police, the FBI, swat teams, and pitchforkers carrying burning sticks would surround my house, ready to take me out.

The footsteps stopped right beside my head.

"Chyna, look at me," my dad said in the gentlest voice he could muster.

I must not have done a good job of covering myself. If only I had written down a spell to hide myself better. I should have thought ahead.

I lifted my head to face my dad. There was no trace of anger in his gaze. Only a profound sense of sadness at the sight of me huddled and vulnerable under a thin pile of leaves. His shoulders slumped with the weight of unspoken words.

With a heavy sigh, he sat down next to me and reached out to rub the back of my head, a silent offer of comfort and understanding.

Disappointment hung in the air, but beneath it, there was love.

"I'm sorry. I didn't realize how bad you felt. I guess I misunderstood the gravity of your situation. I thought it was typical teen girl drama. Had I known…" He paused, letting out another heavy sigh. "Your aunt told us that you had a busted lip that she healed. I wish you'd told us about it. But I also wish we would have been more attentive. I'm sorry, baby girl."

The tears came instantly. I couldn't hold them back even if I tried. Each one felt like it was carrying all the pain, guilt, and pressure I'd been trying to keep bottled up.

My dad reached out, his comforting arms enveloping me. A wave of emotion washed over me as tears spilled down my cheeks uncontrollably.

In that moment, I felt the weight of the world pressing down on me. The guilt and fear threatening to suffocate me. But having my dad present, knowing he had my back, gave me comfort.

After crying for what felt like an hour, we sat in the silent woods, listening to the sound of birds chirping and taking flight from the branches above us.

"I'm sorry, Dad. I didn't know what to do. I just wanted her to stop bothering me. What's going to happen now?" I asked between sobs.

"I know, baby girl. Right now, your mom and aunts are fixing everything."

"What? How?"

My mom and aunts had begun the cycle of cleaning up my mess. My Aunt Crystal, of course, didn't see this as a big deal. She wanted to erase the entire town's memories of the incident, replace them with memories of an average day, then get back to watching her TV show and go about her day.

My mom, on the other hand, along with my Aunt Celestine, saw this as a bigger issue. My aunt wanted to reform me so I wouldn't need them to "fix" every issue I had.

So, the townspeople who knew what had just happened had their memories erased—but that included all their memories of me and my parents too.

My mom wanted us to have a fresh start which meant we had to move to a new town about an hour away from our former friends and family. With a heavy heart, I watched as the familiar landscape of my hometown faded into the distance, a blur of memories and regrets left behind in my wake.

The incident that had forced my family to uproot our lives still loomed large in my mind today. It was a shadow that trailed my every move.

Now, as I sat before Chicago, my past and present colliding in a whirlwind of emotion, I couldn't help but wonder if history was doomed to repeat itself.

Old habits die hard.

CHAPTER 37

It took about three hours to "clean up" the mess from the dinner I ruined, but I enjoyed every moment of it.

I was finally working alongside my mom, using magic and learning the spells I'd always wanted to learn.

She refused to teach me the spell to erase memories, but she taught me other spells that repaired broken dishes or removed stains.

She erased everyone's memories of the dinner conversation and replaced them with a pleasant version where we talked about sports and barbeque.

My mom desperately wanted to erase my existence from Chicago's mind, but we were too deep into the relationship for that to go smoothly. So, I was relieved when she didn't go through with it.

"This should do it," she said with a sigh as she erased the last memory from the chef's assistant.

My dad placed everyone back into their seats at the table and moved the chef and his assistant to a couple of chairs in the kitchen.

There was no way to avoid the chef experiencing major back pain after being tossed against the wall, but hopefully he would associate it with regular back pain due to his age.

"Thanks, Ma and Dad. Sorry again for what I did," I said with genuine regret as we took our seats.

"Chyna, you have to learn how to control your emotions. You can't keep doing this. What if we weren't here to save you and clean up your mess? What would you have done then?" my dad said impatiently.

I realized I had seriously messed up. Had this happened when my parents weren't around to save me, I would have been screwed.

"I don't know what I would have done. I'm trying to control it. I was doing so good. Even at work when I was being harassed by my coworker, I didn't..."

Suddenly, I remember.

I hadn't gone to the extreme, but I had used my magic on him. I couldn't help it. Justice had to be served in that case.

My mom shook her head and rolled her eyes.

"This is exactly why I never wanted to teach you magic. Ever since you were a little girl, you were too curious and would use it without restraint after learning just one spell. You would use the spells publicly too, and I just knew that you wouldn't be responsible," my mom said.

"I was a child at that time, Ma," I said in my defense.

"And apparently, you still are. Your cousin, Ameri, on the other hand, was the opposite as a child. Even with my crazy sister using her magic all out in the open, your cousin was very disciplined, like me until recently. Now, that child is just..." my mom stopped talking when she heard Chicago groaning as he came out of the spell coma.

She gave me and my dad a pointed look then whispered her spell to wake everyone up at the same time. As soon as she finished reciting the spell, we picked up our conversation from the fake memory and talked about the game and how well Chicago had played.

Chicago and his parents snapped awake after hearing the spell, then they looked around the room, confused.

They had just woken up from a spell coma that altered some traumatic memories, so it would take a while for them to come back to themselves. My family guided them through a conversation that would make their transition smoother, making them think they just had a simple brain fart that made them lose track of the conversation. After a few minutes they began to move normally, eating their food again, and joining in the conversation when prompted.

"You remember that shot you made? You were on fire, baby. I think you were trying to show off in front of your parents," I said, reeling him back into the conversation.

Chicago placed his hand on the back of his head and nodded. "Right. Thank you, baby. I wasn't trying to show off, I was just in the mood. That game was intense, and I've been beefing with some of those dudes for a minute," he said, jumping back into the conversation.

Everything was smooth sailing from then on.

My mom even added a spell that would introduce fond thoughts of me into Jackie's mind so she wouldn't continue provoking me.

Jackie remained quiet for the rest of dinner, but that familiar kindness returned to her eyes—the same look I'd seen the first time we met. She even complimented me on the necklace Chicago had given me.

Once the dinner was over, we all said our goodbyes as both Chicago and my parents were leaving in the morning to return home.

My mom and dad gave me a warm group hug.

"Chyna, please take care of yourself and be careful, baby girl. Remember what we told you. We can't always be there to clean up your mess," my dad said.

"Well, it would help to learn the spell to erase memories, just in case I need it for an emergency," I said, turning to my mom.

"No, you shouldn't need it. Keep yourself in check. Besides you're not skilled enough to accurately use it. There were still a few small cracks in some of the dishes you repaired. Practice those spells," she said as she walked out the door, my dad following behind her.

Chicago came over to hug me after they left.

"Tonight went great. I told you my mom liked you," he said as he kissed my forehead.

CHAPTER 38

Two weeks later, Chicago and I were back to our regular routine. Although, I didn't have the spell book anymore, I still remembered how to maintain the love spell, so I continued to pour it into him.

Chicago started taking me to more of his gym sessions, so I could learn how to use some of the machines to keep my body in shape.

I never really needed to do much exercising growing up, because I was naturally in shape thanks to my genes. But as I had gotten older, I noticed the weight was sticking.

It didn't look bad. In fact, it gave me a sexier, more mature look, but I needed to tone my body, so I could look even better.

We decided to do an early morning workout session before I headed to the salon to work on a few heads.

I hated working out this early in the morning, and Chicago wasn't even giving me a second to dread it. He was constantly throwing different sets and reps at me.

He tried to keep me motivated and make it fun by telling jokes and giving me compliments.

It helped a little—but what really helped was watching him do his workout.

The way the sweat dripped off his body was all the entertainment I needed. It was enticing.

I wanted to wipe the sweat off his abs with my tongue, and I did shortly after our session in the gym shower.

We had arrived very early, so no one else was there to interrupt us.

By the time I got to the salon, I was still thinking about that gym shower moment. I was also excited for the date night we had planned after work.

Thankfully, I only had four clients for the day, which meant I'd have plenty of time to head home and get ready.

My first client went super smoothly.

She just wanted a simple silk press of her shoulder length hair. I was able to finish with her a half hour ahead of schedule, so I chatted with my hairstylists for a little while.

Gee, Leslie, and Tamara were planning to take a huge group trip to Cabo in a few weeks with some of their other friends. They invited me to go along, but I had politely declined.

"Someone has to stay here and keep taking clients," I said, chuckling.

The trip seemed like a super fun idea, but I wasn't ready to take a vacation yet. I was still recovering mentally after what happened two weeks ago.

Besides I hadn't even had a baecation with Chicago yet. If I was taking any vacation at all, it would be with Chicago first, because at least it would be free.

"Chyna, your client is here," Chelsea announced from the hostess bar.

I indicated to Chelsea that it was okay to take my client to my chair, and I would be there shortly.

I watched her walk over with a woman sporting a recognizable twist out. She walked over to my chair and sat down. As soon as the client turned to face the mirror, I saw that the familiar twist out belonged to a familiar face, Sasha Mackie.

I quickly walked over to greet her.

"Hi Chyna, how are you? How have you been?" Sasha asked with a huge grin on her face.

"I've been great. Thanks for asking. And thank you for coming, I didn't even realize you had booked. I saw your name, but it didn't even register with me who you were."

Sasha scanned the salon with her big brown eyes.

"I love this. You did amazing on the decor and design. I'm so happy for you."

"Thanks! How did you find out about the salon?"

"An influencer I follow, Cia Don, got her hair done here and promoted your page on hers. I was so shocked to see that you were the owner. I knew I had to book an appointment and try you out."

"I'm so happy to hear that. I love working with Cia, she's brought me a lot of clientele."

We continued to chat as I started on her hair. She wanted a sew-in with hair provided by me. So, we found the perfect bundles to match her natural blown out hair texture and color.

As we continued our conversation, we began to drop the professional tone we had grown accustomed to using toward each other. In no time, we were talking like childhood friends with no filter.

She filled me in on the details at my old firm. They had won and lost cases that I had worked on. Not that I really cared anymore, but I was all ears when she told me Richard was getting closer and closer to being terminated by the firm.

"Girl, he's constantly messing shit up. We had an important meeting with the client, and he was so unprepared. He was scrambling through papers making a big mess on the table. It's been months since you left, but he still brings you up, talking about, 'if Chyna had done this paperwork correctly when she was here, then I wouldn't be so behind on my case.' Or 'Chyna messed up this paperwork, and I have to go back and fix her mistakes.' Our boss told me in confidence that he's planning on expanding our team with new hires, which basically means he's going to be finding Richard's replacement very soon," she said.

I was loving the news of all of Richard's failures and screwups. I didn't care if he got fired or not. I was just happy that I didn't have to deal with him anymore. He had been the biggest pain in my adult life.

Good riddance.

We continued to gossip and reminisce about the firm until I was almost done with her hair. She was an easy client and was constantly checking herself in the mirror to admire my work.

She was loving the texture of the bundles I provided and was so surprised to see how well it matched her hair.

"Damn, I really want it straightened, but I love how it looks blown out, I just might walk out like this and tell everyone this is my real hair," she said.

"Okay! You really could get away with it. No one would know it wasn't all your," I said, running my fingers through her hair and the bundles.

"I bought it, so technically, it is my hair."

We laughed, and after about two and a half glasses of champagne, I could tell Sasha was opening up even more.

I was enjoying this side of her. We had had some good times working at the firm and had been able to unmask and code-switch when we were by ourselves, but we had never allowed ourselves to fully loosen up because of the environment we were in.

"I still can't believe you own your own hair salon, Chyna. This is crazy, but also so amazing. And you did it so soon after quitting the firm. How?" she asked, her curious eyes looking up at me before taking another sip of champagne.

I took a deep breath, trying to decide exactly how much I wanted to share with her.

"Well, I met a really amazing man who helped me get to this point. He really supported me and gave me all the motivation I needed."

"That's great to hear. But dang, does he have any brothers? Cousins? Shoot, I'll take an uncle," she said, laughing.

"Yeah, if you're down for a long-distance boo, since his whole family is in Houston," I said.

I finished her hair, and she loved it. She told me she'd be back as a regular client. Then we hugged and said our goodbyes.

It felt really good to see Sasha again, to see just how far I'd come in my journey from employee to boss.

Just as I had planned, I finished work right on time, giving me three and a half hours to get ready for my date night with Chicago.

We had enrolled in a salsa class. It was the first time we were taking a dance class like this, so we were super excited to go.

I wore a gorgeous red dress with fluttering ruffles and a high slit that showcased my thigh. It looked perfect on me, and I complemented it by wearing my hair in a short, side-part bob.

Chicago couldn't keep his hands off me, not at home nor at the salsa class.

When I walked into the class that evening with Chicago by my side, my heart tingled with excitement. The longer we stayed, the more I felt like myself again—free, light, and fully in the moment. It had been a while since I felt that way.

Every time Chicago touched me, it sparked something inside that got stronger with each twirl and dip. He held me close as he spun me, just like the teacher showed us.

In his arms, I felt alive, totally in sync with him as we moved to the beat of the salsa. We laughed, danced, and got completely lost in the moment, enjoying every second together. It was one of our best dates yet, leaving us both feeling happier and even more connected.

Chicago had made us reservations at a nearby restaurant, and we went straight there after class, choosing to sit on the patio. The stars were out, and it felt intimate as we looked upon a perfect view of the Valley below us.

Chicago sat across from me, the flickering candle on our table casting a dim glow on his chiseled face.

"Chyna, I can't stop thinking about our family dinner. I'm still happy about how our parents got along. I want to do that more often," he said with a slight smile on his face.

I glanced up at the sky to avoid his gaze, still feeling embarrassed about how the dinner had actually gone.

Even though he only remembered the good times, the entire incident and the way he had looked at me after seeing me use magic still haunted me.

"Mm-hmm, it was a great dinner. I really enjoyed it."

"My mom's still talking about how much she likes you. She thinks we'll have some beautiful babies together."

"I think we will too, but before we discuss kids…" I pointed at my ring finger and raised my eyebrow.

"I know. Don't trip. It's coming," he said smoothly.

We continued to chat about our future, with Chicago insisting he wanted a football team of kids, which I was fully against. After several minutes of debating, we settled on four.

I found myself constantly gazing into Chicago's deep brown eyes. I felt a warmth spread through me unlike anything I'd ever known. His presence filled me with a sense of peace and contentment, and with each beat of my heart, I found myself falling deeper and deeper in love.

His laughter was music to my ears, his touch sent shivers down my spine, and his smile lit up my world like nothing else. When I was with him, I felt loved, cared for, and like someone finally got me.

"If you had the power to do anything, what would you do?" he asked while we ate our dinner.

I pondered the question for obvious reasons. I already had the power to do whatever I wanted, so what should I tell Chicago? Once again, I wished I could come out to him and tell him the truth about who I was.

"You mean if I was a witch?" I asked softly.

"A witch? I guess. They don't really have that much power, though. I meant if you had power like a superhero or something."

"I think witches do have power. They have spells."

"Yeah, but they don't have the power to fly or shoot lasers out their hands," he said.

I studied Chicago's eyes, wondering if it was really time to let him know.

"Witches aren't really about that life. They need spells and potions and shit. They're weak without that. Without those tools, they're just regular people," he said.

I nodded in agreement. "Yeah, they're regular people, aren't they? What would you do if you met a witch? Would you ask for anything?"

Chicago leaned back in his chair and thought about it.

"Nah, I'm good with life right now. I wouldn't want anything to change. That shit kind of creeps me out. But if I had superpowers, I would want to fly so I could score more shots," he said before digging into his meal again.

CHAPTER 39

It had been five months since the hectic family dinner, and my relationship with Chicago had grown stronger than ever.

We experienced holidays together and even took a short trip to Mexico before he had to focus on work. It was the perfect pre-baecation before we went all out for the summer.

We had even survived the NBA Finals together, during which I had to seriously quell the urge to use magic on every woman whose eyes were glued to my man.

They were all over him. Even trying to sneak into his hotel room.

I had to up my spells to make it easier for him to ignore the groupies. But I may have gone overboard and had him so focused on me that he couldn't focus on the game and missed his chance at a championship ring.

It took him a while to get over the loss, but he was recognized as an important player and landed a few new sponsorships.

Now that the basketball season was over, it was time to really focus on getting *my* championship ring: the wedding ring. I was ready to officially be Mrs. Moon. I could tell Chicago was becoming more and more ready and open to it too. He just needed a little encouragement.

"So, how are you going to do it? What spell are you going to use?" Cali asked while we waited for our waiter to come and take our order.

We were dining out at a new sushi spot we had seen all over Pic-Talk.

"All I can do is continue using the spells I've been using. My mom took the spell book, and it's been hard to reach my cousin to get the copy she created. I can keep using the same spells, I just have to up my skills, which I've been working on," I said.

"Well, just be careful. I'm still worried after what you told me happened at the family dinner. That shit was insane and could have ended very badly," she said shaking her head.

I'd had to tell her, but part of me regretted it. Cali judged me hard, but I didn't blame her. I understood that what I had done was very reckless, and I felt guilty about it.

Especially after injuring the chef, who even put out a statement on social media saying he'd be scaling back his business for a while due to back pain.

But I didn't need to be reminded of my mistakes over and over. I had moved on, and things were good now.

I massaged the side of my neck, trying to ease my growing frustration and push those memories back where they belonged— in the past.

"I know, Cali. I got this. I'm not going to be reckless like that again. There's no reason to anyways, because Jackie and I have been in a really good space lately."

"Humph, well that's good," Cali said, dropping the conversation before our waiter arrived.

For the rest of our lunch, we filled each other in on everything new in our lives.

While I had been busy keeping up with Chicago's busy schedule, Cali had been busy solidifying her relationship with Frankie.

They had gone on two baecations and met each other's parents. They were getting really serious, but Cali insisted she wasn't ready for marriage yet.

After lunch, I returned home, delivering the two sushi rolls Chicago had requested.

He was standing in the living room looking out of the floor to ceiling windows, watching the beautiful pink and orange sunset. He turned toward me and smiled as he held his phone to his ear.

"Alright, Mama. Chyna just got back, so I'll talk to you later. Chyna, my mom says hi," he said.

"Tell her I said hi and I hope she's doing well," I said in response.

He hung up the phone shortly after and came over for a hug and a kiss before grabbing the bag of sushi and digging in.

"How's your mom doing?"

"She's doing good. Just checking in on us."

"Us? She asked about me too?" I asked, selecting a bottle of white wine for us.

"Yeah, of course she did. She just wanted to know how you were and how the salon was doing," he said before stuffing a sushi roll into his mouth.

I squealed on the inside, happy to know that Jackie and I were still on good terms.

Jackie and Stephen had been visiting us more frequently, which gave me a chance to finally build a better bond with Jackie now that I felt she no longer hated me. She actually became super sweet and comfortable to be around. She was still a little distant and hadn't fully opened up to me yet, but it felt good to be around her.

I stood at the corner of our kitchen island, sipping my wine and watching Chicago eat.

We chatted briefly about my lunch with Cali and his gym session. As soon as he finished demolishing the sushi rolls, he wiped his mouth and gave me an intense smile.

"Why are you smiling like that? It's weird," I said.

"I have a surprise for you," Chicago said in a voice that sent shivers up my spine.

I was very curious to know what this surprise was given his mysterious tone. He had a playful yet serious look in his eyes as he read my face for a response.

"What? What is it?" I asked, inching closer to him, anxious for him to tell me.

He rose from his seat and walked into the living room where he retrieved an envelope from the coffee table, never once breaking eye contact with me. Then he slowly walked back toward me, looking down and scanning the envelope as if to ensure it hadn't been tampered with before placing it in front of me.

"Open it," he said, keeping his eyes glued to mine.

I held my composure and slowly picked it up, resisting the urge to rip it open as Chicago and I engaged in an intense eye fuck session.

I peeled back the folds of the envelope and removed its contents.

My jaw dropped.

I was looking down at two plane tickets to Paris, France. One in my name and the other in Chicago's.

"Chicago, what is this?"

I was squealing now. No longer able to hold my composure.

"These aren't the actual tickets because they're on the app. I was just trying to do it the old-fashioned way and be a little romantic. I wanted you to know that's where we're going next week," he said.

"Oh, my God!" I couldn't stop screaming and hugging him.

I'd never been to Paris, but it had always been on my bucket list. So, I was beyond excited, thinking about all the clothes I was going to pack and all the clothes I was going to buy while we were there.

"Chicago! What's the occasion? What made you...why are we?"

"Just because I love you, baby. We deserve this, a real extended baecation," he said before kissing my forehead.

"Oui, oui!" I said as I wrapped my arms around him.

CHAPTER 40

The aroma of freshly baked croissants and rich espresso filled the air, mingling with the gentle breeze that wafted through the open doors of the busy Parisian café.

As the morning sun painted the sky with soft hues of pink and gold, I sat across from Chicago, our hands glued to mugs of delicious hot chocolate as we indulged in the array of pastries spread across the table.

The weather was nice. Slightly warm, but I couldn't resist treating myself to a hot chocolate. Just like the ones I had seen numerous times on Pic-Talk, while scrolling for places to go and things to do in Paris.

I was a little disappointed that although the Eiffel Tower was only a few blocks away, I couldn't see it from where we were.

When I finally saw the tower for the first time, it truly took my breath away—its iconic silhouette stood proud against the Parisian skyline. Initially, I couldn't tear my gaze away from the magnificent landmark.

Holding Chicago's hand, I looked at him and saw that his eyes filled with wonder and awe too. A swell of joy rose in my heart, grateful to be sharing this magical moment with the person I loved most in the world.

I had a good feeling about this trip.

Even before he gave me the tickets, I had been pouring my spells into him constantly, hoping it would push him to propose. But without the spell book, I wasn't sure if I was on the right track anymore—or if I was overdoing it.

Chicago knew a trip to Paris was at the top of my bucket list, so it only made sense that he'd want to bring me here for a marriage proposal. At least that's what Cali and I had figured.

"Hell yeah, he's going to propose. I mean, why wouldn't he? That would be the perfect place to do it," Cali said with stars in her eyes.

I'd had my suspicions about Cali. I think she'd known all along Chicago was planning to propose.

Usually, a guy would rope in his girl's best friend to make sure he was planning everything right when it came to the choice of ring and where to propose. After all, Chicago could easily reach out to Cali through her man because they were friends.

But what had really made me suspicious was that, lately, every time I brought up marriage, Cali's eyes would immediately sparkle, and she would get a cheesy grin on her face. So, in response, I had given her hints as to what rings I liked and shown her videos of other couple's proposals in the hope that she would relay the message to Chicago.

We spent our first day in Paris sightseeing and taking tours. We started off with the Eiffel Tower, then had lunch on a boat circling the city as our host pointed out some historical sites.

Next was the creepy Catacombs tour, during which Chicago sped through the tunnels so fast, I had to run to keep up with him. Lastly, we stopped to view the Arc de Triomphe and had dinner at a nearby restaurant.

"Wow, their Louis store is huge. We have to plan a few hours to do some shopping before we leave," I said, the excitement evident in my voice as I thought back to the Louis Vuitton store, we had passed on our way to dinner.

We had found a fine dining steakhouse where we tried escargot for the first time. I was surprised that Chicago actually liked it, he said it reminded him of oysters.

"Yeah, definitely. I need to get a few things from there too," Chicago said.

"So, what's the plan for tomorrow?" I asked, looking for any hints.

Chicago dropped his eyes to focus on his steak, cutting it and taking a bite before answering.

"I have something nice planned that I think you'll like," he said nonchalantly, but his eyes glowed with excitement, which in turn made me excited.

"Well, I can't wait to see what you have in store for us," I said as I shimmied in my seat, unable to contain my enthusiasm.

The next morning, we kicked things off with a cozy breakfast at a nearby café before heading to a macaron baking class. It was a super sweet gesture, because throughout our entire flight to Paris, I had made a list of all the macaron shops I wanted to visit along with all the flavors I wanted to try.

The class was filled with other couples and was taught by an informative French instructor.

My macarons turned out perfectly. I prided myself that I had quite possibly been a baker in my past life. Chicago's macarons turned out better than I would have expected. They were presentable, but nowhere close to mine, which I teased him about.

Afterwards, we wandered around, taking in the buzz of Paris before stopping at the Sacre Coeur Basilica.

We didn't stay out too long because Chicago wanted us to head back to the hotel to get dressed for dinner, stressing that I had to don my best dress because we were going to the most prestigious restaurant in the city. Of course, I had the perfect dress for the occasion.

It was a chic white halter dress with a ruffle hem. It was the perfect look for a night of fine dining in Paris with the possibility of a proposal capping it all off.

I had envisioned wearing this very dress when Chicago got down on one knee to propose to me. I hoped he had hired a photographer to capture the moment.

Once I got out of the shower, I called Chicago, asking him to bring me my after-shower body oil that I had forgotten to bring into the bathroom with me, but he didn't answer.

I wrapped my towel around me and walked into the bedroom, only to find it empty.

"Where the hell..." I grumbled under my breath, already getting annoyed.

My dress was laid out on the bed with a folded note sitting on top of it. I snatched it up and quickly scanned it.

It was a handwritten note from Chicago.

Hey baby,

I left early to go grab something special for our dinner tonight. Let the hotel know when you're done getting ready and they'll have a car bring you to me.

Love Cago

P.S. That dress is going to look good as fuck on you! See you soon.

I regretted my flash of temper, which had instantly been replaced by euphoria. I allowed a few tears to roll down my cheeks since I hadn't started my makeup yet.

It was really happening.

Everything I'd worked so hard for and dreamed about since forever was finally coming to fruition.

I gave myself permission to squeal and cry with joy for a few minutes before pulling myself together to finish getting ready. I wanted to take my time so I would look my best, but I also wanted to hurry and be where Chicago was.

I was convinced that the "special something" had to be my engagement ring that he was picking up before dinner. So, while I used my magic to flawlessly apply my makeup and do my hair, I envisioned what the ring would look like.

Hopefully, he had chosen one of the ten rings I had shown Cali, and it had been custom-made right here in Paris.

The excitement and anticipation were eating away at me.

As soon as I was ready, I snapped a couple of photos and sent them to Cali, telling her about the dinner and asking her if she thought my look fit the occasion.

It was noon in LA, so she responded right away.

"Yes, girl! You look good! Let me know how dinner goes," she texted back, ending her message with a winking face emoji.

Something was definitely up, and I couldn't wait to find out what it was.

I left the room imagining I was in a melodramatic movie, slowly sliding my fingers across the furniture as I walked toward the door. I stood in the doorway looking at the beautifully decorated room and pondered leaving my life as a girlfriend behind and hoping to return as a fiancée.

As the sleek luxury car glided through the bustling streets of Paris, I couldn't help but be mesmerized by the city's transformation under the cover of night. The soft glow of the streetlights cast a warm, ethereal radiance on the cobblestone streets, illuminating the elegant architecture that lined our route.

But amidst the beauty of the city at night, there lingered a faint sense of unease. I felt nervous about the thought of Chicago possibly proposing. I yearned for the moment he'd finally declare his love and commitment to me. I was ready for that fairytale moment. But a small part of me…was scared of what came after.

As we neared the place where Chicago awaited me, my heart fluttered with anticipation, a mix of excitement and apprehension swirling within me. I couldn't shake the feeling that tonight was significant, a moment that could change the course of our lives forever.

The car pulled up in front of a beautiful villa that resembled a castle. The villa stood before me, bathed in moonlight, its ivy-covered walls whispering secrets from centuries past.

I stepped out into the cool night air.

A few sleek cars were parked near the valet, and a couple of men in sharp black attire stood by the entrance. It had to be some kind of exclusive restaurant—perfect for a private dinner.

One of the men approached and gestured for me to follow him inside.

"Bonjour, madame. Do you have a reservation?" the maître d' asked in a thick accent.

"Yes, I believe so. My boyfriend should be here. Chicago Moon."

"Aw yes, Chicago Moon. Right this way. Champagne?"

He offered me a flute of champagne and guided me through the villa to the back yard.

All of the tables had been decorated with flowers and candles. Only three were in use, and I didn't see Chicago at any of them.

The maître d' continued to guide me through the back yard and along a cobblestone path that was lit up with beautiful fairy lights and flowers.

As I followed him down the path, my heart was pounding so hard it felt as if it was going to jump out of my chest, and the knot in my stomach just kept growing. There was no reason to be nervous, I was only going to meet the man I'd been seeing for the past year, but tonight felt so intense.

I was led into an open grassy area where I saw Chicago sitting at a white table with a beautiful array of flowers on it.

I felt myself tearing up as I let out a sigh of relief. My heart felt full in that moment.

And then in the next moment, my heart skipped because I noticed he wasn't alone.

Sitting beside him was his mom, Jackie, with the corners of her mouth quirked up ever so slightly.

CHAPTER 41

"Jackie, what are you doing here?" I asked as I patted the corners of my eyes dry.

I was shocked to see her.

The last time I had heard from her was the day before Chicago and I flew out. She was still in Houston, excited for us to have a great time. She had even asked us to bring her back some chocolates and a bottle of wine.

But maybe she was in on the proposal too.

Maybe she was here to witness the moment her son proposed to his girlfriend. Chicago probably needed the extra support.

Perhaps my parents were here too. I looked around to see if they or Cali were hiding in the bushes.

There was some faint chattering in the background, but I believe it was coming from the other guests at the restaurant.

"Oh wow, you look so gorgeous in that dress. It's beautiful!" Jackie said, wearing an unnerving smile.

"Thank you, Jackie. Do you like it, Chicago?" I asked, spinning around slowly.

"You look beautiful," Chicago said in a flat hushed tone that made my entire body tense.

I brushed it off and walked over to the table to join them.

The only remaining chair was directly opposite Chicago and his mom, who were sitting beside each other. It was an awkward place for me to sit, several feet from Chicago.

But I guessed it might be easier for him to come to my side when he was ready to propose. Possibly, after we ate dinner.

Although, it would be better for me if he proposed before dinner, so I could avoid any bloating or getting stains on the dress which would ruin the pictures.

I scanned the yard again, trying to figure out where the photographer might be hiding. Maybe Chicago had a hidden camera planted in the bushes to really lay on that surprise factor.

"Looking for someone?" Jackie asked.

"Oh, no. I was just looking at the scenery. This place is really beautiful. You did good picking it out," I said, looking at Chicago.

Chicago dropped his eyes and looked down at the table before turning his head toward the villa.

Something was up.

He couldn't be that nervous. I mean, I did look absolutely stunning, but he should be used to it by now. If my proposal outfit made him nervous, then God bless his soul because he would be a basket case when he saw the wedding dress I'd picked out.

"Hmm, I figured you were looking for your parents," Jackie said before taking a sip of wine, locking eyes with me.

A wave of elation washed over me, and my smile slipped out like a secret I didn't mind spilling. She knew exactly what I was thinking.

"My parents? Did you bring them here? And Cali too?" I asked, trying to contain my excitement inside but it was seeping out of me.

I would literally jump for joy if he had flown my people out here to witness this special moment.

Chicago squinted, taking a moment to respond before his mom interrupted him.

"I figured you were looking for your parents so they could bail you out of this like they did last time," Jackie said in a sharp tone.

"Cali is like you too? So, y'all had this planned the whole time?" Chicago asked, furrowing his brows.

"What are you talking about?" I asked, completely thrown off.

"Don't play dumb now. We know who you really are, Chyna Cole. You have your father's last name because it holds no weight and no one would recognize it, but you come from the Louissaint family. A tribe of witches who settled in the Midwest almost two centuries ago," Jackie said.

A jolt shot through me as Jackie's words hung in the air.

Her accusation landing like a thunderbolt, shattering everything I had envisioned for this evening. Shock and disbelief washed over me in a wave, leaving me dumbfounded and speechless.

How the fuck did she know my identity? The family name that I never mentioned to a soul.

My mind raced with a flurry of thoughts, panic rising like bile in my throat.

In that moment, I felt exposed, vulnerable, as if the carefully constructed walls I had built to protect myself had come crashing down around me. And as I searched Jackie's eyes for any sign of deception, all I found was a steely resolve that sent a shiver down my spine.

The truth was out, and I feared there was no escaping it.

"No," I said, my voice faint, chuckling slightly to dismiss her statement.

I looked at Chicago, searching his eyes.

"Chicago…what's happening?"

Chicago adjusted his seat and leaned toward me, a look of frustration and anger brewing on his face.

"Did you really use a love spell on me?" His voice trembled. It was a desperate plea for my answer to be no.

I parted my lips to respond and defend myself, but nothing came out. What could I say at this point to win back his trust and his heart?

Chicago leaned back in his seat, a chilling calm demeanor coming over him before he covered his face and let out a sinister laugh.

"Oh, my God, I can't believe this shit, man. All this shit was a lie. You used the fuck out of me. You came into my life with so much ease I never questioned it. What am I saying? I couldn't question it because you used some fucking weird witchy shit to fuck with my head!" Chicago said.

Each word leaving his mouth hit me like a brick.

I sat frozen, not wanting to believe this was actually happening. Here I was, thinking I was going to get proposed to, and instead, I got exposed.

My mind scrambled for a way out. Maybe I could erase their memories like my mom did that one time. I'd seen her do it, but I still didn't know the spell. She refused to teach it to me, and I couldn't remember the words she used no matter how hard I tried.

"You fucking weird ass bitch! You really had me in my feelings falling in love with you. I don't even really know who or what the hell you are. This shit is crazy," Chicago said as he slammed his hand onto the table.

Jackie placed her hand on his back and shot me a look.

"When I first heard of you…when Chicago first mentioned you, I got this weird feeling in the pit of my chest, but he spoke so fondly of you, so I brushed it off. I was still cautious about you, but I wanted to trust that my son had really found love. But it was when I first met you that I recognized the energy that I felt. My sister…" Jackie paused, looking down at the ring she had on her pointer finger.

"My sister has that same energy as you, because she also practices magic like you. Our mom practiced magic too. It didn't run in our bloodline, but because my mom used it so frequently, my sister and I had become familiar with it.

"My sister followed the same path as my mom, which is why I separated myself from her. That magic is the same magic that killed my mom, so I wanted no part of it. And I was free from it. Until I met you and sensed it all over you. It was like my sister's but way stronger. That's because it's in your blood.

"I just knew something wasn't right when I met you and I'm happy I trusted my intuition.

"That night when I didn't go to dinner, I was in contact with my sister. I hadn't talked to her in over twenty years. It took some time to find her and get a hold of her. We did a lot of catching up that night, so in a way you helped us rekindle our relationship. I thank you for that, Chyna," Jackie said as she raised her wine glass to me before taking another sip.

She cleared her throat and continued as I sat silently, still speechless.

"We talked for hours and hours about Chicago and then about you. In all that time away from her, my sister had really sharpened her skills because she was able to get a sense of what you were immediately. So, for the remainder of that trip, I had you pegged, but I played it cool.

"But when I got home and my sister called to check on me, I was so confused that I almost cursed her out. I was yelling, 'Why are you calling me after all these years? How did you even know I went to LA?'"

"And she said to me, 'Sister, you called me the first night you were in LA. You reached out to me.'

"But I didn't know what she was talking about because I didn't remember any of that happening. And why didn't I remember? Because your mom wiped my memory clean of any suspicions I had about you and from that night you exposed yourself. Unfortunately for you, my sister was able to restore my memories for me, and we soon figured out what you had done to Chicago.

"So, every time I came back to LA to visit him, while you were feeding him love spells, I was countering those spells, so that he could easily break free. We removed the spell on him months ago, and he was so distraught when he found out. We decided on a plan to put him back under your spell but hide the part of him that knew what you were doing so you wouldn't be suspicious.

"I bet you really thought he was going to propose to you tonight, huh?"

"What the fuck?" was the only sentence I could murmur as I sat there with tears rolling down my face.

As Jackie's revelations shattered my world, a chill swept through me, freezing me in place as if time itself had come to a standstill.

Embarrassment flooded my cheeks, hot and prickling, as the realization that I had been completely exposed washed over me like a tidal wave. Anger simmered beneath the surface, a seething fire threatening to erupt, but it was overshadowed by a growing sense of dread. I felt trapped.

With Jackie's eyes boring into mine like daggers, I felt a suffocating weight pressing down on me, squeezing the air from my lungs.

The shock of her words left me reeling, my mind racing to find a way to rectify this, even as I knew there was no way out.

I was in a different country, alone and exposed.

I hadn't bothered to tell my parents where I was going, because I was hoping Chicago would if this had turned out how I had imagined. So, there was no one here to save me, and for the first time, I felt utterly powerless.

CHAPTER 42

We sat there in silence for a few minutes. Anger, frustration, pity, and disbelief written on both Chicago and his mother's faces, mirroring the emotions I felt in my soul.

"Not much to say for yourself?" Jackie asked.

I stayed mum, still processing, trying to come up with any explanation that might suffice.

"That's alright. Take your time. Just know that we're protected from any kind of magic spell you try to cast on us from here on out," Jackie said, rising from her chair. "Come on, son." She nodded at Chicago as they gathered their things.

"You can keep the hotel room, I already got my shit out. And you can keep your flight back. But when you get to LA, your shit will be in the lobby. Depending on how long they'll allow it to sit there," Chicago said as he walked out behind his mom.

As soon as they were out of sight, I let out the ugliest cry ever.

My heart was shattered into a thousand jagged pieces, each one stabbing me in my chest and throat, making it hard for me to swallow my own saliva. The pain was raw and unrelenting, tearing through me with a merciless intensity.

Each breath I took felt like a struggle, as if the weight of my torpedoed dreams was crushing my chest.

It took a full hour before I was finally able to stand.

I tried to hide my puffy eyes from the maître d' as he ordered a ride to take me back to the hotel. Fortunately, I had brought my shades with me, because I thought it would look cool to wear them for our engagement photos.

When I arrived back at the hotel, my voice was too hoarse to even say *"merci"* to the driver as I had done earlier when he dropped me off at the villa.

Once inside my room, I looked all over for Chicago's belongings.

Gone.

Every trace of Chicago that had been in that room was gone. The only thing of his that remained was the hotel bathrobe.

The hotel had provided us with a matching set, and Chicago had worn his the night before. And there it was, lying on the bed.

I'm not ashamed to say that I wrapped his robe around me, burying my nose in it so I could savor his scent before crying myself to sleep.

In the morning, I was awakened by the housekeeper who I rudely shooed away. I wasn't ready to get up. I wasn't ready to face the day or even to eat, never mind explore Paris. I wanted to rot away in this bed for eternity, and that's exactly what I did, if you could call twelve hours an eternity.

By evening, I couldn't take my stomach's intense growling anymore. Since I hadn't eaten the night before, my stomach felt completely empty. So, I ordered some room service and indulged in the finest dining the boutique hotel could provide. It was actually scrumptious.

My phone had died, but I saw no reason to charge it.

The thought of Chicago reaching out crossed my mind, but it was quickly dismissed when I remembered the glare he had shot me before walking out. That look sent shivers down my spine.

After I finished eating, I spent the rest of the night crying my eyes out again until they ran dry.

By morning, I knew I couldn't leave yet. I couldn't leave Paris on a note like this and be haunted by the memories forever. So I decided to extend my trip by a week, just enough time to build myself back up again.

I finally charged my phone and tried to muster up the energy to get my shit together.

A short conversation with some of my stylists at the salon helped to cheer me up. They were unaware of the situation with Chicago, so they sent us their best wishes for a safe and fun trip. I went along with it, feeling slightly ashamed that the trip had already gone to ruin.

Next up was a conversation with Cali. She had called me over a hundred times, but I couldn't find the courage to answer any of her calls. It took every ounce of me to finally call her back. And as soon as I heard her voice, tears poured from my eyes again.

"Chyna, what happened? I've been calling you for days! Chicago came back to town without you, and I've been worried ever since. Girl, I thought y'all were going to come back engaged. Instead, he came over questioning me, asking me if I was a witch too. He was tripping out, and Frankie had to take him outside to calm his ass down. Did he really find out? How?" Cali asked, her voice raised in disbelief.

I explained how Chicago and Jackie had ambushed me. As we spoke, her shock and surprise led to multiple outbursts.

"What the…? So how the hell is he mad at you when his own damn aunt is a witch? Yo, this shit is crazy! Girl, I'm so sorry this happened. Do you think there's a way to fix it?"

"I don't know, Cali, it's bad. The look on Chicago's face that night…his mom even said they're protected from my spells. It's over. What if they expose me and ruin my salon…my family?"

My sobs broke through as I cried to Cali. "I'm sorry I got you involved in this. I know how much you love Frankie, and I don't want this to affect y'all."

"Girl, no. Frankie will be fine. He's honestly confused and thinks you cheated on Chicago or something, and that's why he's calling you a witch bitch as an insult."

"He called me a witch bitch?"

My fears had come to a head.

I had to let my life move forward in the short amount of time I had left in Paris. I couldn't let a broken heart ruin the rest of my trip or my life, I reminded myself, thinking back to what Cali said before we hung up.

So, during the last few days of my stay in Paris, I sought comfort in the vibrant tapestry of the city's culture. I was eager to lose myself in its enchanting allure.

With every step I took through those winding streets, I felt lighter as if I could finally breathe. Nobody knew me out here, and that was the best part. I could be whoever I wanted. And with how beautiful everything was around me, it was like my problems didn't stand a chance.

I used my magic freely, casting spells on the locals so they would trust me and tell me all the best spots to go to for food, fun, and unique shopping experiences. From savoring decadent pastries at quaint cafes to exploring world-renowned museums and galleries, every moment was a testament to the richness of Parisian life.

It felt amazing to live life as if I was in a movie, and I did just that up until the last day.

On my last night in Paris, my heart was heavy with the burden of impending farewells. I didn't want to even think about how I was going to pick up the pieces of my life once I returned to LA. Assuming there were any pieces left to pick up.

My mind began imagining all the different ways Chicago could destroy me. Given that he was often on live TV and had access to journalists, he could run to the media and blab. He could try to destroy my business.

I was sure all of my belongings at the condo were long gone by now. All of my designer clothes and bags. I sulked at the thought of starting over.

Before I went to bed that night, I booked a hotel room for a month. Just until I figured out my next living situation. I knew I needed to get back to the salon and do more heads, so I could build up my savings and get a nice place to stay permanently. A home that no man could remove me from.

I had just set my phone down and was trying to fall asleep when it pinged. I was reluctant to check and see who it was, but curiosity got the better of me and I caved.

The bright light from my phone blinded me, making me squint as I tried to read the text on the screen. As I began reading, I gasped and shot upright.

The text was from Chicago.

"Hey, I know shit ended really badly but I need to talk to you. It's weird not having you around. I want to trust that you did what you did because you love me. Part of me still loves you, even with the spell reversed. Your stuff is still here. Come see me."

In an instant, the few small pieces of my heart that I had glued back together shattered once more. I didn't know how to feel. I was conflicted.

Was this real? Did he still love me, even without the spell? I had always hoped that would happen. I'd planned to remove the spell myself one day, believing that he would still love me without it.

I couldn't sleep that night, wondering what I should do. Should I go see him? Could it be a trap or a setup?

Part of me wanted to start over with a brand-new life, but another part of me wanted to be with Chicago again. Him discovering that I was a witch could turn out to be for the best. It had worked out for my mom and dad. Maybe it could work out for me and Chicago.

I sent my response that morning, confirming we would meet back at the home I had grown to love.

CHAPTER 43

Even though the flight was super long, it wasn't long enough for me to sort out my feelings. Throughout the entire flight I contemplated my next move.

Did I want to go back to Chicago or start over fresh?

I went through pages and pages of a pricey Paris-designed notebook I had bought at the airport, listing the pros and cons of being with or without Chicago. The bottom line was that he knew I was a witch and might be willing to accept it. That was a better pro than having to start over and hope that my next man would accept me.

I sat uncomfortably in my first-class seat still remembering the last look he had given me and how horrible it had made me feel.

Could he really want me back after making a face like that? Or could this be a setup to sell me out to the government? Or have me locked away or burned in the middle of town for the world to see?

"But that could backfire on him. I mean, not only is his aunt a witch, but if the public knew his ex was a witch, it would affect his career because people would think he made you use magic to give him an unfair advantage during his games," Cali said, the voice of reason.

We were talking on the phone as I waited for my plane to board.

"That's true, but still…what the hell's going on? Why would he send that text?"

"I'm really not sure, girl. The last time I saw him was the day he accused me of being a witch too. But Frankie has seen him recently and said he seems to be in a better headspace. He won't give me the details, though."

"I'm really sorry you got caught up in this. The last thing I want is for my shit to affect what you and Frankie have going on. Y'all are so cute together."

"Don't worry about it. We'll be fine. But what are you going to do? I think that if you really want to see him again, meet his ass in a public place for safety?"

"So, everyone can record us on their phones while the pitchforkers haul me away?"

"Girl, people don't pitchfork anymore! I'm telling you, if that man is as smart as I think he is, he will not expose you like that. If anything, I'm more worried about him trying to lock your ass up and force you to be his magic genie. Frankie was just telling me the other day that if I really am a witch, then I need to use my powers to make his bank account bigger. Girl, I wouldn't put it past Chicago to try to use you like that, 'cause he didn't win his championship ring this year."

That conversation added even more stress to my plate.

Would Chicago use me like that? But why would he when he could go to his aunt? I didn't think they had much of a relationship, though, so maybe he would come to me for magic. Maybe I could even convince him that he needed me. I could easily learn some new spells to help him win games. Then we could truly be a power couple.

By the time my flight landed, and I disembarked, I still hadn't made up my mind. So, I decided to order an Uber.

My plan was to check into my hotel and go over my decision one more time. But somehow, before I could type in the hotel's address, I found myself typing in Chicago's.

Not long after, instead of unloading my luggage at the hotel, I was unloading my bags in front of Chicago's high rise. Even though I knew I needed more time to fully think things through, I desperately wanted to see him again. I was beyond anxious to know if he had meant what he said in his messages.

I had let Chicago know that I was on my way, but he never responded so I wasn't sure what to expect and hesitated before entering the elevator. I shook off my worries, and within a couple of minutes, I was inside the condo where—to my surprise—I could hear several voices in conversation.

I rounded the corner into the living room and came face-to-face with Chicago, his parents, and a man I had never seen before.

This new guy had a shiny bald head, a beard full of gray hair, and a serious look on his face.

"Chyna. Come in," Chicago said, his tone normal as if nothing had happened.

I didn't budge. I remained where I was, within running distance of the door in case I needed to make a quick break. I wasn't sure what was going on, but I didn't have a good feeling about it.

"Chyna, please. We just want to talk. We have no ill intentions," Jackie said, raising her hands in surrender.

I crossed my arms, losing patience. There was no sitting down and talking after what had happened. We were past that.

"Hi, Ms. Chyna Cole. I'm Desmond Harris, and I'm Chicago's personal lawyer," the stern-faced man said as he rose from his seat and walked over to me, reaching out to shake my hand.

I didn't move a muscle. The only response he got from me was a raised eyebrow.

He clasped his hands together then nodded. "Okay, I'll be blunt. I know who you are and what you did to Chicago…the spells you used. Luckily for you, the Moons aren't going to press any charges."

"Press charges? For what exactly? What can they prove?" I asked in defense.

"Young lady, we can absolutely find proof of what you did. We could expose you and…" Jackie said before being cut off by Chicago, who also rose to his feet.

"Mama, stop. Chyna, we aren't trying to press charges or expose you or anything. What we're trying to do now is work out some sort of deal with you," Chicago said, his voice weary.

"Like I said, there's nothing to press charges about. Also, you wouldn't be able to expose me without exposing your own aunt."

"Look, we won't go back and forth about this. We have a proposition for you. Please take a seat and hear us out," Desmond said.

"No, I'll stand right here. Talk."

"Okay. Like I was saying, the Moons want to avoid going against you. Instead, they want to work with you. You scratch their back, they scratch yours."

"I'm listening," I said as I unclenched my jaw.

"First, before we get into this, I have a question. What was your goal? Why did you use the love spell on my son?" Jackie asked.

The atmosphere in the room shifted palpably. Silence hung in the air, thick and charged with anticipation as all eyes turned to me.

I stood there frozen like a statue for a moment, trying to steady my breathing.

"I really love Chicago. A lot. But it didn't happen overnight. At first, yeah, I wanted to use him to build a better life for myself…but then I got to know him. Chicago has been so perfect for me. He's so kind and loving, I grew addicted to him.

"I was so comfortable being with him that I didn't want things to end. But I wanted to tell him exactly who I was so many times. I couldn't, though, because I was scared of his reaction. I didn't want him to look at me…the way he did when he found out," I said, pouring my heart out along with a few tears.

I turned toward Chicago, hoping my honesty would reach his heart.

Chicago shook his head. I couldn't tell if he was angry or frustrated or maybe both.

"You could have told me at any moment. I did shit for you that I've never done for any other woman before. My aunt said she undid the spells on me, but a part of me still feels love toward you. I don't know what that is. I don't know if it's your magic still running through me or if these are real feelings I have toward you. This shit is so messed up, I don't even know how I really feel," Chicago said.

"Not only did you mess up my son's head with this love spell shit, but it's also messing up his game. His last few practice sessions have sucked. I don't know if this is a reaction to all these spells or what, but he needs to focus. So, we need to get this shit settled now, so by the time he gets back on the court for the season, he's back in beast mode," Stephen said, his voice laced with disgust.

To me, it seemed like he was more upset about his son potentially messing up his basketball contract than he was about the love spell that had been cast on him.

"What can I do to make this right?" I asked, as I tried to dab at the tears that were rolling under my chin.

"This is why we have you here, Chyna. Are you ready to hear us out now?" Desmond asked, extending his arm to guide me toward the couch.

This time, I obliged, and as I sat down, I noticed a slim stack of papers that looked like a contract resting on the coffee table.

"Alright, so like I said, I'm Chicago's personal lawyer. I'm a friend of his aunt, so I'm not new to any of this magic shit. I don't care what you did. It's done. Cat's out of the bag and now we're here. What I care about is Chicago's future.

"You two have already made the news as a couple. People see you as a new, young power couple...Chicago, the up-and-coming basketball champion and future MVP, and his girlfriend who's a successful businesswoman. It sells. That's why you two need to stay together and keep up this image, because this relationship could take both of you very far.

"The image of Chicago as a stand-up guy in a committed long-term relationship, especially if it ends in a marriage with kids, would make him beloved by millions of fans, increasing his sponsorships and longevity in the industry. People would love him on and off the court.

"And of course, that would boost you as well. Think of all the Magical Touch Hair Salons that could pop up all over the country.

Think of all the clients you could get. And all the money you could earn to achieve the life of your dreams. That's what you want, right? I mean that's initially why you went after Chicago in the first place, before you fell in love with him. It's a win-win situation," Desmond said as if he was pitching the sale of a new car.

I sat there trying to wrap my head around what he was saying. It did sound like a win-win situation. Chicago needed me just as much as I needed him.

And this was what I truly wanted, right? To be with Chicago. For him to know I was a witch and accept me. To build my salon empire.

It was exactly what I had always wanted.

Desmond pushed the pile of papers toward me.

"We created a contract for you and attached a binding spell to it that his aunt will cast on you both. This contract requires the two of you to be in a relationship for six years. This will give the media just the right amount of time to cover you both, which will solidify you as a couple. During this time, you will be THE power couple that everyone wants to win, wants to be, and wants to hate on because they aren't you. So, you two cannot separate until the six years are up.

"By the end of those six years, if the love is real this time, you can either continue with the relationship, get married and have kids, or you can separate amicably. However, in this contract, you're not allowed to have any public scandal that could ruin your image. In exchange, like I mentioned before, you would live the life of your dreams.

"By the time the contract is over, you'll walk away with your dream life. You'll have lots of salons and enough money to take care yourself and your future children with or without Chicago. How does that sound?" he asked with a sly grin.

"It sounds amazing. Is this what you want too?" I asked, turning to Chicago with hope in my eyes.

"It's the best decision for my career," he said, his demeanor stoic.

I picked up the papers and skimmed through them.

"So, what happens if we don't last until then?" I asked.

"That's what the binding spell is for. You won't have a choice. Physically and mentally, you two won't be able to leave each other's side for a long period of time. The spell will allow for short absences when Chicago has away games, but if you're apart for too long, you'll experience a very uncomfortable tugging in your body.

"You also won't be able to speak publicly about anything that would potentially ruin your public image. Nor will you be able to show this contract to anyone else. All they will see is a blank document. No need for the law to get involved. The binding spell is all we will need.

"I know it's a lot to take in. So, we will give you some time to read over the contract in detail. We just need it back in three days or it will be void."

"Void?"

"Yes. We only included you in this because you already have an image with Chicago. If you don't want to participate, that's fine. We'll find someone else immediately to start building up his image. At least with someone new, we wouldn't have to add in any binding spells or magical clauses. And that new woman would, of course, reap the benefits. Think it over, Chyna."

CHAPTER 44

"I knew it! I knew his ass was going to try to use you!" Cali said, panting and sweating as she navigated the last stretch of our hike.

I nodded as I tried to focus on my breathing.

For some crazy reason, we had decided to take a more difficult trail today that involved us basically climbing a mountain to see a tree. Our conversation was necessary, but it was going to have to wait until we found a resting spot.

It was a challenging hike, but we made it to the end. The views were amazing, but we questioned whether it had been worth Cali almost passing out.

A sense of accomplishment washed over me as I indulged in the beautiful panoramic views of the city that stretched out before me. I looked down upon a vast expanse of rolling hills and verdant valleys bathed in the warm glow of the rising sun.

We sat and admired the view from the summit for a short while before we were joined by other hikers, who were also seeking a rest from their laborious trek.

In that moment, as I sat on the ground underneath this tree that had survived a wildfire years ago yet remained tall and strong, a profound sense of relief settled over me. I deserved this moment. I deserved to feel the breeze cool my hot face after such a journey.

With each breath of fresh mountain air, my worries melted away, and they were replaced by a calm, lasting sense of peace. The quietude of the wilderness enveloped me, wrapping me in its gentle embrace and offering solace from the disarray of life. Solace from the choice I had to make. Solace from Chicago and that freaking contract.

I threw myself backwards onto the ground and soaked up the warmth of the early morning sunshine.

"Chyna, don't do that. Don't lie on the ground like that. An animal probably peed right where your head is lying," Cali said in a nagging tone, bringing me back to reality.

"Leave me alone. I need this moment," I said, snapping back.

But as soon as I felt something crawl across my finger, I quickly jumped up, dusting off my hair and making a mental note to wash it later.

We found a secluded spot away from the growing crowd of hikers where we could still enjoy the view.

"So...are you going to sign it?" Cali asked.

"I don't know. I thought a hike would help clear my mind, but it's still foggy. It sounds like a really good deal. Just imagine me opening more salons, being the business woman I've always wanted to be. And on top of that, getting to keep my relationship with Chicago, with him knowing who I am and accepting me. That's something I've been dreaming about since the day I met him. I just...I just don't feel completely sold for some reason. It still feels kinda scary, you know?"

"What's scary about it?"

"I don't know. Maybe the fact that my dreams are really about to come true. It's bittersweet and scary. What happens next? What will my future dreams be?"

Cali tilted her head back and took a deep breath.

"You'll always find new dreams. That's the exciting thing about life. We'll always have something new to look forward to. New desires and new dreams. But it sounds like you've made up your mind already.

"I'm not sold on the whole contract and binding spell. That part sounds scary. I know you don't want to, but maybe you should ask your mom before you sign it. She probably knows about that spell binding stuff."

I shook my head vigorously.

"Absolutely not! I haven't even told her Chicago and I broke up. I don't need her judging me and telling me she told me so. Not right now."

"Okay, okay I get it. I do think you need to really sit with this, though. I know it sounds good'n all, but to me it sounds too good to be true. And you know what they say about that."

"I know all that and I agree with you, but I only have three days to think this over."

"Doesn't it worry you that they're trying to make you rush into this? Three days isn't enough time to decide if you're ready to be bound to someone for six damn years. That shit sounds crazy!" Cali said throwing her hands up.

"So, you think I shouldn't do it?" I turned to study Cali's face.

Her mouth dropped at the question, and she took a few moments to answer, furrowing and unfurrowing her brow as she gave it some serious thought.

"I can't tell you what to do. And even if I did, I know your ass wouldn't listen anyways. I'm pretty sure you're going to go through with it. But since you have experience as a paralegal, do your due diligence and read over every single word in that contract. Mark that shit up if you have to. Make sure it works in your favor. That's all I'll say about it."

I knew Cali had her doubts.

I had my doubts too.

But she hadn't told me not to do it. Maybe because she assumed it was a good deal just like I did. Or maybe she was right, and I'd already made my mind up.

Whatever the case, her advice was solid and helped to ease my conscience.

Later that day, I took Cali's advice and read every single word of the contract. It was exactly as Desmond had indicated. I couldn't find anything that would leave me at a disadvantage.

The contract stated that all financial gains I accumulated during the relationship, including partnered sponsorships and other ventures I planned to undertake, would not be forfeited once the relationship was over. Nor would Chicago have the right to sue me for any of my earnings.

There was also a nondisclosure clause that would prevent either of us from speaking publicly about our relationship once it had ended. In other words, no tell-all books or interviews. And once the relationship was over, we would never need to speak to each other again. I was fine with all of that.

The only thing I didn't see in the contract were terms guaranteeing me additional salons. I needed that in the contract, so I sent an email to Desmond requesting he add that in.

The next day, I received a revised contract by email which stated that Chicago would personally invest in three new salons in any location I wanted.

In his email, Desmond wrote that by the time those salons were up and running, the publicity and fandom generated by our relationship would help them become so profitable that I would have enough money to open more salons on my own.

I took the rest of the day to truly think it over.

Cali was right. I knew which way I was leaning, but I wanted to be absolutely sure. So, I meditated, created pages and pages of pros and cons, and even prayed. I slept confidently that night knowing exactly what I was going to do the next day.

Even though I hadn't spoken to Chicago in the past two days, I knew I was making the right choice. He and I just needed time to process everything.

CHAPTER 45

On the morning of the third day after receiving the contract, I started my day as usual and headed to the salon to take care of my regular clients. Even with my heart spiking throughout the day in anticipation of what was to transpire later, I played it cool as if everything was normal.

Some of the stylists invited me out for drinks later, and as much as I wanted to go to calm my nerves, I declined. I needed a clear head going into this.

I made the excuse that tonight was a date night with Chicago, which elicited a bunch of "aws." I was relieved that they didn't sense anything was wrong with my relationship. Especially given the way Chicago had acted in front of Cali when he returned from Paris.

I was very happy he hadn't done the same in front of my stylists.

I felt sick to my stomach when I got the text with the location for our contract signing. It was the same house Chicago's parents had rented for the family dinner.

The same place where I'd lost control and used magic, forcing my mom to step in and erase their memories. It felt like a cruel joke, but apparently, they always rented that property when they were in town.

When I arrived, everyone was waiting for me in the dining room: Chicago, Jackie, Stephen, Desmond, and a new woman I had never met before.

She was somewhat heavy set and had a sweet face that was familiar. Seeing her next to Jackie, I realized they looked a lot alike. She was probably Jackie's sister, the one who had undone the spell on Chicago.

I began to feel ashamed and hurried to sit at the empty seat next to Desmond.

"Hi Chyna, I'm Tammy, Jackie's sister and Chicago's aunt. I know a lot about you already, so don't feel ashamed. What's done is done. And now we are here, falling deeper into the rabbit hole," she said with a laugh.

"Hi Tammy, it's nice to meet you too," I said, trying to shake off the eerie feeling that had come over me.

I was ready to be done with this. It was all beginning to feel somewhat sinister. I was ready to fast forward to six years from now when I would reap the harvest of the seeds I was sowing right now.

"Alright, let's get started," Desmond said, pulling the contract out of his briefcase. "Chyna, this is the official contract we agreed on. Feel free to read it over again."

I skimmed through the contract, comparing it to the copy Desmond had sent me by email.

Everything matched up. It was legit, and I nodded in approval.

"Chicago, do you need to look through it again as well, or are you ready to sign?" Desmond asked as he passed him the contract and a pen.

Chicago shook his head and signed the contract right away.

His aunt pulled out a small black dagger which she handed to him.

"In order to bind this, we need your blood. Just use the tip of the dagger to make a prick on your thumb to draw your blood, then stamp your thumb on the contract," Tammy said.

Chicago did as he was told and then passed the contract and dagger to Desmond, who passed it to me.

I sat there with the contract in front of me, thinking over my decision for the last time. I took a few deep breaths before glancing over at Chicago.

He hadn't said a word to me since I'd gotten here.

Was he still upset with me? If so, then why did he sign the contract?

Everything felt as if it was moving at a fast pace, along with my heart rate. I took several deep breaths as I tried to calm my heart.

"You don't have to do this if you don't want to," Chicago finally said, his eyes meeting mine.

"Is this what you want, Chicago? I still love you and want to be with you again, but is that something that you really want? Do you want to be with me again?"

Chicago took a moment to answer, placing his head in his hands and rubbing his eyes.

"I told you, I still don't understand these feelings I have for you. Yes, I do miss you, but I'm still messed up by what you did." He shook his head then peered at his bloody thumb before putting it to his lips to stop the bleeding. "I signed, so...I think that should tell you something."

I nodded then picked up the pen and planted my signature on the contract. Then I sliced my thumb and stamped my blood onto the contract to seal the deal.

"Okay," Tammy said as she stood up and began reciting a spell.

Almost instantly, a wave of lightheadedness hit me.

I watched as the blood signatures on the contract dried instantly, sealing the spell.

"And now it's done," Tammy said with a smile on her face.

My stomach dropped.

That's when I realized why her face looked so familiar. It wasn't just because she resembled Jackie. It was because I'd seen her before. Many times. She was the same woman with the sweet face and blue dress who had haunted my dreams.

"Oh, do you recognize me now?" she asked with a sly edge to her voice.

I grabbed my things and ran out the door to my car, stopping only to vomit in the bushes that lined the driveway. I couldn't tell if it was an after effect of the spell or the shock of realizing who Tammy was.

She had known who I was this whole time and had been monitoring me in my dreams.

Even more shocking, she had known what I was up to from the very first day that I used the spell on Chicago.

My mind was racing with a thousand questions as I got into my car and sped away. I drove straight to my hotel. I didn't want to be around those people anymore.

Once I made it there, I felt exactly what Desmond described as the tugging. My body felt as if it was being gently pulled on from the inside out, like the pull of gravity when you're hanging upside down.

So, this was what I'd have to deal with for the next six years anytime I wasn't near him?

My buyer's remorse kicked in immediately, and I wondered if I had made the right decision.

Those thoughts were abruptly interrupted when my phone began to ring. I checked the screen—it was my mom.

Now was not the time. I tossed my phone onto the passenger seat and buried my face in my hands, waiting for it to stop ringing.

A few seconds later, it finally did. I breathed a sigh of relief.

"Chyna! What did you do?" my mom's voice erupted from the phone.

I picked up the phone and saw her face on the screen.

Once again, she had used a spell to force my phone to answer.

She couldn't even allow me a few moments to fully process what had happened before demanding answers.

How did she even know?

"Chyna, you did a binding spell didn't you? I felt it! Who did you bind yourself to? What have you done?" she asked, her eyes welling up with tears.

I let out a long breath, feeling overwhelmed.

I didn't feel like arguing, but I needed to talk to someone. So, I told her everything.

She sat silently on the other end of the phone, staring off into space. I could tell she was upset. But more than that, she looked tired and defeated.

"I can't believe you would do that. You want that life so badly. I don't know why, but it's..." She shook her head then looked at me. "It's okay. It's done, and I'm sorry baby girl, but I can't get you out of this one."

CHAPTER 46

S hortly after the binding spell was placed on me and Chicago, I moved back into his condo, but I'd been staying in the guest room. We'd been slowly trying to get back to how things were before everything went down, but I could tell he was still fighting it.

At first, when we got back together, I would cook breakfast every morning, making all of his favorites. But he'd skip it, saying he wasn't hungry or that he'd grab something on the way to wherever he was headed.

After a while, he started eating the meals I cooked again. He even began complimenting me like he used to. But anytime I tried to start a real conversation, all I got were dry, uninterested responses.

He was incredibly hard to deal with. I felt like I was living with a stranger. It stung even more because I knew Chicago, and he knew me, but now he was so distant.

By the second month, I'd had enough. I found myself begging my mom to help me figure out how to break the contract and undo the binding spell.

I went back home to visit my parents, and the second I stepped off the plane, I felt that tugging feeling again. But this time it was stronger than that first day.

It almost made me nauseous at times, especially if I was standing really still.

I remembered that the contract stated that Chicago would feel the tugging too unless he was at a game. When he was on the court, he wouldn't feel it. I should have added a similar clause to my contract too.

When I was working at the salon, I didn't notice it unless I was taking a break while waiting for the next client.

But now, in a different state and miles away, I could really feel it.

My mom was very excited to see me and gave me a much-needed hug.

"I've missed you. You look a little worn down. What's going on?" she asked.

"It's this contract, Ma. I don't think I can go through with this anymore."

I explained that I was having my buyer's remorse and hated that I had rushed into it.

"I really thought Chicago and I would be on the same page again. I thought our relationship would morph into something like what you and dad have, and he would forgive me and accept me for who I am," I said as I broke into tears.

"I know, but you can't force things to be how they were. I've told you this many times, Chyna. Actions have consequences, especially when dealing with magic. And because we have these magical abilities, karma hits us back even harder.

"Sweetheart, I never wanted you to have to go down that path. That's why I always tried to steer you away from magic, because I had seen this scenario play out with others before, and I didn't want that for you. I know I may have come off as a bitch and a nag, but I only wanted to protect you.

"In this day and age, magic can really go to some people's heads. It's the power that makes people do some strange things", she said in an effort to console me.

I pulled out the contract so she could read it and see if there was any way to undo it. It would've been great to have a magical lawyer on our side, like the Moons.

Maybe I should've taken my paralegal job more seriously.

"Chyna, these are blank pages," my mom said as she flipped through the contract in confusion.

"No, it's all right there," I said, taking the document from her and reading some of the terms out loud.

My mom sat and thought for a second before reciting a spell I had never heard before. Once she finished speaking, she was able to see what was written on the contract.

"It's a spell to hide information, almost like invisible ink. Whoever did it must not be that skilled, because it didn't take much to remove it," she said as she began reading through the pages.

For a moment, I had a glimmer of hope that since Tammy was not a born witch, then maybe her spellwork wasn't that strong after all. If my mom and aunts teamed up like they had in the past, then maybe they could break this contract.

Unfortunately, that glimmer dulled to nothing very quickly.

"I'm sorry to get your hopes up baby, but I don't think there's anything I can do. The magic she used to hide the contents of this contract are weak, but the actual binding spell is pretty strong because it's tied to blood magic. It would take a lot of time and skill to undo that."

"No, there has to be something. You and Aunt Crystal and Aunt Celestine, the three of you are way stronger together. There has to be something that can be done," I said, pleading with her again.

My mom thought for a while. "I don't know. The three of us could maybe do something, but Celestine is away right now, and who knows when she'll be back.

In the meantime, though, I could work with Crystal to find a spell or something that could help. But you know you'll have to pay that woman with something really nice."

"At this point, she can have my car," I said, only half joking.

I stayed with my parents for a couple more days before returning to LA as quickly as I could to avoid any more of the tugging I was experiencing.

As soon as I stepped into the condo, I was greeted by Desmond.

"Welcome home, Chyna. How was your trip?" he asked.

"Where's Chicago?" I asked, refusing to take one step farther.

"He's out. He said I could wait for you here until you got back. Tammy was flagged immediately once the invisibility spell on the contract was broken. I just wanted to remind you that there is nothing that can be done to break this contract. It's unbreakable until the time is up. But hey, feel free to waste your time and your mother's," he said, slipping on his suit jacket before walking out the door.

CHAPTER 47

After a year of being bound to the contract with Chicago, things were finally starting to pay off. Chicago started getting invited to more lavish and exclusive parties with other celebrities and the upper echelons of society. Of course, as his plus one, I was extremely happy to go.

Before attending any of these events, Chicago would take me shopping anywhere I wanted to find the perfect dress to impress. I loved these little shopping dates. They felt like old times.

Each time we went to the shops, we got closer to each other, falling back into our old rhythm.

It became more and more common for the media to spot us out together looking like the perfect couple, whether it was at a celebrity birthday party, a sporting event, a charity event, or even when we were out on our regular date nights that Desmond encouraged.

Chicago was always reluctant at first, but once we arrived at the event, he would be back to his old cheerful self.

We were even invited to be interviewed for a popular sports magazine. We weren't going to make the cover, but it was a first step.

The magazine sent a writer and photographer over to our condo to snap some photos of us together and interview us about Chicago's career and our relationship.

"Everyone is looking at you two. You've been labeled the new 'couple goals.' How does that feel?" the writer asked.

Even though we had been prepped on how to respond, I barely spoke because I was too nervous. So, Chicago took the lead and handled it smoothly.

"It feels good to know that people are looking at us as goals for their relationship. It means we're doing something right. I'm very fortunate to have Chyna by my side. She's an amazing woman who has truly supported me in every aspect of my life," Chicago said as he held my hand.

"Yes, I agree and the reason why we have such a beautiful relationship is because we communicate. We have trust and mutual respect for each other. That's very important for a thriving relationship such as ours," I said, chiming in.

Chicago turned and squinted at me, all while maintaining a smile on his face. I could tell that he was trying to say I was full of shit.

When the article came out, the photos from the interview went viral and were reposted on many different blogs, cementing us further as 'couple goals.' Which was a job well done in Desmond's eyes.

He was trying to maneuver himself into being our manager. Still, I wasn't sure why he was allowed to start having so much say.

"I'm just making sure the contract is being fulfilled. You can't just say you're a couple. The media has to believe it. And when the media believes it, that's when the money will start rolling in. And when Chicago gets his money, you'll get yours, Chyna," Desmond would say.

I hated to admit it, but he was right. The more we were covered by the media, the more the opportunities came knocking at our door. That included red-carpet events, movie premiers, big sponsorships for Chicago, and even brand deals for me.

The first brand deal I had was with a popular fashion brand that worked with a plethora of celebrities. They sent me a huge haul of clothes to promote on my Pic-Talk account, which had grown in popularity and now had triple the followers.

And because I had increased access to celebrities, I was able to magically "convince" some of them to let me style their hair, which brought more buzz and hype to my salon.

In no time, Magical Touch Hair Salon was booked out months in advance. My stylists and I watched our finances grow tremendously.

We were growing a little too fast, though, as Chelsea constantly had to turn away walk-ins. We simply had more clients than we could handle. I had also received a fair number of inquiries from talented hairstylists who were eager to have a station in the salon, but we didn't have any available.

That's when I decided to open a new location.

Chicago had the funds readily available, so we immediately started the process, and I worked with my previous realtor to find a new location.

We found the perfect building in West Hollywood: an old hair salon, which made it easier to renovate because all we had to do was install new equipment and update the decor. The second salon was up and running faster than the first.

The soft opening started off as one of the best days ever.

We had a DJ on site plus catered food and a professional photographer.

Unlike the last time, this soft opening included lots of bloggers, big social media stars, and some celebrity pop-ups.

After a few hours, the event turned into a full-blown party. Everyone was still on their best behavior, but you could tell folks were having a great time.

The event was a success and took my business page from two hundred thousand followers to almost five hundred thousand in just one day.

But, unlike my last soft opening, Chicago and I didn't go out afterwards. Things were still rocky between us, so he left early. I stayed until the end and helped clean up, which gave me a chance to get to know my new staff a little better.

I didn't get back to the house until after midnight, which hadn't been the plan. I had wanted to get home earlier, hoping Chicago and I could celebrate in private.

It had been a while since we'd been intimate. The last time was right after our first magazine interview. We had been so horny and caught up in the moment that we didn't even make it to the bed. We had sex right there on the couch, the same one we'd sat on during the interview. It was what we needed. It was long overdue, just like it was now.

I crept into the condo just in case Chicago was asleep. I was going to wake him up anyways, but I wanted to freshen up and change into the something sexy first.

As I tiptoed down the hallway toward the bedroom, I heard noises and saw a dim light glowing from beneath the door. I figured he must still be up watching TV.

Had he waited up for me? How sweet.

Once I got close to the door, though, I realized that those noises weren't coming from the TV, and my heart dropped to the pit of my stomach.

Chicago's familiar moans and groans filled my ears until I detected a moan that wasn't his. I swung open the door to witness my worst fear: a naked woman bouncing on top of Chicago. They were having sex in our bed!

The worst part was, they didn't even notice I was standing there in the room with them.

"What the fuck?" I snapped.

They both turned their heads toward me, but didn't even stop gyrating.

The woman, who looked Hispanic, cocked her head in confusion.

Chicago's face, which moments ago had displayed sublime pleasure, turned into an ugly glare.

"Who is she?" the girl asked, turning back to Chicago.

"Shit, my bad, Chyna. I thought you were going to be back later," Chicago said, his hands still gripping the woman's waist as she slowly swirled her pelvis against Chicago's manhood.

I felt completely disrespected and disgusted. Rage boiled in my blood. I was hurt. The heart that had fallen into my stomach was now shattering into a million pieces.

"Your bad? What the fuck do you mean, your bad? Who the fuck is she?" I was yelling now, my voice cracking with each question.

"Is this your ex? I thought y'all broke up?" she asked, finally bring her hips to a rest.

"How the fuck can we break up when we were just at my salon launch today? Chicago, you're cheating on me? You're really cheating on me?"

"Don't act surprised. We ain't been on good terms in a minute," Chicago said, completely unfazed.

"We have a fucking contract!"

I could feel my hands shaking and my breathing becoming erratic.

"Just go to your room. We'll talk about this later," he said, shooing me away.

Now I was beyond livid and immediately whispered a spell.

"Look, I don't know what y'all got..." the woman began to say before being plucked off of Chicago and slammed into the wall. She twitched twice before passing out.

"Yo, what the fuck!" Chicago said, jumping up from the bed and running over to the girl. "Lina, are you alright?"

I tried to strike at Chicago as well, creating a dark purple ball of energy in the palm of my hands as I recited a spell aloud. I threw the ball at Chicago, but it dispersed before it could hit him.

"You're trying to attack me? My aunt already told you that you can't use any more spells on me! Now get the fuck out!" Chicago said, his eyes reflecting the fury I felt.

"Fuck you, Chicago!" I said as I stormed out of the room, slamming doors, and swiping everything resting on a surface onto the floor as I fled the condo.

CHAPTER 48

I watched as my mom and both my aunts gathered around me to perform the ritual required to break the binding spell the contract had placed on me.

My mom was preparing a potion for me to drink while my Aunt Crystal drew a symbol on the ground. She then came over to me and drew smaller symbols all over my body with white clay.

My Aunt Celestine rolled her eyes as she sprinkled herbs on the ground. She didn't want to participate in this ritual at all.

The night before the ritual, at our family dinner, she made her feelings very clear.

"Chyna is a grown woman now and made this decision all on her own. She should clean up her own mess," Aunt Celestine protested.

We had sat at my parents' dining room table, enjoying a delicious spread prepared by my dad that featured all of my favorite dishes.

After the cheating scandal with Chicago, I hadn't wanted to be around him any longer. So, I had caught the first flight back to my hometown.

Chicago was an asshole, and I cursed him the entire plane ride, lobbing spells at him that I knew wouldn't touch him, but which eased my aching heart.

I also cursed each tug I had to endure because I was away from him. I hated that I had agreed to this stupid contract.

"I should just go up there and beat his ass for what he did," my dad said. He was usually the mediator, but now he looked like he needed one himself.

"Calm down. We should have seen this coming. I told you, Chyna, that nothing good comes from casting spells on people like that," my mom said.

"Exactly, and that's the reason why she needs to just endure this contract. She signed it. With blood too," Aunt Celestine said with a grunt.

"Well, what's done is done, and my niece wants out. So, I'll help in any way I can. But I'll need a new car. Auntie wants to look fly in a new Mercedes," Aunt Crystal said, chiming in.

"Of course, whatever car you want. Just please help me," I said, clasping my hands together as if in prayer.

My mom had really come through for me. She had been able to find a ritual that had been used successfully to break spells bound by blood. It took a lot of skill, which all three of them combined could provide.

But this still wasn't a guarantee, because sometimes breaking a blood spell required a sacrifice, which none of them had been willing to do. So, we were betting all odds on the basic ritual being the fix.

"Most people were able to break the spell without having to do any sacrifices. Sorry Chyna, but we don't owe you that," my mom said.

"I understand," I said.

"But the ritual has failed many times, whether it was done with sacrifices or without," Aunt Celestine said.

"I want my brand new white GLE SUV Mercedes, whether we break the spell or not," Aunt Crystal said.

Now, all three of them stood together, holding hands, as they prepared to begin the ritual in my moms' lair.

"Okay, Chyna, drink the potion and we'll begin," my mom said.

I took my first sip of the potion and immediately gagged. It was disgusting.

I hated that I had to go through this, but I hated even more that I had to put my mom and my aunts through this. The ritual would drain their magic, leaving them weakened and unable to use their powers for days, maybe even weeks.

But I desperately wanted out of this contract and out of this bullshit relationship with Chicago.

Whenever I was away from Chicago, I could feel the tugging with each hair on my body, throughout my bones, in the flow of my blood, and even in the shattered pieces of my heart.

I couldn't believe Chicago had cheated on me. I never would have guessed he was that kind of guy.

In all the months that we were dating, I hadn't had even an inkling that he was like this.

But it was now clear that without any spells controlling his actions and feelings, this was the real Chicago. This was how he felt about me, and I no longer wanted to be a part of his life anymore.

It had been a week since the cheating incident, and he hadn't called me once, but I had received numerous calls from Desmond and even a call from Jackie.

I replayed the night I caught Chicago cheating in my head, then I chugged the rest of the potion, gagging and coughing as I tried to keep it down so the ritual would be a success.

"Alright, let's begin," my mom said.

The three of them squeezed each other's hands tightly and began to recite the spell.

I started feeling lightheaded and began to wobble as I struggled to remain upright, but I soon fell to the ground.

As their chants grew louder, I realized the markings on my skin were glowing bright green while the markings on the ground were glowing purple.

Then purple smoke emerged from my mom's and my aunts' mouths and forced its way into my mouth.

I felt extremely hot as I laid on the ground, feeling energy running through my body as purple smoke swirled around me. The tugging was replaced by a whirling feeling caused by the energy I had just absorbed.

As my body grew hotter, I shrieked and started sweating like crazy.

Then, suddenly, a huge purple smoke ball began to pour from my mouth, the tail end of it was still inside me. Inside the purple ball was a neon green orb that was being pulled from my body by the purple smoke. The green orb must have been the binding spell, and it was putting up a good fight to stay inside me.

I cried out in pain as my mom's and my aunts' chanting grew to a feverish pitch as they tried desperately to strengthen the purple smoke.

The purple smoke ball continued to tug its way out of me, inch by inch, dragging the green orb along with it. The orb bucked and ricocheted furiously, refusing to let go.

Then the green orb began to vibrate, and the purple smoke surrounding me evaporated in a whoosh.

I gasped for air as the green orb threw itself back into my body.

The markings on my skin, along with those on the ground, were now smeared. And just like that, the tugging returned.

My mom dropped her head while my aunts shook theirs.

"It didn't work," I said as I sobbed.

CHAPTER 49

In two hours, it would finally be six years since Chicago and I signed the contract.

I was sitting on the patio of a beautiful new French bakery that had opened down the street from my third salon in Santa Monica. I took another bite of my buttery croissant and looked over the planning details for my next salon which was being built in Houston, TX. It had plans of being ready for business in the next few months.

So far, Magical Touch Hair Salon had eight locations across the US in LA, New York, Atlanta, Miami, Dallas, and Houston.

Business was booming.

I had solidified myself as a celebrity hairstylist, having worked with some of the biggest A-list celebrities for red-carpet events and even touring with them.

I had also launched my own hair care line. It was a dream accomplishment. The ingredients were magically beneficial, so my products were always flying off the shelves as soon as they were restocked.

Sitting beside my laptop was a popular hair magazine featuring my face front and center on the cover. I glanced over at it for the hundredth time, not only to admire how good I looked, but because I was so proud of myself and my achievements. I had landed the cover because the powers that be wanted to commend me for my influence in the hair industry.

The cover showcased my radiant smile and my big, bouncy curls that took me hours to style.

Inside the spread, there were various pictures featuring me with different hairstyles I created on myself, along with styles I'd done for my clients.

One photo even captured me styling Beyé's hair for a red-carpet event—a shot I had enlarged and hung in the living room of my New York City condo.

Even though Chicago and I were still together, I had my own place that I would stay at occasionally.

He, on the other hand, owned several properties throughout the US, which he stayed at when traveling for games or other events.

He had even bought a sprawling estate in Italy last year, where we spent the holidays together. It was a beautiful mansion with a lush garden bordering the house, a large pool, and breathtaking views of Lake Como and the mountains that surrounded it.

I could still remember the first day I visited.

"Damn, this is beautiful! I'm going to come here every year!" I said as my heels clinked against the marble flooring in the foyer.

"We'll be here every year. It's our vacation home. I even got us a boat so we can cruise around the lake," Chicago said peering through the grand front doors where part of the lake was visible.

He gave me a tour of the whole estate that day, and I oohed and aahed at every site and feature. By the time I finished seeing everything, the sun was setting, so we had a late dinner on the boat as we toured the lake.

Chicago had hired a private chef to prepare our dinner, something that had become a norm for us now.

The chef brought out two large plates filled with pasta and two fat lobster tails. We wasted no time digging into our meal and enjoyed every bite.

I sat across from Chicago, admiring how much he had matured since we first started dating. He still looked pretty much the same, but his body was leaner and more toned—the perfect frame for a basketball player. His eyes were softer, with thin age lines settling around them.

Chicago and I had really been in a good place over the last few years. At the beginning of the contract, things had started off extremely rocky.

After catching him cheating on me and trying to break the spell (with no luck), we separated for about two years. I had moved into a condo not too far from his, which Cali helped me find, because I needed to stay close to avoid the tugging caused by the contract.

Throughout those two years, we would only see each other at events or occasionally at a game when it was suggested that we be seen together to maintain the façade of our relationship.

During that same period, I was hooking up with a rapper, and Chicago was hooking up with any groupie he found outside his hotel room at away games.

It was a dark time, but we managed to keep our affairs out of the media.

One time, I was spotted out on a date with my rapper boo, but we were able to easily spin the narrative that we were only having lunch because I was styling his hair on the set of one of his music videos.

Chicago and I were "spotted" out many times after that to convince the public that we were still together.

About a year after that, we were able to come together and somewhat rebuild our relationship, starting off with our friendship. Building a strong friendship and partnership eventually led us to where we were now: talking almost every day and sharing everything with each other.

It had been a slow buildup, but I was so glad that we had gotten to this point. It was essential, especially given we were both victims of this contract.

The time we spent away from each other was hard on both of us, mainly because the contract put an incredible strain on our bodies.

It messed up Chicago's game after a while. But once we rekindled that spark, we moved back in with each other, and I attended more games, which helped weaken the binding spell and improve Chicago's throws and dunks.

I even cast a few spells for him to trip up the other team during the championship game, which allowed his team to win the game and earn him that championship ring he longed for. It was our little secret.

I gathered up my things, walked out of the French bakery, and jumped into my cherry red, drop top Maserati that I had bought a year ago. I started the engine, then peeled off toward Chicago's old condo.

The old condo where everything had started.

We hadn't been there in years because Chicago had rented it out after he started buying houses. But the previous tenants had just moved out, so Chicago figured we would use it as the meeting place to end our contract.

Just as I got on the highway, I got a call from Mrs. Sullivan.

"Hey, girl!" I said as I rolled up my drop top to hear her better.

"Hey girl, hey!" Cali said, her voice blasting out of the car speaker.

Cali, the now pregnant wife of Frankie Sullivan, had just left her doctor's appointment after her six-month checkup.

"I'm so ready for this baby to come up out of here! I'm ready to hold him or her in my arms, but I'm mainly ready to get my body back. I need sushi!" Cali said in a whining voice.

"You're almost there. I'll be at the hospital with a sushi boat the minute you push my little niece out."

"You're going to have to fight Frankie about that. He swears it's a boy. I don't care what it is. I'm just ready to meet them."

"Me too."

"So, you headed to Chicago's old spot for the contract release?"

"Yes ma'am. Headed that way now."

"Wow! I can't believe it's been six years already. How do you feel?"

"I don't know how I feel. I was just reminiscing about everything. So much has happened. From all my salons coming to fruition, to both my and Chicago's careers taking off. I even started reflecting on the bad stuff, like the cheating and the affairs. I can't believe all of that actually happened. But one thing I do know: I'm ready for this pulling and tugging to be over."

"I bet you are! That shit always sounded awful. I remember when we went on my bachelorette trip to Turks and Caicos, and you were sick almost the whole time. I hated that for you. But now, it's about to be over. We have to have a contract release party afterwards! Let's go out! Let's go to the club!" Cali said with excitement in her voice.

As if she would be able to last through a late-night party in her pregnant condition, especially since she always dozed off before 8pm.

"Have you made your decision yet? I know Chicago has to decide too, but when you're asked, will you stay with Chicago or not? I mean he did give you that engagement ring. Does that mean y'all will get married?"

I took a deep breath. I hadn't wanted to answer that question yet.

The way Chicago and I had begun our relationship was messed up, but now we're in a really good place.

He had proposed to me when he won his championship ring. At first, I assumed he'd done it for the cameras…for the publicity.

But I honestly think he meant it and that he really wants to be with me now, given how close we'd grown to each other.

He always said he still had a lot of love for me, and I've always felt the same about him.

We were practically in a committed relationship now anyway, because we lived together and slept together. Something I never thought would happen again when we first signed this contract.

Chicago had changed…but I knew he still had his issues.

For instance, I knew he was still sleeping with other women. But I wasn't fully bothered by that anymore because I was still seeing my rapper boo occasionally too.

I wouldn't leave Chicago for Rapper Boo, though. Things with him weren't serious enough to go that far.

Besides, just the thought of leaving Chicago made my heart flip-flop. I felt comfortable with him. He knew exactly who I was and what I was capable of doing, and that was something I had always wanted in a partnership.

But I didn't need him anymore.

If Chicago and I split up today, everything would be fine. I would keep my businesses and my homes, and he would keep his. It would be a clean break followed by a little PR cleanup. Then he could be with whomever he wanted, and I could focus on myself.

I handed my car keys to the valet at Chicago's old condo, and made my way to the elevator, then I pushed the button for his floor.

I was still on the phone with Cali, and she asked me again.

"Chyna, what are you going to do? What's your answer going to be? Are you going to stay with Chicago or not?"

I took another moment to think things through.

As soon as I opened my mouth to answer, the doors of the elevator slid open and there stood Chicago, his warm inviting smile and kind brown eyes making me question everything all over again.

"You ready?" he asked holding his hand out to me to lead me into the living room where Desmond, Tammy, Jackie, Stephen, and my mom and dad awaited.

"Yes."

ACKNOWLEDGMENTS

First things first, I must thank God for helping me push through and finish this book. It was a very long journey, full of many learning curves and changes along the way.

Special thanks to all the readers who took the time to read my first book. Whether you loved it or not, your support means everything to me. This book was something I originally wrote for myself—to laugh about and reread for my own joy. I didn't care if I sold one copy or none at all. I was simply proud to have created and published something of my own, and doing so has definitely healed my inner child—the one who used to daydream different scenarios and make movies in my head. It felt good to finally bring one to life.

With this book, I wanted to create something fun and straight out of my wildest dreams. Literally—it came from one of my dreams, and I expanded and added more to it. I know the character of Chyna will be both loved and hated (according to my beta readers—half of them loved her, the other half, not so much). Honestly, I have mixed feelings about her too, but I enjoyed the process of bringing her to life. She was a headache, but an interesting one. If anything,

I hope this story shows what *not* to do. Please, do not use magic or spells to force love from anyone—haha. And while I know she probably deserved more karma, at the end of the day… she gets witch she wants.

I have to thank my dear friends, Julie, Brandon, and LaDarria, for encouraging me throughout this journey. Thank you for your support, your excitement, and all the joy you shared when I told you about the book. It truly meant a lot and helped motivate me to finish.

To my family—my mom, my dad, my sisters, my brother, and my grandparents—thank you for all the love, support, and excitement you showed for this book. Thank you for all the hype you gave me. Your persistent, "When is the book ready? When can I buy it?" definitely kept me going. And no, I didn't write about anyone in this book, so y'all don't have to worry—haha. I was also so excited to learn that my dad wrote a book before. I'm proud to follow in his footsteps.

Lastly, to my editors, Andrelle Quammie and Tee Tate—thank y'all so much for all the guidance and care you poured into this book. I know my first manuscript screamed that it was my first time writing a book, but I really appreciate you for not critiquing me too harshly. Thank you for your kind words, encouragement, and the countless hours you spent working on this story. I'm truly grateful for your thoughtful feedback and the care you put into helping me shape this story. I couldn't have asked for a better editing experience.

Once again, thank you, everyone, for your love and support!

ABOUT THE AUTHOR

 Ciara Hall is a first-time author, with SHE GETS WITCH SHE WANTS being her debut novel. Currently living in Houston, TX, Ciara loves to explore new restaurants and things to do in the city while posting fun pictures on her Instagram. Ciara has always been passionate about reading and writing. She was writing scripts for her made up TV shows when she was younger. With many ideas of interesting stories roaming inside of her head, she is ready to be the next best-selling author.

Instagram: author_ciarahall
TikTok: author_ciarahall
Website: https://authorciarahall.carrd.co